first

BOOK ONE OF THE LIVE ONCE TRILOGY

Laura,
I hope you enjoy
my "first" book!
- Chanda
Stafford!

chanda stafford

First
A Red Adept Publishing Book

Red Adept Publishing, LLC
104 Bugenfield Court
Garner, NC 27529
http://RedAdeptPublishing.com/

First Print Edition: May 2013
ISBN-13: 978-1-940215-01-3
ISBN-10: 1-940215-01-3

Cover and Formatting: Streetlight Graphics

"DON'T SAY A WORD."

adrian

THE ROOM SMELLS MUSTY, UNUSED. Kind of like the back storage buildings on the farm, or the old cellar the Chesanings don't use any more where we explore and play games. Shafts of sunlight slant through the cracks in the heavy, dark red curtains, and when I take a step, more puffs of dust cloud the air. Chairs covered in white blankets line the walls and tower over me in stacks almost as high as the ceiling.

"What do you think they're doing out there?" I whisper, but it's so quiet, I could be shouting.

My servant, Will, shushes me. "If you listen closely, I bet you can hear your First talking."

I creep over to the door and press my ear against it. Nothing. As if no one's on the other side. "Isn't this the Release Ceremony? Shouldn't I be out there with him?"

Will nods, leaning against the wall, crossing his arms in front of him. "That's normally how it happens. This is... odd."

"Did I do something wrong? Did I make Thoreau mad?" I bite my lip to keep it from trembling. *Grow up, Adrian. Stop acting like a baby.*

"No, of course not." He flashes me a quick grin, but I can tell he's nervous.

"Are you sure?" I hate it when my voice is all shaky like a little baby's.

"Definitely. I would know if there was a problem." He shrugs, and a bar of light illuminates his carefree smile. "I bet it's to save you from having to sit out there for the whole ceremony. Some of them can get pretty long."

On the other side of the door, I hear clapping. An old man's voice rises up as the applause dies.

"There, you see?" Will says. "Nothing to worry about." I turn away and tune him out so I can listen to Thoreau.

"Thank you, my friends, for this most welcome reception. As a First, I've lived for hundreds of years, influenced this country in ways the average person can't even begin to comprehend. With your continued support, and that of Princeton, I will use your gift to change the future and create a better tomorrow. Thank you."

A dull roar follows his words, and I fidget in my seat, watching the door. My eyes dart to Will.

"This doesn't make any sense, Will. I should be out there."

"I'm sure they'll call you shortly, Adrian. Maybe the usual waiting room was unavailable and—"

A loud boom shakes the room, and I almost fall down. The chairs weave back and forth in their towers, and millions of dust particles rain down. Will shoves me away from the wall and pushes me toward the back of the room.

"Move, now!" he shouts, but my ears are ringing, and I cough from the dust. He looks behind us at the door and forces me to move faster.

"Murderer! Child killer! Free the Second!" a loud, mechanical voice shouts from the other room. "Free the Second! Free the Second!"

There's more yelling, but I can't make out what they're saying. Another, quieter boom. Will pushes me to a narrow closet.

"In here," he hisses and shoves me inside. We stay like

2

that for what feels like a couple hours before the door to our main room bangs open, and I hear the heavy clomping of boots.

"You in here with the Second, boy?" Will stays silent. There is a general grumbling outside, some swearing my mother would never approve of, then the deep, gravelly voice speaks again. "Alpha Code One, this is Underground Robin. Is the cargo safe and accounted for? I repeat, is the cargo safe and accounted for?"

Apparently these are magic words for Will because relief washes over his features.

"Who wants to know?"

"Papa bird." The men march over to our closet and slide open the door. "Good spot, boy." The head guard, an older man with a pinched face and a permanent frown sheaths his Artos. The other guards keep theirs out. Why? Is it still dangerous?

"What's going on out there?" Will asks.

"Nothing we didn't expect. Stupid rebels, always doing things half-assed." He grins. "Let's go." One of them reaches out for me, but I jerk away.

Will touches my shoulder, reassuring me. "It's okay, Adrian. We're safe now."

I shake my head and step back. "Where are we going?"

"Someplace safe." The head guard takes my arm roughly in his. "Don't worry. We won't let anything happen to you." One of the other guards laughs, as if that's somehow funny.

"Is... my First all right?"

"He's fine, boy." He drags me from the closet. "Now let's go."

"Where?" My feet skitter, trying to find purchase as the guard forces me to follow him. The other men glance at each other, at me, then away again. Even Will won't meet my eyes. Fear freezes me, and I dig my shoes into the thick carpeting. "Will? What's going on?"

"Nothing," he answers too quickly. "Just a trip down to

3

the medical center, to make sure you're all right." He tries to give me another smile, but he's lying about something. I can feel it.

"But I'm fine," I protest as the guard pulls me to the side of the room, behind the curtains where, instead of a window, there is another door. "Can't you just tell them that? I'm fine. I just want to go back to my room."

Will shakes his head, sadly. "I'm sorry, Adrian, I really am."

"What's going on? Why are you sorry? Will?"

"Let's go," one of the other guards growls from the rear of our group. "We don't have all day. Some of us have work to do."

FIRST OF THE FIRSTS

mira

Two years later

"**S**TOP IT, MAX. I'M COMING!"

My five-year-old brother bangs on the bathroom door again. "Come *on*! We're going to be late!"

"I don't know why you're so excited. Nothing ever happens at these things." Kicking aside my brown coverall, I peer into the mirror. It'll have to do. Who cares if I smell as though I've already been working for four hours taking care of the hunting dogs and cleaning out the stalls in the barn? I have. Not everyone can sleep until noon and avoid work like the girls in the manor.

"Hurry up. Mom said we have to go *now*."

I roll my eyes, run my fingers through my short, spiky brown hair, then wet it again, trying to bring some order to the mess. Impossible.

"I'm coming. I'm coming." I pull on a soft white tunic and pants, then tie the faded yellow belt around my waist, cinching it tightly so that the billowing folds of the tunic collect pretty much in the middle. Good enough.

As soon as I open the door, Max bursts in, his old blue baby blanket wrapped around his newly tattooed arm. I grimace. The memory brings back the pain of my own tattoo, the throbbing soreness that came after the numbing cream wore off. I rub my hand across the top of his bare head, barely able to see the shadow of the rich, black hair that used to curl past his ears. *Poor little guy.*

"Aren't you too old for that?" I nod at his blanket and chuckle when he scowls just like our father used to, and then slams the door in my face.

I wander into the kitchen and grab a piece of toast from the plate on the counter. The stuff tastes like cardboard, but it looks like real bread and supposedly has all the nutrients necessary for a person to work at peak performance. Personally, I'd rather eat the wood shavings in the barn. I bet they'd taste better. Real bread is reserved for special occasions—like Christmas—so the Chesanings can feel good about themselves for giving us a treat.

My mom pushes buttons on the drink dispenser in the opposite wall, ordering coffee. Her worn, once-pink robe clings to her generous frame.

"Good morning." I try to kiss her on the cheek, but she swats me away with a dishrag.

As soon as the dispenser's sliding door opens, she grabs the steaming disposable cup and sets it on the counter. "What took you so long? The First will be here soon."

I shrug. "I had to work, remember? The Chesanings want to go hunting in a couple days. They ordered in another dozen hounds, since apparently the ones we have are too old. Tanner said they've got a fox in the barn. Must have cost them a fortune. Besides, it's just another visit. I don't see why I can't stay home the way Anna does."

"Mira Marie, that's enough. We've been over this before, you're going. Even though the likelihood of you being chosen is slim to none, your brother still has a chance."

I roll my eyes as Max rushes out of the bathroom, tunic crooked, belt tied in a lopsided yellow bow. I put down my toast and fix his uniform. "Do you remember your lines?" I smile and tweak his belt.

He stops fidgeting and nods solemnly. "Do you think they'll ask me?"

"They might. You never know, so it's best to be ready."

"Do you think I'll do okay?"

"Well." I pat the sides of his tunic up and down and make a big show of searching his pockets. "As long as you're not hiding any frogs or chickens in there, I think you'll be fine." His sudden wide, gap-toothed grin makes me chuckle. As soon as I let go, he darts away.

Mom glances at the blue metal clock above the kitchen sink, effectively ending the conversation. "You're late, both of you, and this is your brother's first visit. He needs you there. It's your job to take care of him."

A shadow crosses her eyes, and in my mind, I see a different small hand clutching mine. I scrunch my eyes shut, trying to chase away the ghost. It never works. Dead little sisters are particularly persistent.

"Can't you say I have a fever or something? It's stupid. Firsts always look at us like we're animals. Besides, there are plenty of other kids for him to see. No one's been picked from our farm since—" *Oh yeah, my cousin.* When I blink, his fair hair, light blue eyes, and ready smile flash behind my eyelids.

Mom sighs, and the worry lines etch the sides of her mouth into deep grooves. "This discussion is over. You need to get out there and support your brother." She points her index finger, poking me in the chest. "He needs you. Do *not* skip this time." The front door to our apartment slams shut. Apparently Max got tired of waiting for me.

Grabbing my half-eaten piece of cardboard, I leave the apartment, taking the steps two at a time, and exit the steel-sided complex. Instead of going around the proper way, I sneak through the red climate-controlled barn, shoving the rest of my breakfast in my mouth.

I stop at the other side of the barn door, behind the row of children standing at attention. There are about a dozen of us today—all wearing the customary white and yellow—ranging from barely five to seventeen years old. Most of the kids are related, tanned skin, deep dark eyes, stick-straight dark hair and slight, athletic builds. I'm the standout. I never figured out where my blondish-brown hair came from.

Max rushes to the end of the line and stands next to Bran, a frizzy-haired redhead whose time in the program is almost finished. He tries to stand as tall and still as Bran, puffing out his chest with importance, but after a few seconds, he fidgets, holding his arm as if trying to cover up his birthday present.

I rub my own brand, what the Chesanings call a barcode, tattooed in faded blue ink on the inside of my wrist like a crooked half of a bracelet. Anger fills me. We shouldn't have to be here. We're kids, not livestock at an auction.

From the house, a short procession makes its way toward the courtyard. The Chesanings are there, along with one of their servants, Tevan, a jerk who does Mr. Chesaning's bidding and makes Tanner's life a living hell. With them is a portly middle-aged man with balding white hair and a pencil thin mustache, and two unsmiling, dark black-clothed military officers. They walk discreetly behind an ancient man dressed in a crisp black and white suit, leaning over a knobby wooden cane. At his side walks a leggy black and brown shepherd mix.

Huh. He has a dog? Just then the old man misses a step and stumbles forward. The dog instinctively leans into him, helping balance his master. *It must be his. I've never seen a First bring a dog before.* A memory from school, or rather a picture of an old man with a dog seated next to him, swims to the front of my mind. Yes, I know this man. Only one of them travels with a dog: the first of the Firsts, Socrates.

WELL PAST MY EXPIRATION

socrates

aHANDFUL OF CHILDREN SLOUCH IN a ragged line in front of me. The littlest ones monkey around a bit, as they always do, and a boy at the end—one of the youngest—sucks his thumb. I bet if I look him in the eyes, he'd cry. Not that I entertain myself by making young children cry. I'm not that much of a monster. From the corner of my eye, I see an older girl slink to the end of the line. *Hmph. She's late. Thought they taught them better than that.*

"A lot of younger ones this time." I turn to Mr. Chesaning, who joins me.

Wearing a clean, pressed brown suit, he looks uncomfortable. I have a tendency to do that to people. Maybe he just doesn't like wearing a suit. Fashion doesn't matter much when you're surrounded by servants. Anything the master and mistresses of the house wear must look like riches to the children waiting in front of me.

"Yes." He nods. "I like to think we have the best Texans there are. Sweet and docile, that's our goal. We've had a couple light years here—fewer visits—so we haven't produced as many as we used to. Most of the ones we keep close by are younger children. The older kids are out working the fields. If you want, we can call them in.

Harvesting season is just starting, you know, so we have every hand out there we can."

"No, it's fine. If anything, the mistake is mine. I've been to five farms, and I thought I would have been able to choose a suitable candidate before now."

"Well, sir, I'm glad you came here. When we heard you were sick, we didn't think you would be able to make it out this far."

I smile tightly and nod at him. "Yes, that old nemesis, cancer. According to the doctors, it's not serious, and I do have some time left, even though there's no cure for getting old. However, this is an important decision and not one I want to make lightly. If you're ready, Mr. Chesaning, my companions and I would like to get started."

"Sure, sir, of course." He nods, and I glance at the portly man next to me, my friend, Edward Flannigan.

Edward nods, swipes the back of his hand on his glistening forehead, smearing thin swaths of pale red hair and waddles over to the line of children. "My name is Mr. Flannigan, friend to Socrates and teacher to those fortunate enough to be Absolved. We've selected your farm as one of a very few that we believe would have a candidate who meets the high standards Socrates has set for his next Second.

"Every year, several esteemed members of our society choose a Texan child from the farms to be Absolved of the crimes of their ancestors. This is an amazing opportunity, because if you're selected, you'll be allowed to travel the world with your First, go where they go, explore exotic places, and meet people you'd never have the chance to meet here at the farm. As an Absolved, you will have the opportunity to be free from farm life." He smiles at the children.

"All your life you've prepared for this day. You've worked hard, studied, and learned everything your teachers have asked of you. We are confident that you can make your farm, your family, and your people proud, whether or not you're chosen for this great opportunity. Are you ready to begin?" The children nod and answer in a chorus of yeses.

"All right, then." He claps his meaty hands in front of him. "Let's see if you're worthy of this honor." Several of the children smile nervously, a few look bored, and the girl on the end looks like she'd rather be anywhere else.

"Who can tell me what started the Immigration War?" A tiny hand shoots toward the sky. The girl, around six or seven, fairly bounces with excitement. Edward nods at her.

"We did, sir," she squeaks.

"What is your name, girl?"

"Analeise, sir."

"Thank you. You are correct. Your ancestors were unhappy with the New Patriot Act of 2297. Does anyone remember what was in that act?" The girl's hand rockets skyward again, but he looks over her. No one else volunteers. He nods to a stick-thin boy about halfway down with tight blond curls. "You, over there. What's your name?"

"Hector, sir."

"Well? Do you know what was in that act?" Hector rolls his eyes before answering.

"The New Patriot Act of 2297 made it illegal for anyone to be found without a V-chip, and only people with state issued I.D. could get one. Anyone caught without one was immediately deported to the nearest border checkpoint."

"Very good, Hector. Now why did Texas choose to betray our country and rebel?"

"They thought that it was wrong to discriminate against people who didn't have a V-chip. They also claimed that the government arrested people who disagreed with them and sent them to prisons in other countries."

"Was this true?"

Hector shakes his head. "No, sir. Of course not. Our government would never arrest anyone without a good reason."

11

"Very good. During that war, your ancestors chose to become terrorists and attack innocent people. Can anyone tell me what happened?" Analeise raises her hand again, but he ignores her once more and points at a young boy on the end next to the girl who arrived late. "You there. What happened?"

The young boy jumps. His newly bald head shines pale in the sunlight, and his arm still bears the redness of a new tattoo. "Th-they sent suicide bombers to attack the White House and the..." his brow furrows in concentration. The girl leans down and whispers something in his ear. "... Pentagon on the anniversary of the Immigration bill, sir." He puffs out his chest and grins.

"Very good," Edward says. The girl next to the boy puts her arm around him and squeezes his shoulders. The boy beams up at her. "What's your name?"

"M-Max."

"Good. Thank you." Edward gestures to the girl. "What happened after the war?"

The girl straightens a bit before answering. "The government had no choice but to bomb most of Texas and the Southwest and move the leftover people to working farms for their own safety. Any remaining rebels were killed by bioengineered viruses released into the air."

"Thank you. And your name is?"

"Mira."

"Excellent. What happened with the viruses?"

The boy next to Mira raises his hand, and Edward nods at him. "The rebels used their own people to take the virus to big cities around the world, and it got everybody sick."

"Did a lot of people die?"

Max nods. "Yes, millions and millions of people died."

"Good. Thank you, Max." Mira smiles down at him and rubs her knuckles on the top of his head.

"What does it mean to be Absolved?"

Analeise raises her hand again, bouncing on the tips of

her toes in excitement. Edward sighs and shakes his head before calling on her.

"It's the best thing in the world, sir. I... I would be so happy, and I know my momma and daddy would be so proud of me. I'd be the best Absolved there is." Edward winces, and I chuckle.

"Thank you, Analeise. That was very good." He turns back to me, smiling tiredly and opening his arms to encompass all the children. "I present to you, the children of Chesaning Farms."

We all clap appropriately. The dull sound echoes across the open space.

After the meager applause dies down, I limp toward the line of children, relying more than I would like on my old mesquite cane. My other hand lightly grazes the scruff of Ben's neck. I try not to, but on every other step, I lean a bit into his canine strength. It's harder, these days, to do things I used to take for granted, like walking.

As I hobble down the line, I pass a tow-headed boy with scarred hands clenched in fists at his sides. His eyes are an earthy brown, and his nose has a crooked bend. I also pass the ones barely out of diapers. I need a Second with more presence. A five-year-old doesn't command much attention, no matter how old the person's soul is.

I look over the heads of the younger children and focus on the older girl at the end, the one who got here last and congratulated the boy after he answered his questions correctly. What was her name again? Mira. Yes, that's it. She is about as tall as I am—which isn't saying much— slim, with short brown hair that's barely within regulation guidelines and messily out of control. When her eyes meet mine, I see resentment, anger, and pride. Her chin tilts up, and she stiffens her spine as if preparing for an attack. *Interesting.*

Her robe is clean, maybe a little wrinkled—she must have been in a hurry—and she appears to be at the age for graduating out of the system. I study her eyes. She has potential. I make my way over to her. Ben wags his tail and sniffs the hem of her pants. *Hmm, what does he like about her?*

After studying her for a few seconds more, I walk down the line again, my sandals scuffing up little puffs of dust that cling to my robes. I stop at a boy around twelve with chocolaty-brown hair and big dark eyes. He glances up at me. I smile, and he ducks his head. *Am I that terrifying?* I'm just an old man, well past my expiration date.

He sniffles, and when the boy looks up again, he's trembling. I turn away. I don't have the luxury of taking the time to reassure a weak Second, though I suppose it's a lot to ask of any child, especially the younger ones, not to be afraid at a time like this. I walk back to Mr. Chesaning just as he's joined by his wife.

The woman wrings her hands. "I'm sorry, sir. We have a few more kids out in the field, but this is most of them."

I smile and shake my head. "It's fine. Normally, I have an itinerary created months in advance, but I was unable to find the child I was looking for anywhere else."

They nod.

"Well, there's always the Anderson and Dawson farms." Edward leans toward me, his bald pate shining in the sun.

"Let me think for a moment." I look back at the children fidgeting in the heat.

The girl on the end stands silent, staring at me as if daring me to say or do anything, but then she looks down when the young boy, Max, tugs her sleeve. She gently touches his back, murmuring to him. Ben whines at my side, shifting from foot to foot as he looks at her. He's never acted like this before. Is it a sign? He ignored the stocky youth at Lawrence farms and the young girl who bounced on her heels and reached out to pet Ben as we passed. He paid them no mind, so maybe this one is different. I glance back and see my advisor, the Chesanings, the guards, and the staff all eyeing me impatiently. Waiting for this old man to make a decision. So I do. Yes, I nod, this one's as good a guess, better perhaps, than any of the others I've seen. "There's no need for that. I believe I've made my decision."

I walk back to the line of children. As I reach the end, the girl looks up at me, meeting my gaze, and I let myself fall into her gray eyes—my future eyes—and see myself reflected there. I turn away from her to face the Chesanings, my friend, and the assorted servants and guards.

I point at the girl. "I choose this one." My voice echoes as the children's whispers and the quiet voices of the adults fall silent.

The girl gasps. "No."

For a second, I think she'll run. Then resilience returns to her gaze, and I know I've picked the right one.

Smiling, I repeat the same words I've repeated six other times. "I choose you to be Absolved of the crimes of your ancestors. Do you accept?"

Indecision flares in her eyes. After a second, she bows her head and whispers, "Yes."

LUCKY

mira

"I CHOOSE YOU," ECHOES IN MY head, but I'm too numb to feel anything. Is this really happening? Only three months left until my birthday and now this? I don't want to go. Never seeing Max again, or Tanner, it'll kill me.

I scowl all the way back to our cramped apartment and stomp my way into my closet-sized room with its sterile white walls and lumpy old mattress. I sigh. Looking around, even I have to admit that being some old man's maid must be better than this. I rip off my tunic and sash, slip on a comfortable gray shirt and pants, and tighten a belt around my waist.

"Mira!" Max rushes in, tears leaving wet tracks down his chubby baby cheeks. He grabs me around the hips and buries his head in my side. "You can't go!"

I totter backward. "Whoa, Max. It's going to be all right." I pat him awkwardly on the back. "It's okay."

"No, it's not. Tommy said you're gonna die. He said that's what happens when you get picked."

"Don't be ridiculous." I sit down on my bed. "You know that's just a story they tell to get us to behave. You know what our teachers said; it'll be a great opportunity."

"You can't go."

"I have to." Anger rushes through my veins, and it's all I can do to keep from smashing a fist through the wall. *What example am I setting for Max?* Gritting my teeth, I fight for calm. "I don't have a choice. It's not that bad, right? I'll see all sorts of places, meet different people. Besides, since they picked me, you don't have to stand anymore." My hands shake, so I fist them in my pockets so he doesn't see. "It's a good thing, Max. Trust me."

He shakes his head, eyes red and bottom lip trembling. "I don't want you to go."

"I'm sorry, Max. I have to."

His eyes widen. "Did you tell Tanner?"

Damn. "No. It just happened. I haven't had time to tell anyone." I close my eyes and see Tanner as I did yesterday, leaning against a tree at the edge of the clearing, our secret place, sun shining off his reddish-brown hair, laughter sparkling in his eyes. Dread fills me. He should have been the first stop after being chosen. I bunch up my uniform and throw it into the corner.

Max lets go of me just as suddenly as he latched on and rushes for the door. "I'll go tell him."

"No, don't. It's all right, I'll do it." But I'm speaking to an empty doorway. "Max?" Nothing. *Little brat.* The door slams.

Just as I'm about to follow him, my mother rushes in and envelops me in a tight hug. No one else is around, so I'm not sure why she's bothering to act as if she cares. The last time my mother hugged me was right after Rosie died. Right after she said it wasn't my fault.

"This is so wonderful." She kisses my cheeks and clutches me to her chest again. *Wow, she's really putting on an act.* "I can't believe it. Someone from our family was chosen! I never would have thought. I always knew you were destined for great things." *Wait, didn't she say this morning that there was a slim to none chance?* I raise my eyebrows, but she doesn't see it, she's hugging me

17

so tightly. Her heaving breaths and the dampness of her tears almost make me believe she's genuine. Almost.

I push myself away. "What if I don't want to go?"

"Nonsense, Mira. This is a great opportunity for you and for our family. You know what happens to Absolved Texans. It's the closest any of us ever get to being free."

"I don't want that. I just want to stay here. Tanner and I—"

"That's enough. That part of your life is over." Her eyes narrow, and her mouth sets into a firm line. "You're not a child anymore."

"What if I want to stay here?"

"Stop it. Socrates chose you for a reason." She smoothes my hair, a gesture that would have been downright maternal coming from anyone else's mother. With her, it's just another way to criticize my shortcomings. In this case, my unruly hair.

I pull farther away from her. "You and I both know that if Socrates knew about me, he never would have picked me."

"Mira, you are the most amazing daughter a mother could ask for. Of course your First knew what he was doing."

"Right. You're just saying that because you're finally getting rid of me. We both know I'll be a terrible Second. I skip visits like the Chesaning girls skip their chores. I even had to spend three days in the box. I've been written up so many times it's a wonder I haven't been kicked out or shipped off to another farm."

She shakes her head. "We all make mistakes, sweetheart, but we can be Absolved of our sins. Your father would be so proud of you."

"I thought he hated the Firsts."

"Of course he didn't. You wouldn't know, Mira. You were so young when he died."

"Five years isn't that long." But I'm arguing to her back as she walks out of my bedroom. Once again, I'm alone.

I can't stay anymore. The walls close in, and I feel like any moment my mom will come back, or Max, or Tanner. Oh yeah, Tanner. Guilt hits me hard, and I shove my feet into shoes. I should see him. Really, I need to see him, talk to him, beg him for forgiveness. But from what? It's not like I asked for this. It's not like I wanted this. It's not my fault, right? But there's no answer, only the echo from the empty walls. *I have to get out of here.*

Sneaking out is pretty easy—there's no one home—but somehow, it still feels wrong, like I should be working or at school or something. Passing around the edge of the courtyard, I notice that it's recess, and Max is out playing.

"Mira!" he shrieks and runs toward me, grabbing me in another hug. "What are you doing out here?"

"I'm going for a walk." I gently break free and smile as I scrub my hand on the top of his head. He ducks, just like he always does.

"Going to see Tanner? You looove him, don't you?" He bounces up and down on his heels in that excited, hyper way only little kids have.

"No! I don't love him." Right? My cheeks burn red hot. "He's my best friend, all right?" I chew on my bottom lip and look out toward the field where Tanner works.

"But you have to! Tanner said he'd come over after work."

"Umm, just... just tell him I can't see him. That I'm tired or something."

Max's eyes get huge. "But you're leaving! You want me to lie?"

I wince at the message I'm sending. Some role model I am. "Please Max. If you tell him I'm gone, he'll come looking for me, and I, I need some time alone right now."

He sticks the tip of his tongue out the corner of his mouth as he thinks. "But Mom said—"

I pull him to me, and he squirms. "I know, I know. It's wrong to lie. But just this once, can you do it for me?"

Max thinks for another long stretch of seconds, still with concentration.

19

"Please?"

Finally he nods, and I feel a relieved grin stretch across my face. "But it's your fault, right? If Mom catches me, I'm gonna say it's your fault." He narrows his eyes at me, so I know he's serious.

"That's fine." I chuckle. "I deserve it if she gets mad at me."

After Max leaves, I head out past the edge of the fields and cross over a small hill.

Nestled between the shadows of that hill and the edge of the forest is a sacred place. Little wooden houses rise above the ground on spindly stilts. Dolls have tea at the edge of a little tiny sandbox. Stuffed animals romp with each other, their weather-beaten hides gray from the elements. My eyes linger on the little brown teddy leaning against the swing set. I placed it there after Rosie died. The creature's lopsided bow droops, once bright red, now pale silver. The rusty swings clank against each other in the lazy summer breeze, and if I concentrate, I can hear laughter and nursery rhymes, and see tiny hands making hopscotch squares on the rough-hewn boards. Little invisible feet climb the ladder, and ghostly children shriek as they speed toward the earth on the slide.

The playground had been a paradise for the little ones until the Chesanings banned it many years ago. They said it was too dangerous having children that close to the forest, but there was nowhere closer to the apartments to put it. I think Mrs. Chesaning just didn't like the sound of the kids laughing and playing. She sends her own brats out often enough with their nannies.

But no matter how much she tries, Mrs. Chesaning can't banish the ghosts. Everywhere I look—behind the slide, underneath the tire swing, sitting next to the doll drinking tea, and nestled between teddy bears and ragdolls—are tiny handmade wooden crosses. Where the playground was once filled with laughter, it's now a place no mother ever wants her child to visit.

Living on the edge of the wilderness, we have more than our share of losses. But we're Texans, the losers of a long-ago war, so it doesn't really matter what happens to us, as long as there are enough workers in the fields and kids in the Second pool to fill the lineup whenever a First comes to call. It seems as though a kid dies at least once a year. Sometimes, it's because they get lost in the woods, like my sister; other times, it's a farming accident, like getting kicked by a horse. Then, there's the plague. My family's been lucky. We've been spared the coughing, bloody vomit, and the bone-jarring seizures. Others, not so much. The last time disease hit our farm, it was pretty bad. Twenty-eight people died. Nineteen of them were kids.

I make my way through the knee-high weathered crosses, some leaning, some missing their crossties altogether. A few stand tall, obviously recent. Many of the names are worn smooth from the elements, their identities lost like the children who disappeared, faded away, or breathed their last, only to be taken away by blue-clothed cleaners in the dead of night.

The cross I stop in front of, Rosie's, is like that. Lopsided and gray, the wood doesn't even display the barest etching of her name, but the letters weren't worn off from snow or the rain. I rubbed them away myself by running my fingers over them, as if that could somehow bring us closer together. It hasn't worked yet. I kneel and pull up the tufts of grass surrounding the cross. By its base, a small patch of clover sprouts. I run my fingers over the soft white flowers and leave them to grow.

"I'm sorry I haven't been back to see you in a couple days," I murmur as I sit in the grass next to her marker. "I know it's not an excuse, but I was chosen by a First. And, well, I'm going to have to leave. I don't want to, but I don't think I have a choice." My eyes sting, and I pluck a blade of grass from the ground, letting it go when an evening breeze picks up and whisks it away.

"I never thought anyone would pick me, not after what happened." The wind picks up, and I can almost hear her laugh the way she always did, even though the sound of her voice is fading. It's been so long. "I'm so sorry, Rosie. I never meant for you to die."

"IT'S NO MISTAKE."

socrates

"**Y**OU KNOW, SOCRATES, IF YOU don't feel up to it, I'm certain they can do the grand opening without you." The sun slants through the narrow window slits of the huge air-bus, shadowing Eliot's face. On her white suit, it reflects a brilliant, blinding glow. The smooth hum of the vehicle slows as we reach our destination, the National Museum of American History.

"Nonsense, Eliot. It's not every day someone creates a museum exhibit in my honor. And we'd best not forget the reporters and how they love their photo opportunities." My head throbs, and I rub the old, round scars that dot my skull, but the pain doesn't go away. If anything, it gets worse.

"Just for you, is it?" She chuckles, a throaty, masculine sound incongruent with my memories of her former raven-haired beauty. I suppose that's to be expected since she chose a male this time around. Despite that, she's still my wife, and even though our physical bodies have changed more times than I care to contemplate, our souls remain the same. Briefly, I think about voicing my analogy to Ellie, that even though we replace the engine every eighty years or so, the mileage just keeps adding up. Somehow, I don't think she'd appreciate it. Probably think I'm referencing the fine lines by her eyes or the grooves starting to deepen the sides of her mouth. Youth even flees from us, the immortals, with time.

"Well, I was the first one to survive, my dear, and I think we were all a bit surprised by that."

Eliot shakes her head. "Don't sell yourself short, Soc. You were chosen to be a First for a reason."

I slant her a lopsided smile and laugh. "I volunteered, remember? Back when it was mostly poor saps and criminals. The human trials had too many casualties. Scientists were running out of inmates to practice on. I had nothing left to live for, after my son..."

Eliot remains silent as the bus comes to a stop on the ground. The slight bump wakes Ben. He lifts his head and thumps his tail on the ground.

"Sirs, are you ready? We're here." The pilot's tinny voice echoes through the belly of the ship.

"Yes, we're ready," I answer, and the thin, metal door slides open. Lightweight steps fold out and lower to the ground.

I stand up, legs wobbling, and reach for my cane. Ben trots over to my other side, and I grab his harness for support.

Two nondescript black-uniformed security guards, both wearing mirrored visors with thin bands around their heads that allow their supervisors to see and hear everything they do, stand at the foot of the steps. They keep their hands behind their backs and wait in silence while I make my way down the stairs. A third guard stands behind them, holding on to an old-fashioned wheelchair with a worn, cracked black seat and metal wheels.

"Haven't seen one of those in about five hundred years. Have you, Ellie?" The thing looks so rickety. Will it even support my weight?

"No, it's been a while." She and Ben join me under the scorching sun. The guard pushes the chair forward for me to sit in it before stepping back and standing at ease, casting a practiced glance around for any threats.

"This isn't necessary, you know. I can walk just fine on my own." My hand shakes on the head of my cane, and the guard stifles a snort. Cheeky brat. When I was his age, I'd never have dreamt of treating my elders in such a manner. The antique design must be the museum's idea. I'll never admit it to Ellie, but I also prefer it to one of the more modern hover chairs that interface with the user's fine motor skills. Maybe I just like to know how things work, and these antique chairs are pretty easy to figure out.

She shakes her head. "You can barely make it from the ship to the ground. Just sit down so we can get this three-ring circus over with," she says, meaning the reporters and their antics, I think.

Muttering "wench" under my breath, I hobble over to the chair and lower myself into it, wincing at the pain in my joints. My breath comes out in short, agonizing bursts, and I lay my cane in my lap. Ellie raises her eyebrows in concern, but I look away, focusing instead on the lines in the cracked gray asphalt landing strip. A little weed, just a pair of leaves, really, springs between the cracks. Honestly, I'm surprised the gardeners didn't take care of that. Usually, the grounds around our capital are impeccably maintained.

One of the security guards reaches out for the handles, but Ellie shakes her head. "I can get that." As the guard folds his arms in front of him, I glimpse the faded tattoo on his wrist. It's kind of ironic, really. Only two hundred years ago, the government sought to segregate the Texan rebels who tried to destroy the very fabric of our nation so they couldn't do any more harm, and now, well, they're guarding two of this nation's arguably most important people.

Eliot pushes me down the wide sidewalk toward the front of the pale white building, not even exerting herself a little, which I suppose is normal, considering she's only forty years old and in peak physical condition. Ben trots along next to us, and I keep a light hand on his harness. The guards fall in behind us. As we near the front of the building, we hear a commotion, like a deep roaring interspersed with higher-pitched screams and shouts.

"The service entrance is closer," Eliot says. "I should have asked the pilot to land in the back. We could have avoided the crowd."

"And the reporters, you mean," I quip. She snorts. "Because, you wouldn't want to deprive our adoring audience of our presence, would you?"

"I doubt those are fans, Soc. Adoration wouldn't put a bullet in your head the way these people would." Right. Lifers.

As we approach the off side of the half-moon walkway in front of the building, about two hundred people of all races and ages—most of them young—strain against a low police barrier, chanting and holding up signs. A couple of reporters who probably came for the dedication perch outside. Cameras float in the air above the protestors' heads to get better angles. A few of the more adventurous ones zip in and out for close-ups. At least they're ignoring me for now.

"I hate it when you're right."

"I'm always right." Ellie pushes me forward.

In front of the crowd, a ring of police officers—who look identical to our guards—stand elbow to elbow, waiting for trouble. For a country that still prides itself in freedom of speech, there sure is a significant military presence at all protests. If I didn't know it was illegal, I would have guessed them to be clones. They hold the Artos, the latest model laser gun, a better deterrent than the waist-high fiberglass barriers hastily erected to keep the protestors at bay.

Our guards move forward and fall into position around

us, but their presence can't block out the chants of "Live Once, Only Once" that echo off the tall stone buildings. As we get closer, I can read the signs, printed in blood-red letters, mostly spelling out the same chant with variations like "Serial Killer," "Child Murderer," and "Die, Socrates."

At the front of the crowd, a paunchy, narrow-eyed, middle-aged man with thinning dark hair cups his hands to his mouth, trying to shout above the crowd. It works. As soon as the onlookers hear his voice, the yelling dies down.

"Where is the honor in killing a child? Where is the justice? Where are her rights? Doesn't the Second get a choice?" As we pass him, the group leader's voice fades, and the protestors' chants grow once again. As we reach the edge of the crowd, a dark-haired teenaged girl breaks free of the crowd, struggles over the police barricade, and rushes toward us, pulling something from her pocket.

"Bomb! Get down!"

The girl screams wildly, maniacally, and I freeze. Ellie jerks the chair back, and two guards jump in front of us. The one on the right fires his Artos at the child. A static-charged electric blue arc of light shoots through the air and hits its target with deadly accuracy. The girl collapses to the ground and convulses. A strangled cry rips from her throat.

The guards try to block my view, but around their shoulders, I can still see the girl thrashing weakly, heels drumming erratically against the cracked pavement. One of her small, pale hands opens, and a round silver disk rolls out and rests a few feet away.

More guards pour out of the surrounding buildings and force the crowd back using pulsating stun shields and waving their guns in the air. Carefully, one approaches the girl with a clear bomb containment cube and places it delicately over the object. He backs away about ten feet and then pushes a button on his wrist unit. The small disc ignites, and the box flashes with bright white light before filling with smoke. The would-be bomber lies motionless, her blank eyes staring into the distance. Her fingertips twitch on the dusty ground.

"Is she dead?" My heart seems to stop in my chest. Her empty eyes stare across the space at me. Through me.

"No, just knocked out. By the time they get done with her, though, she'll wish she was." The guard chuckles. A trio of officers from around the perimeter approach the girl and fasten sticky cuffs around her wrists and ankles. As they pick up her unresponsive body, several protestors from the crowd surge forward and attempt to break the blockade. The stun shields quickly quell their heroism, and they fall back, their more cowardly comrades catching them. After the protestors back down, the officers carry the girl roughly to the first of three jet-black police cruisers hovering in front of the museum and toss her into the back seat before slamming the door. Just like that, she's gone, as if she never existed.

Ellie jerks on the chair, a silent warning for me to keep quiet. She knows me too well. Ben leans against my legs, and my fingers find the scruff of his neck before instinctively scratching him right there in his favorite spot. His skin tenses up, and I can feel him kick out his back leg in that quick-fire way dogs have when you find their favorite spots.

The crowd is quieter now, more subdued, and the protestors disperse. Their leader disappears into the crowd. Maybe even they, the voice of the resistance, don't want to be associated with the arrest of a child terrorist. Yet, as I glance at the front of the crowd, the reporters are still there, cameras still filming. So much for my grand entrance. Largely forgotten, we make our way around the crowd to the wide, white cement steps leading to the museum's front doors. At the base of the stairs, I shift the tip of my cane to the ground and grip the armrests of the chair before forcing myself to my feet.

Eliot puts her hand on my shoulder. "Soc, stop. There's a ramp on the other side of the stairs."

"Let me do this at least, woman."

"Don't be foolish. You don't have to prove anything to anyone. The reporters aren't even watching you."

"It doesn't matter." I grit my teeth with the strain of forcing weakening muscles and bones to support my weight.

Pushing away from the chair, I force myself to remain upright, and after a while, I glance back at Eliot. "I walk just fine, see?" I snap my fingers and almost immediately Ben pushes his back against my hand. My fingers dig into his rough coat until I feel his harness then lift my left foot to the first step. Using Ben and my cane, I make it up a couple more steps before turning around. Eliot's still standing at the base of the stairs, leaning one hand on the wheelchair, a slight, exasperated smile on her face. "Are you coming?" I arch an eyebrow.

She shakes her head. "You're a pain in my ass. You know that, right?"

I grin. "And you wouldn't have it any other way."

Her sigh and following silence are her only response.

Two more guards stand at attention on either side of the main doors, and the one on the right nods in deference and leans over to open the door. I incline my head in thanks.

When we get through the door, I dig in my front pocket, pull out an old, braided black leather leash and snap it on Ben's collar. Eliot chuckles and shakes her head. She'd gotten me the latest gravity-based lead for our anniversary last year, but I've yet to take it out of the package. Damn technology. Hell if I can figure out how to use it half the time. Tried and true, that's what works best for me. Back in my first life, we called dogs like Ben service animals. That was back before modern medicine made blindness and deafness—as well as a host of other debilitating diseases—go the same route as leprosy and smallpox. Cancer too, if you got the vaccine. I never did. Hindsight, they say.

A white-haired man with a nametag that reads "Chief Curator Alfred Ruger" looks down at Ben and stiffens as though he's going to say something. I tighten my hand on the leash. *Go ahead. See how quickly I leave.* Ruger glances at Eliot, and she shakes her head in warning. He briefly closes his eyes and takes a breath. "Right this way, please."

"Thank you for inviting us," I reply as the door closes behind us, shutting out the crowd. There are reporters in here, too, and I have to keep from groaning. I am the guest of honor, I suppose.

"The pleasure is all ours." He bows deeply and gestures to the left. "Socrates and George Eliot, please, follow me."

Entering the museum, I always notice the vast space. The ceilings stretch up to meet enormous windows, flooding the entire room with light. White walls paint everything clean and fresh and emphasize the artwork displayed there. This is, of course, only the public portion of the museum. Most of the real action takes place far underground in the original History building.

A pale, hook-nosed tour guide in an almost colorless beige suit leads a group of red-and-gold-uniformed school children, probably from around the third grade, past one of the exhibits. Their teacher, an obviously enhanced redhead in her twenties, follows, balancing precariously on four-inch heels.

"You'd think that, in the last five hundred years, women would have finally chosen comfort over appearance," I murmur to Ellie.

"Hush, you," she admonishes. "You're a man. You wouldn't understand." She pushes me a little faster past the group.

"Technically, my dear..." I cast a grin in her direction. "So are—" She jerks the chair, cutting off my breath and further commentary.

Oblivious to our presence, or at least pretending to ignore us, the tour guide gives the children a history lesson. "After the Texans bombed the White House and the Pentagon during the Immigration War, there was nowhere for our government to go. They looked everywhere to find the best place to make their new base so they could finally defeat the rebels." A few of the kids glance at us, snicker, and point.

A young blond boy tugs on his teacher's arm. "Are those Firsts?"

"Yes, dear. Don't stare." The teacher takes the boy's hand and leads him away, but the child cranes his neck to gawk at us anyway.

"He's so old. What are they doing here?"

"Shhh. I don't know, Kellen. They probably have important business."

The tour guide's voice drones on. "After considering several locations around the country, President Hughes decided to use the abandoned Smithsonian Institution. He assessed all of the various buildings, demolished the ones in too much disrepair, renovated the ones they could use, and safely stored away most of our nation's treasures. After all, it would be a terrible thing if the Texans got their hands on something as important as our original Declaration of Independence. After the war, they reopened small exhibits in each of the buildings, so people could still see some of our most amazing historical artifacts."

We finally pass out of their range, and I let out a deep sigh. Even though that kid treated me more like an exhibit than an actual person, I'd much rather be over there than on my way to give a speech. You'd think I'd be used to public speaking by now, but no, that was Eliot's forte.

"Socrates?"

I turn back to Ruger. Shoot, I'd forgotten he was even there. "We're here, sirs."

We stop at one side of a small crowd of reporters in

31

front of a darkened, cordoned off hallway. Many of the parasites are so focused on the front of the building, probably itching to be out there where all the action is, that they don't even realize Ellie and I are here. Heaving a tired sigh, Ruger leads us to the front of the group where an old wooden podium sits.

He turns to face the semicircle of reporters standing around the mouth of the hallway. "Good afternoon. Welcome to the National Museum of American History. We are very pleased all of you could make it to this, the grand opening of our newest exhibit: The History of Firsts and the Release: Our Nation's Key to Peace. Joining us is our esteemed guest, the first of the Firsts, Socrates, and his companion, George Eliot." He steps back and bows deeply, gesturing for me to speak to the crowd. Ben and I take the podium. When I stop, he sits promptly at my side.

I glance back at Ellie to see if she's going to follow me, but she shakes her head.

"Ladies and gentlemen, thank you all for coming today. Project ReGenesis has been a cornerstone of our country for nearly five hundred years, and because of it, we have enjoyed a period of peace and prosperity unequalled in human history..." *Well, unless you're from Texas.* "We have prevented war and famine, kept our country in order, and created stability envied by our allies and enemies alike." I pause for effect. "There are nearly 13,000 of us around the world, but I was the first person to survive the procedure and unlock its key to success.

"Our work, however, is far from over. My brother, Leonardo, stands at the cusp of a breakthrough that will allow sustenance farming at the bottom of the ocean. My sister, Marie Curie, has just published her findings on a study reversing radioactive effects on the human body. We still have much to do, but with the help of the Smithsonian, we are pleased to bring some of our past to you."

One of the reporters, an older dark-skinned man with

white hair buzzed short in the front, but long in the back, wearing a silver and black suit, steps forward. Five hundred years, and some people still insist on wearing mullets. Never a good idea. "Is it true you've chosen a Second from Chesaning Farms?"

"Yes." *So much for keeping the leeches on topic.* Ellie moves behind me and takes my arm in support, squeezing it, keeping me grounded.

"Isn't that hypocritical?" *Damn. I'm going to need all the grounding I can get.*

"How so?"

He gestures at Eliot. "Your life mate isn't taking another Second. He has openly shown his disapproval of the entire program. You're even supporting a bill to free the Texans. Yet here you are, choosing a seventeen-year-old girl as your Second."

Ellie's not taking a Second? I turn to her. She has gone pale, and her mustache twitches.

"Socrates, I... I'm sorry. I should have told you sooner," she murmurs quietly, so only I can hear her.

The reporter's voice takes on a sarcastic edge. "You didn't know about George Eliot's decision? Don't you find that strange, considering you've lived together for two hundred years?"

Panic reaches out its filthy, slimy hand and chokes me. *Life without Ellie? No. I can't do it. I could never...* My hand tightens on Ben's harness, and he leans into me, offering his support. His long tail thumps against the back of my legs, and I feel myself relax a little. *Pretend like you already know, that's the best bet. The easiest way to get those vultures off your tail.* "Of course I knew about it." I smile widely. "And I fully support Eliot's decision in this matter. Even though we've given our heart and souls to each other, we are still two separate people, and we have our own paths to travel. I merely didn't realize she'd already made the announcement public knowledge."

Another reporter, a short, svelte, chestnut haired artificial beauty on impossibly high heels, steps forward, her surgically enhanced lips parting with excitement. "But you've got to feel something, sir. She *is* your mate, after all. I know if I were in your position, I'd try anything to change my mate's mind."

I twist my lips in a sarcastic semblance of a grin. "You're not me, though, so the question is moot. My personal beliefs are that every citizen has the right to make his or her own decision as to their mortality, even us Firsts."

Another reporter, young, big brown eyes, and a bust to match, aggressively pushes the woman aside. "What about your Second? Doesn't she get a choice? Is it because she's a Texan and not a free citizen?" What the hell? Don't they vet these people before they let them in? What is she, a Lifer plant? Wouldn't be the first time.

I smile pleasantly and shake my head. "Please refrain from topics that don't relate to this exhibit. We have much to do and less time to do it in."

"Just one more question, please." The first reporter raises his hand again to get my attention. I squint at him.

"What's your name?"

"Franklin Jarvis, sir."

"Fine, then, Mr. Jarvis. Get on with it."

"What about the protests? How do you feel about those? A girl out there tried to kill you, and reports say she almost succeeded."

At my side, Ruger wrings his hands, clearly in a panic. Ellie remains motionless, letting me fight my own battles. "I'm sorry, but I have no comment as to what may or may not have occurred outside. However, I can assure you, I'm quite alive and unharmed, and I thank you for your concern. This question and answer period is over."

I step back, and the reporter shouts something else, but I ignore him as I turn and face the darkened entry to the new exhibit. *Stupid reporters. They don't really care about the past. It's already been reported on, written about, done to death, so it's not really interesting any more. This article? It's just a fluff piece.* Above the hallway opening, "Our Immortal Past" is engraved. Ruger reiterates that there will be no more questions from the vultures waiting for more scraps.

Stretching across the hall, a long golden ribbon glints in the dilute sunlight. When Ruger joins us, he carries a large pair of gold scissors. With a flourish, he hands them to me. At about ten inches long, they're not particularly spectacular scissors, but just large enough that I will have to use both hands to open and shut them. Ellie steps forward, holding out her hand. I carefully pass her my cane, and she grips my elbow to keep me from falling.

After a couple tries and a bit of fumbling, I'm able to snip through the ribbon. My eyes follow the twin streaks of gold as they fall away from the blades and pool on the floor to either side of us.

"After you." Ruger gestures for us to enter the exhibit.

"Might as well get this over with." I grin at Ellie. She returns it with a smirk of her own.

We make our way down the dim hallway, a sharp contrast from the bright, natural light of the main museum. Waist-high displays line both sides, and spotlights illuminate portraits on the walls. The first display focuses on the scientific exploration into the procedure, back in the twenty-first century. Brightly lit, colorful dioramas break down the theory behind mind-uploading and the animal experiments that eventually led to the first voluntary human test subjects, most notably, death row inmates.

On the second long glass case, the engraved brass label on the front reads "Socrates, the first of the Firsts." In it, a variety of artifacts are displayed on dark blue velvet: an old leather wallet, a high school diploma, an ancient pocket watch. What do these matter? What is their significance? They have no relevance to the actual scientific procedure.

These items, save the diploma which has my name, could have belonged to anyone.

"They're supposed to make you look more like everyone else," Eliot whispers in my ear, as if reading my thoughts. She has always been good at that. "Normal."

I snort and pause at a wrinkled picture of a young child in a white baptismal gown. "What's that picture doing in there? Who is that?" I turn to her.

She raises her eyebrows. "What are you talking about? You know who that is."

"Is it me?" Where would they have found a baby picture? I don't think any of those exist anymore.

She narrows her eyes in concern and touches my hand. "Are you feeling all right?"

I huff and peer closer at the picture. "If that's not me, who is it? Why would they have a picture of someone else in a display case dedicated to me? They must have made a mistake." I try to look around her to catch Ruger's attention.

As I raise my hand to beckon him over, Ellie takes a step to the side, blocking my view. "Stop. It's no mistake. See?" She points to a display tag next to the picture.

I bend closer, straining to read the tiny text. "I can't see letters that small, woman. I'm five hundred years old, remember?"

Sadness enters her eyes, and she takes a deep breath. "That's your son, Adam."

"YOU'RE NOTHING."

mira

WHY ARE WE GOING TO the fields? I thought you had to go to the Manor today?" Max asks as we leave the apartment building the next morning.

"Because I want to, that's why. I thought you loved exploring. Besides, I don't have to go there until later. Would you rather stay in our stuffy apartment or go to school?"

He shakes his head emphatically. "School's dumb. The fields are boring. Let's go to the woods." He walks alongside me, scuffing at the dusty ground with his shoes.

I stop. "No. The woods are dangerous. We're not supposed to go in there."

Max turns to face me. "Why not? It's much more fun in the woods. There are trees, and the stream, and stuff to climb on, and bugs and chipmunks, and deer." He pauses. "Is Tanner in the fields today? Is that why we're going there?"

I turn away. Everyone's always trying to paint us in some stupid romantic light, but it's pretty hard to feel starry-eyed about someone who's like a brother to you. "I don't know, and it doesn't matter. That's where I want to go to think. If you'd rather, I can drop you off in the kitchens so you can stay with Mom. You know how much she loves it when you're with her at work." Maybe we *should* just skip the fields or at least walk through the woods so I don't get caught cutting corners, but I want to see Tanner as soon as possible. He is my best friend, after all, even if the way he looks at me is certainly not very brotherly.

"No, please don't." Max hurries to catch up as I turn around the side of the gleaming red barn.

We walk through the packed-dirt yard toward the wheat fields that stretch out for over three hundred acres behind the buildings. Ahead of us, the Chesanings' four girls lounge lazily in the grassy yard behind the plantation-style manor house. Alessa, the eldest at my age, has long, curly blond hair and a wicked smile. Vienna and Vanessa are boy-crazy twins and always dress alike and wear their dark brown hair in the latest fashions. The youngest, Gloria, is only a year older than Max. She is wearing a pair of VRI goggles on her head, one of the older models that don't interface with your brain, and reaches out, as if to touch something only she can see.

I grab Max's arm. "Let's just go back home."

"No, I want to go to the field. You promised." He digs his heels into the ground and refuses to move.

"I never promised anything. Besides, you didn't want to go just a minute ago. You're right. It's a bad idea. Let's do something else."

He jerks free and runs ahead a few steps.

"Max," I plead. "Come on." I hurry after him, but it's too late.

Alessa sees us and gets to her feet. She brushes off her totally impractical pink and white ball gown—as if her Prince Charming is going to ride up on a white steed and sweep her off her feet—and saunters toward us. Her artificially bright hair glows in the sun, and she looks about as real as the dolls that line the shelves in Gloria's bedroom. "What are you doing over here?" The disgust in her voice is undeniable.

Max freezes and darts his head down.

Scowling, I shove my brother behind me. "Nothing. I'm sorry. We shouldn't have come this way." I look down in deference when all I want to do is spit in her face. Even though that would be satisfying, at the very least she'd have me thrown in the box, at the worst, banished or executed. "Come on, Max. Let's go." I grab his arm again.

"Hey, I'm talking to you. Don't you walk away from me." I freeze, hating that I have to but doing it anyway. "You're the chosen one, right?"

I continue to look down without saying a word. Maybe if I'm boring enough, she'll lose interest and leave us alone.

"I'm talking to you, scum." My hands tighten, and Max whimpers. I immediately release my grip on his arm.

"Sorry, Max," I whisper and force myself to look away from Alessa. It takes everything in me not to rip that glowing yellow hair out of her head. I take a deep breath, then another. "We... we were just going to the fields. We didn't mean to come through here." I grind my teeth together, and in my head, I can see them turning to dust in my mouth, along with the words I wish I could say.

"That's right, Texan. You go *around* the yard, not through it. You don't deserve to set foot on our grass. You're not worthy." She stomps her ridiculously high-heeled shoe and steps forward, forcing me back.

Max wrenches his arm away from me and sticks his finger in Alessa's face. "You can't talk to my sister that way."

"What do we have here?" She leans down, putting her soft, dainty white hands on her surgically diminished waist. "Are you her little protector?" Max puffs his chest out with importance. "Do you know what's going to happen to your sister, little boy?" She pokes him.

Max nods. "She's going to be free. She'll get to travel and talk to people, and help her First."

"Free?" Alessa cackles. "That's a laugh." She leans

39

down even closer to Max, so close that her brightly painted lips are only a couple inches from his ear. "Let me tell you a secret, brat." He looks up at me, wild eyes begging for help, but I can't do anything. "Your sister is dead," she whispers.

"No!" Max rears away from her and pummels her with his little-boy fists. I can barely get my arm around him and wrench him away, he's suddenly that strong. Her words sink in. I'm going to die? *What if she's right? No, she can't be.*

Alessa jumps back, outraged. "You little brat. How dare you attack me? Is the truth too hard to handle? I could have you killed for hitting me. Don't you remember what happened the last time you messed with one of us?" She raises her hand.

I jump between them, and her hand cracks against my cheek as I take the slap meant for Max. My face burns. Anger turns my vision red, and I look down at the ground, grinding my teeth to keep from lashing out. It's better to do nothing. Anything I do can and will be used against not just me, but Max and my mom long after I'm gone.

She leans into my face, red and puffed up with self-importance. "It doesn't matter if you're Absolved or how important you think you are." Spittle from her mouth flecks onto my face, but I dare not wipe it away. "You're nothing. You'll never be anything. Don't forget that." She turns and stalks away.

My anger simmers, building up until it's all I can do not to wipe the sneer off of her face. "Max, come on."

For once, he doesn't argue.

WITHOUT BLAME

socrates

mY OLD LEATHER CHAIR CREAKS as I lean back and stare out at the stars through the bay window in my study. *How could I have missed it? What kind of man doesn't recognize his own son? He was my child, my Adam. How could I not know who he was?*

The shrill ringing of the phone startles me, and I nearly tip all the way back in my chair. *Be careful, old man. Wouldn't do to break a hip at this stage.*

Maggie, my housekeeper, knocks softly on the heavy oak door. "Sir, George Eliot's on the phone from the Smith, and she wants to talk to you."

"I'll take it in my office. Thank you." Using my hands for leverage, I force my weakening legs to bear my weight. The light briefly catches on the faded bar code marring the inside of my left wrist. It was Stephen's. Many have them removed. It's strongly encouraged as a healthy step toward starting a new incarnation, but I never have. Someone sacrificed his or her future so that I can help create a better one for everyone, and every time I see those strange lines, almost alien in color, I am reminded of that.

"Would you like some help?" Her brown eyes soften as she watches me struggle.

"No, my dear. I'm all right."

She nods, and her weather-lined face wrinkles into an exasperated smile. After nearly forty years of service, she knows when I'm lying. Ben stretches, gets up, and trots to my side, leaning against me until I grab his harness. He knows, too.

"Good boy." His tail thumps, and I dig my crooked hands into his thick coat.

My office is decorated much like the rest of the house with dark, antique wood-paneled walls and rich, thick curtains. Glowing lights gleam from recessed ports along the walls and ceiling. With a simple voice command, screens silently slide down from the ceiling, and a high-powered console rises from a desk made to resemble aged teak.

I lower myself into a white leather chair that predates my aged body by a good one hundred and fifty years. My knees protest with a loud, cracking sound. I pick up the old-fashioned handset.

"Hello?"

"Socrates? How are you feeling?" Eliot's voice is anxious; we haven't talked since the exhibit opened.

"Better, now that I'm home." I exhale and force myself to relax, rolling my neck, hearing the crack of old bones protesting.

"You know, if you'd just gotten the vaccine like everyone else, you would be just fine."

"I know, I know, but as foolish as it sounds, I don't trust the new technologies."

"You were a product of new technology once, my love. Back then, you were the apple of the scientific community's eye. Of course there wasn't a cure for cancer back then. But now, well, everyone gets one, Soc. It would have saved you all this trouble." She's frustrated, and I don't blame her. I tend to be a stubborn old man. "Demosthenes asked me if you were going to request a med-ex permit."

"A Medical Exemption Permit? For what, chemotherapy? You know they made that illegal over a hundred years ago.

42

Besides, doctors never grant those if you're over eighty. It costs more for the treatment than to take a new body. Or, well, die if you're not a First. Most people don't have much working use left after that age. At any rate, it's too late now. At my age, the doctors would just tell me to take a Second anyway, which is what I'm going to do. No use fixing the old body if there's a newer, upgraded model."

"I thought they gave you at least six months?"

"They did. I think I'm just feeling my age. Maybe I'm just cranky, finally going crazy after all these years. There are no rules, no medical textbooks for what people should be like, mentally, at my age."

Silence. "It's all right to be angry at yourself for what happened at the museum." Her voice is a quiet hum over the suddenly echoing telephone line.

I shake my head, the abrupt motion setting off more aches and pains. "I thought we were talking about the cancer?" She doesn't respond. "Besides, what kind of father doesn't recognize his own son, Eliot?"

"A father who hasn't seen his child for over four hundred years."

"That's no excuse! If nothing else, heavens, I lived in his body for longer than he did. I looked in the mirror and saw his face every day for nearly seventy years. Every. Single. Day. That face should have been as recognizable as my own."

"It was an honest mistake, my love. I don't think anyone else noticed."

I open the top drawer of my desk and pull out a pair of old, metal dog tags and run my fingers over their softened edges.

"It was merely a terrible shock. You haven't been feeling well, and you didn't expect to see anything like that in the museum." Eliot tries to sooth me, and if she were here, I imagine she'd be stroking my hair or holding me loosely in her arms.

I clear my throat. "That still doesn't make it right. He was my son. My first child. How could I forget him?" I rub my thumb in a circle around the face. God, five hundred years later and she still has the power to take my breath away.

"I wouldn't worry too much, my dear. It's probably a combination of the stress and your illness."

With a sigh, I slip the dog tags back into my drawer. "Next, you'll say I'm just getting old."

"You're only eighty-eight. That's hardly prehistoric. Besides, no one can be expected to remember everything."

"When you measure time by the number of lives you've started over, of course eighty-eight isn't a lot." I chuckle, the raspy sound deep and gritty even to my own ears. "If this was my first eighty-eight, I'd hardly be a toddler. But it's not. And it's not just his face that I've lost, either. Somewhere deep inside of me, I know that Adam was an amazing child, but I couldn't give you three reasons why. I can't tell you what his first words were, or when he learned to walk, or even what he wanted to be when he grew up. That picture there, that one little picture in the museum, is one of only two photographs that still exist from my first life, and I didn't even realize it was missing. I even probably took the damn thing, and I didn't remember it existed until I saw it in that display."

On the other end of the line, I imagine Ellie biting her bottom lip, a habit she's had since I married her the first time. "Maybe." She pauses, choosing her words carefully. "You're just cutting it too close. Perhaps you should have picked a Second earlier. The doctors said the drugs can only slow down the disease, not stop it, and some might have negative side effects on your mind."

"I've cut it close before with no ill effects. Remember? That's what we all used to do. It's only a recent trend to choose Seconds so early. We always used to wait until the last minute before picking a new body, and you know me,

I refuse to take the first Second I see. It's got to be the right one."

"It's always been about chemistry with you, Soc." She chuckles. "You know it doesn't really matter, right?"

"I know." I pause. "But for some reason, it's important to me that we click."

"Always the romantic one. When are you heading back to Washington?" Maggie pokes her head in and mimics drinking a cup of coffee. I nod, so she knows I'd like one, too. I don't even have to tell her what I'd like in it—nothing—because she knows me so well.

My laugh has an empty, hollow sound, and I slowly lean forward so I'm sitting upright again. My old back doesn't like that very much. Hell, most of me doesn't like moving, period. At least my leather chair is as comfortable as eighty years spent molding to the same backside can render it. "No sooner than necessary. It's nice to be home in Santa Fe. I've been travelling so much I've barely had any time to relax."

"You deserve it. The mountains have always been a refuge for you. A balm for your soul. And with the bill coming up—"

"I've had a lot on my mind, is that what you're implying? I know you want it to pass, Ellie. That's the main reason I'm supporting it." Maggie brings me a steaming cup of coffee, brewed the old-fashioned way, of course, and sets it on a small wooden coaster she's picked up from another spot on my cluttered desk. After setting it down, she waits for me to tell her if I need anything else, and I shake my head. She bows her head—I never could train her out of that habit—and leaves the way she came. She's surprisingly quiet for a woman of her age and girth.

"What, you don't think it's the right thing to do? Don't you think the Texans have been imprisoned long enough?"

I take a sip of coffee barely cool enough to drink, while Ellie continues her tirade.

"You, of all people, should know that what the government is doing is wrong. What they've done in the past is wrong. If something doesn't change, what they will do in the future will be worse."

"Now you sound like a Lifer," I quip, unable to help myself. Her silence is my answer.

"Do you want me to come home, or would you rather I wait for you in D.C.?" I can always tell she's angry with me when her voice becomes formal, stone cold and emotionless.

"Might as well wait there. No sense teleporting over here if you're just going to go back anyway in a few days." I let my eyes half close, and I start to drift away on the warmth of the coffee. Maybe Maggie slipped something in it to help me sleep. It wouldn't be the first time.

"What if I want to see you? Talk to you?" Her voice grows deeper, huskier. I have to chuckle.

"About what? There's nothing you haven't seen a million times before."

"There's always something new with you, Soc."

"Aren't you teaching? I thought the new semester started soon?" *Did she mention this before?* I mentally scratch my head. *No, I would remember her talking about it.*

"I decided to take a sabbatical. Maybe I'll take a cue from you and write a book." She pauses, but when I let the silence stretch too long, she sighs. "Okay, fine. The board and I came to the decision that it would be mutually beneficial if I took the spring term off." In her silence, her sadness is nearly palpable. But there's something else, too, something she's not telling me.

"Is this in regard to your decision to leave the program?"

"Yes, no. I don't know. Don't worry about it. You have more important things going on."

"That's where you're wrong, my dear. You've been the most important person in my lives since we met."

"Flattery can't change my mind. You know that, right?"

"But—"

46

She cuts me off. "Let me explain, please."

"I'm listening." I steeple my fingers in front of me.

"When Project ReGenesis started, it was portrayed as a way for a select few to live forever so that their talents wouldn't die when they did. It was a noble calling. Five hundred years later, where are we now? What gifts have I really given the world? Sure, I was the first female president, but there have been six since, and most of them much better candidates than I ever was. Out of all of them, only one took a Second, and she only chose one more lifetime."

"Stop selling yourself short. Because of you, we were able to build the first moon space station. You paved the way for space travel and exploration for the next two hundred years, Ellie. That's definitely an achievement."

"You mean the resort for the rich and famous?" she retorts.

"It's not your fault NASA ran out of funding. That war took a lot out of us. After it was over, the government had to put all of their money into rebuilding." Images like old-fashioned snapshots blur through my mind. Ruins, rubble, bodies strewn across the ground. Dust streaked with blood on a child's brow as he sprawls, unmoving, on the ground. Me, a different me, younger with burnt auburn hair, reaching down, hands shaking, to check his pulse, but there's nothing there. I never even learned his name. I should have.

"Well, they did a piss-poor job of it."

"The rebels did a lot of damage." The dead boy's hand is curled in a fist that will never open. His fingers will never again reach out to graze a blade of grass or cup a handful of water from a stream for a mid-adventure drink.

"They weren't the only ones. Our side killed innocents, too." The boy's hand fades away. In his place, I see a line of kids, baking under a white-hot sun, waiting to see if any of them would be chosen to die. A little boy, near the end, fidgeting with his new tattoo. His sister trying to protect him, even now.

"Neither side in any war is without blame."

"Honestly Soc, I don't even know why we're having this conversation. It doesn't really matter. None of the scientific breakthroughs, decisions I've influenced, or treaties I've written, negate the fact that I've killed four kids. Three girls and one boy. Dead, all because I wanted to live forever."

"Isn't that what we all want? Besides—" My voice takes on a sullen tone, audible even to me. "It didn't seem to bother you the last time."

She pauses, and I imagine her face flushing, the warm tone of her skin turning a darker, deeper red. "Last time was different."

"How so? What changed in thirty years that didn't in the last two hundred?"

Silence. "I just... I just can't do it any more, Socrates. Please don't ask me again."

"I'm sorry." I take a deep breath and close my eyes. "I guess I'm just trying to understand. I know we haven't been as close as we used to be, with our busy schedules and all, but I never thought you'd want to leave the program. That you'd want to leave me."

She pauses for so long I wonder if the connection's been lost, even though that's supposedly not possible with today's technology. "I suppose I just don't want to do this again, get attached to people, watch them get old and die while I live and move on. I can't take it anymore," she whispers. I cram the phone to my ear to catch every word.

"So you're just going to stop, then? Live a normal life and then die?"

"Something like that, except for the normal part. Yale pretty much owns me, since they paid for my last procedure. But you get the gist of it. I'm done. It's time to let a new generation, one not held back by the past, have a shot."

HALFWAY THERE

mira

tAKE A DEEP BREATH, MIRA. *You can do this. He's just another teacher. It's not as if you're a complete idiot.* I twirl the thin ivory porcelain cup around in my hand. It's almost completely full. Pale blue birds dance along the outer rim, and if I turn the cup fast enough, they fly.

Gerald, the Chesanings' butler, clears his throat, and I jump, almost dropping the teacup, sloshing the watery liquid over the side. Swallowing my frazzled nerves, I carefully set the cup on the end table next to my chair.

Exhaling slowly, I dart a glance at Gerald, and he scowls at me over his puffy, chipmunk cheeks and heavy hooded eyes. In his starched black and white suit, he sits as stiffly as the flightless birds we read about in school. He'd probably have killed me for wasting tea if Socrates hadn't picked me as his Second. Maybe my new position does have some perks. My eyes stray back to the cup as a thin, clear ring spreads slowly along the white cloth.

"He's here." Gerald's deep voice is the kind that puts kids to sleep.

I jump from my seat. The chair wobbles behind me, and I quickly snake a hand back so it doesn't fall over. Gerald rolls his eyes. I guess I'm making all sorts of good impressions today.

The man who must be my teacher barely fits through the doorway, and I recognize him as one of the guys who stood beside Socrates the day I was chosen. He huffs and pants, red-faced, with thinning, shoulder-length sweat-slicked carrot-colored hair plastered to his head. Cosmetic gold-rimmed glasses encircle his beady brown eyes, and he squints as he openly inspects me. He's wearing an old-fashioned khaki-colored suit with damp stains around the collar and beneath his arms. I've always wondered why, with the technology to genetically correct vision and hearing problems, they haven't done something about sweat, maybe even make it smell better if they can't stop it completely, but I guess that's low on their priority list. He carries a paper-thin tablet in one hand, and I'm surprised he doesn't drop it with all the sweat dripping off of him.

"You must be Mira." His translucent lips pull into a fake smile. "I am Mr. Flannigan, your teacher from Washington. My job is to get you ready to go to Washington. I will teach you proper etiquette for your interview and the acceptance banquet, as well as the importance of basic manners in general. You see, life in our nation's capital is very different from life here at your little farm. There are important customs and traditions that must be adhered to. Most of all, I will teach you *not* to embarrass Socrates." He looks me up and down. "Heaven help me."

I smooth the palms of my hands flat against my pants.

He narrows his eyes at me. "Is there a problem?"

"Not at all, sir." I grit my teeth. "It's just that my mother taught me that if I don't have anything nice to say, I shouldn't say anything at all."

"Is that so?" A faint smile curves his lips. I purse my lips. "Good." He nods. "You're halfway there already."

Now it's my turn to smile. Maybe he's not so bad, after all.

"Do you have any questions?"

"Now that I'm Absolved, will I get my own last name?"

He looks at me in surprise. "What do you mean, girl?"

"Well, as Texans, we take the name of our farm, but you people, you get your own last names. Do I get one now?"

He scratches his head. "I don't know. That... that's never come up before. I'll have to talk to Socrates." He makes a note on his tablet.

"Umm, I was also wondering what my job will be, exactly. I mean, there are so many rumors going around, but in school they teach us something totally different."

Mr. Flannigan grunts and lowers his sweaty bulk into one of the spindly wicker chairs, which creaks under his weight. I eye his chair doubtfully as I sit down in the other one.

"What exactly have you been told?" he asks, avoiding my question.

"Well, our teachers say we go and learn from our Firsts, so that when they die, we get to take over where they left off, so that their knowledge can be preserved for another lifetime. That's why they have a Release ceremony, so we're released from our past lives and can start our future. We'll be making history." A shadow crosses his face, and his thin mouth presses into an even thinner line.

"Is that so?"

"Yes, but I heard something different. Today Alessa, the Chesanings' daughter, told my brother I was going to die."

Mr. Flannigan shakes his head. "And you believed her?"

"I... I don't know. I mean, they wouldn't do that, right?"

He pauses. "Look at it this way. Do you implicitly trust the source of your information?" I shake my head. "Well, there you go. Your teachers would never intentionally lie to you, would they?" I shake my head again, slower this time. "Good. There you have it. Hold fast onto what you've learned throughout your entire life, not the heresy of a spoiled little rich girl."

"But—"

"No buts, just... just believe what your teachers told you, and you'll be fine." Why does he look like he's in pain when he says that?

A thought hits me. "Are you a First?"

Mr. Flannigan looks shocked at first, then laughs, a deep guttural sound like he's never heard anything funnier before in his life. "Me? No, of course not." What's that in his voice? It's like he thinks I'm crazy for asking.

"Why not? You're a teacher, right?"

He shakes his head and folds his hands on his ample stomach. "Much in the same way as your teacher here is. My role is so limited, being a First is... different."

"What do you mean?"

"Well." He looks stuck for a minute, like he can't really find the words. "Firsts are supposed to... they're supposed to lead the world, help pass on useful knowledge and information that would be lost without them."

"So what's Mr. Socrates going to do, teach me all this before he dies?"

Mr. Flannigan tilts his head on his nonexistent neck, like a fat chicken, thinking about going after a worm. "Yes, that's it. But I can't tell you any more. It's not my job. My position is merely to make you more acceptable to those you'll meet in Washington. I'm not... permitted to speak about anything else."

Now it's my turn to look confused. "Why not? I mean, it's not some big secret, is it?"

He hesitates. "No, of course not. However, the law states that the only one who can give you that information, besides the President himself, is your First, Socrates. You'll have to ask him, yourself."

I let out a huff of frustration. "When will I see him next?"

"I'm glad you asked." He smiles. "In three days you'll leave this farm forever. You'll be heading to Washington for a thorough physical evaluation and to be vaccinated."

"Against what?"

"Everything, silly girl. We can't have you getting sick now that you're chosen, can we? There are so many diseases out there in developing countries that modern medicine hasn't been able to cure yet."

"Why bother? We were hit last year by a pretty nasty bug, and no one in my family got sick. Obviously, I'm immune."

"One thing I can tell you is that, in your new position, you'll be travelling around the world. You'll be exposed to different cultures and, therefore, a wide variety of diseases from countries less advanced than ours."

"So why don't all of us get vaccinated?"

Flannigan shrugs. "There are limited quantities of the more common vaccines from what I understand, and there are so many of you."

"So what you're saying is that we're expendable."

He shakes his head. "Of course not. The vaccine is also expensive, and since your people don't travel, the government deemed it unnecessary."

I stand up and pace between the chair and the window. "Kids die, Mr. Flannigan. Every few years, some new disease hits us and kills a few of the younger or sicker ones, then disappears. I know we're servants, but almost all of the ones who die are just little kids. Babies in diapers. If they vaccinated us like the free citizens, none of that would happen."

He opens his mouth, like he's about to agree with me, then stops.

I turn and face him, hands on my hips. "You talk about Socrates like he's this all-powerful guy, like the President." It's a statement, not a question, but Mr. Flannigan treats it as such.

"Yes, he's the first of the Firsts, the oldest of them all."

I shake my head. "I don't know what that means, but if he's as great as you make him out to be, he can do this. He can get his hands on some of that medication."

"The vaccine?"

53

"Yes. I want enough for all of them. For any disease that might strike the farm. Especially now that I know diseases can be prevented." I give him the evil eye as I watch his lips stretch. He curtly nods. "They deserve to be safe."

He settles back in his chair, a faint respect in his eyes. "I don't know if that's possible, or whether you're in any position to make demands, but I'll ask him." He holds up his hands when I open my mouth to speak, to tell him that asking isn't good enough when kids are dying every few years. "You have to understand, Mira, I can't make any guarantees, okay?"

"All right. I understand."

"Do you have any other questions?"

I narrow my eyes at him, at his begrudgingly respectful tone, and bite my bottom lip. "Out with it, girl, what else is bothering you?"

"Nothing..." He raises his eyebrows at me. "Okay, fine. But I'm warning you, it's stupid."

He lets out a hollow laugh. "Duly noted," he says, wryly.

"Why am I still here?" My voice is quiet and sounds young, more like Max's than mine.

"What do you mean?"

"When my cousin was picked, he left immediately." I shift in my chair, crossing my legs then uncrossing them.

Mr. Flannigan looks out the window. "Well, Socrates likes to give his Seconds time to say goodbye to their families, since they'll never see them again." I can feel the blood drain from my face. "Surely you knew that." I shake my head, for once without words. "Your cousin has been gone what, a couple years, right?" I nod. "Then, you've noticed that he hasn't returned, nor will he ever. It's against the law for a Second to return home after being Absolved." His eyes seem sad, creased at the edges.

"Why?"

Flannigan shrugs. "It's the law, and it's not my place to question it."

He's lying. I can feel it. But why? What good reason could he possibly have to keep this from me?

He clears his throat. "Regardless of that, you will be able to affect a great change as Socrates's Second that you would never be able to even hope to achieve living here on this farm." Flannigan touches the thin computer and grimaces. "You'll have to straighten up, Mira, from what I've seen here." He arches his eyebrows at me over the edge of his glasses. "And according to your file..." He waves the thin tablet at me, and in my mind, I see it arcing through the air as he loses his slippery grip. "You could cause quite a bit of trouble once you get to Washington, and Socrates doesn't need that."

I feel myself flush. How would he like if I looked up his past and all of his faults? "I'm not that bad."

Another faint grin touches his lips. "Let's start on the first page." He peers down at the screen. "Leaving the farm without permission. A few times, in fact. Arguing with your teacher. Leaving the farm again." He looks up at me again. "Looks like you take your little trips quite often. Where do you go?"

I lift my shoulders before dropping them as if it doesn't matter. "Sometimes I just need to get away. We kind of live in each other's pockets here."

"Let's see. Here's one for talking back to a supervisor."

"He was trying to feel me up! This is ridiculous. I can't believe they wrote that in there. The man had a serious thing for us girls. I'm glad he's gone."

"What happened to him?" His face is impassive, but there is a dangerous glint in his eyes that I hadn't seen before.

"Shipped off to do construction at another farm." I smile with satisfaction. At least that disaster ended rather well, for our farm at any rate. Now he's someone else's problem.

He looks down at the list again. "Skipping a visit and getting three days isolation?" He waits for me to say more, but I don't elaborate. "Why did you do that?"

"It's a long story."

He waits, fingers strumming on his thick, meaty thigh.

I sigh, letting all my breath out in a big whoosh before smoothing my hands on my pants again. A nervous twitch. "All right, fine. Max was caught watching the news, and Alessa turned him in. But Gloria told him to come with them into the house and watch it with them—"

"Max is your brother, right? How old is he?"

"He just turned five."

Mr. Flannigan nods. "And Alessa and Gloria are...?"

"Spoiled little rich girls," I say, borrowing his earlier words. I smooth my palms on my pants so I have something to do other than relive that day.

His lips twitch. "Ah yes, and watching any sort of video broadcast is strictly prohibited, so he was punished. What did they do to him?"

"He got one day in the box."

"The box?"

"It's a metal box with a slot for food capsules and water tablets because they don't let you eat or drink anything while you're in there, and a hole in the corner for you to go... well, you know what I mean. And there are three small holes in the bottom on one side for fresh air. That's it. It's torture, especially for a little kid, and Max was only four."

"Was it worth skipping the visit to stay with him?"

I nod. "I'd do it again in a heartbeat. He didn't do it on purpose. Like I said, they invited him in there. He never would have gone into the manor on his own. They did it to be mean."

"Hmmm." He sets the tablet on the end table, far away from my cup of tea and steeples his thick fingers before him, as if contemplating my words.

"Besides, who throws a four-year-old kid in a six-by-four metal cell anyway? The only light comes from those little holes in the bottom. I spent the whole day talking to him through those air holes so he wouldn't be alone."

Flannigan raises his eyebrows. "So then they sentenced you to the box, for helping him."

"Yes, though I didn't make him stay with me. He tried, but I made him go home at night. He tried feeding me through the little holes but..." I smile, remembering the mash of composite toast, bugs (because that's what people in the olden days ate, Max had said, proud of himself for knowing that), and twigs he'd tried to force in there. It wasn't pretty. Nor did it smell especially pleasant.

"Where were your parents?"

"My mom was working, and my dad's dead." I spit out the words as if they were venom sucked from a snake bite. "She didn't know until after it happened. As the oldest child, I'm supposed to take care of Max, get him ready for school, make sure he doesn't screw around, that sort of thing."

"I see. Was that your greatest infraction?"

I look away, the old anger slowly leeching from my system. "According to the Chesanings, yes."

A faint smile tugs at the corner of his lips.

What is this guy's deal? Is it his job to dig through my past and find reasons why I'm not qualified? Is that it? Is he looking for reasons to kick me out of the program? Hope kindles deep inside me. Maybe everything isn't so hopeless, after all. "Are you going to tell Socrates about all this?"

Flannigan shrugs. "He does expect an update after I've met you."

"Great. Is he going to reject me?"

"Is that what you want?"

"Yes!"

He arches his eyebrows. Apparently that wasn't the response he expected. "You're very candid about this. Most Seconds jump at the chance to serve their country in this manner."

I bite my bottom lip. *Am I doing the right thing? I don't*

57

even know him, so I'll give him the safe answer. "I just... I don't want to leave the farm. I want to stay here with my mom and brother. With Tanner. It's the only place I've ever known." Maybe if I tell him I was responsible for the death of my little sister, he'll let me go. *Is it worth it? No, I can't.*

"That's perfectly understandable. I don't think you have anything to worry about. Socrates is not like the other Firsts. He does things a bit differently. I expect he'll take this information in stride, but I doubt it'll alter his decision."

Gerald knocks on the door. "Mr. Flannigan, sir?"

"Yes, is there something I can help you with?"

"No sir, but there's a call for you from the press secretary at the Smith. He wants more information regarding the Second's arrival. Do you have time to take the call?"

"Certainly, Gerald. Thank you." Flannigan glances at me. "You may leave now. I think I've learned quite a bit from our first day together." He gets up and strides from the room as fast as his short little legs can carry him.

NOTHING LEFT TO LOSE

socrates

i HUNCH OVER THE DESK IN my study, fingers tapping out the next words to my newest book, *Life Throughout the Ages,* on my ancient keyboard. Another antique, just like me. The manuscript contains vignettes describing important historical events from the point-of-view of people who lived through them and are still here to talk about it. Honestly, if it sells more than a handful of copies to people other than university patrons or other Firsts, I'll be impressed. The common man doesn't care much for what he can't see, feel, or experience, but the university asked me to write a book, so I tap away.

The phone rings, and I pick it up, hand shaking. "Hello?"

"Socrates, it's me, Edward."

"My dear friend." I smile and lean back in my chair. "To what honor can I attribute a call at..." I look at the grandfather clock tick-tocking in the corner of the room, "... ten thirty-two in the evening?"

"You wanted an update. Don't get snippy with me, either. I can tell you're still awake."

"You're quite right. How did the first day go?"

"She's trouble, that one. Defensive and making demands already."

Sitting up straighter in my chair, I chuckle. "What could she possibly want? She's already Absolved."

"Vaccines. For diseases that sweep through the farms every few years. Do you know anything about this?" He sounds angry. His words' staccato notes clang in my ears.

I pause, and it must be too long, because Edward clears his throat. "Socrates? Are you still there?"

"She'll be vaccinated when she gets to the Smith." Does he notice my slip-up? My avoidance of his question?

I hear him sigh over the line, as if I have truly betrayed him by not telling him the truth. "Not for her, for her family and everyone else at the farm."

"Hmm..."

"And you didn't know anything about this?" He doesn't believe me. I can tell it in his voice.

"I've heard rumors..." I lean back in my chair. "Of experiments. Ways to lessen the population crush by testing new disease combinations and mutations on the farms. Just like they did during the Immigration War."

"I had no idea." His words are measured and even, as if he's not sure he believes me or not. I don't blame him. Anyone who spends years teaching kids who've been picked to die must have a healthy set of mental walls.

My chuckle dies shortly after leaving my lips. "Why would you? You weren't there."

"Are you going to do anything about it?"

"About what? All we have is a disease that mutates and hits farms randomly across the country. Not exactly sensational news or a huge government cover-up, here."

"I don't know, but it seems you should do something." He sounds frustrated, his voice gravelly. "Report it, perhaps?"

"To whom? Let's just entertain your government conspiracy theory for a moment. Who would I report it to? The media? They're controlled by the government. The most I can do is give the girl the vaccinations."

Silence reigns on the other end of the line, so I take the opportunity to save the manuscript file. "Look Edward, I know you're frustrated. Believe me, I'd tell you more if I could, but I can't. I don't have any proof, so I'd appreciate you not mentioning it to anyone else, if you don't mind."

Edward chuckles. "I don't think you have to worry about that, Socrates. And thank you for the vaccines. I know your girl will appreciate it."

I smile and pull open the top drawer on my desk, withdrawing a worn, red pen with most of the silver rim and cap rubbed down to the plastic. Holding its cool plastic shell, I push the button on the top a couple times. Still works. Well, if they still made ink for it, it would. "How is everything else at the farm?"

"Quiet. Not at all like Washington. Even all the way out here, I heard about the incident at the Smith. Are you all right?"

I stand up, knees creaking under my weight. "Of course. You honestly think Eliot would let anything happen to me?"

Edward chuckles. "She's better protection than the military."

"You've got that right. If I even sneeze wrong she tries to bundle me into bed. Speaking of which, it is getting late, and she'll have my head if I stay up too much longer, and I know Maggie will tell on me the first chance she gets."

Edward chuckles. "Anything else?"

"Just more rebel activity. They sure have been making their presence known. Shut down a shipping yard east of Boston. Blew up the transport pods, but no one was killed, so that's a plus."

He pauses for a second too long. "Do you think there is anything I should be worried about? You only picked the girl yesterday, so they've hardly had time to mobilize."

"You never know. We've all seen the propaganda. They could be anywhere, anyone, remember? Just to be safe, let's put a few guards in the forest surrounding the farm."

"Do you think they'll try something?"

I pick up the pen and put it back in the drawer, just to be safe. It is, after all, the only real pen I have left. "Don't underestimate people with nothing left to lose. They're the most dangerous of all."

After Edward hangs up, the pain in my head and my bones returns with a vengeance. With thick, twisted fingers, I fumble for the bottle of pain pills and twist open the cap. Another old-fashioned relic. Maybe I should get those painkiller implants Eliot mentioned. The top of the bottle skitters across the top of my desk, and I shake out a few pills. How many? Two? Three? Doesn't matter. All that matters is relief.

"I THOUGHT YOU LOVED ME."

mira

ROUGH WOOD SCRATCHES MY ARMS as I lean over the stall railing next to the old metal shipping crate. The terrified fox inside bares its teeth and hisses. Realizing I'm not going anywhere, it flattens itself, shrinking into the afternoon shadows. Except for its blinking, black beady eyes, I can't even see it.

"It's okay," I whisper. "I'm not going to hurt you." It growls again, a low noise rising up in the barn's stillness. *It's a wild animal, you idiot, of course it can't understand you.*

I kneel down in the dusty, unused stall next to the cage, letting the dim sunlight from the open barn door bathe the cage. In the faded space between light and dark, the poor creature's sides heave with terror. Its ribs stick out against a tattered, patchy hide. It looks awful, not at all like the softly furred plump foxes the Chesanings usually hunt.

Slowly, I pull a small paper-wrapped package from my pocket and open it. Then, even more carefully, I take out a piece of brownish-gray composite meat I saved from my breakfast and drop little bits of it through the bars. It tastes only marginally better than the toast. Hopefully the fox won't care. After a few seconds, its shiny coal-black nose twitches. "Yeah, I know, it doesn't smell the greatest either, but it's the best I can do." I back away from the stall.

Behind me, there's a crackling, shuffling noise, the kind that only comes when someone walks on fresh straw. I jump and spin around. Nothing. As my heart beats faster than the fox's, a familiar shape steps out of the shadows by the back door to the barn. "Tanner, what are you doing here?" I gasp, my breath coming out in a short burst. *What's wrong with me? It's only Tanner. I've known him my whole life.* I grin nervously, trying to get rid of my panic. *What's he doing here? Is he looking for me? He should be out in the fields, working.* I rub my palms on my pants and try to straighten my uniform, smearing dirt and dust from the barn in long streaks.

Sunlight glances off his face and gives him a golden red halo. He's dressed in the dark brown coverall all the field workers wear and holds a worn, green horse lead in one hand. His eyes, normally sparkling with light and easy laughter, are cold and stony, like a stranger's. "Spartacus stepped in a gopher hole, sprained his ankle. I'm bringing Tomas out to take his place. What are *you* doing out here? Shouldn't you be in the Manor, working with that teacher they sent from Washington? It's dangerous for you to be out here alone." He holds himself stiffly, watching my reaction. As if he doesn't know me anymore.

"Nothing," I say, but then I glance back at the stall. Tanner's eyes follow my gaze. When I look back at him, I feel myself standing up straighter, taller. I don't have anything to be ashamed of. I'm not doing anything wrong... well, okay, I probably am, but this is such a minor thing, it's almost non-existent. "It's not like I'm out in the woods, Tanner, this is the barn. I'm perfectly safe out here."

He shakes his head. "Not all danger walks on four legs, Mir."

"Present company included?" I quip.

A grin tugs at the corners of his mouth. He strolls over to me, only to stop a couple feet away, as if there's some invisible wall standing tall and firm between us.

Tears burn the back of my eyes. "Tanner," I whisper. The name I've said a thousand times before sounds almost foreign on my lips, as if it belongs to a stranger.

Even dusty from half a day in the fields with dirt streaking his temple and sweat staining his collar, Tanner is still the most handsome guy at the farm. *Oh Tanner, I'm never going to see you again. I'm so sorry.* My breath catches in my throat, and a feeling strangely like the beginning of a sob catches up to me. *No, I can't.* Lip quivering, I blink away more tears. *Relax Mira. Look at Tanner, does he look upset?* That's the part that shakes me the most. He's just standing there, like one of the bleached white columns on the Manor house, like it doesn't matter. The only way I can tell he's even bothered the least is that his hands clench into tight fists at his sides, his knuckles turning white.

Leaning back against the stall door, I try to act relaxed. "Nothing, I was just feeding the fox. I thought it might be getting hungry."

"It doesn't matter, you know that, right? Those hunts are brutal. It's not like it's going to get out of this alive." The way he says it is mocking, as if there's more to it than just a fox, and he jams his fists, including the one holding the horse lead, into his deep pockets.

"It's not right."

"No, it's not. Capturing something so beautiful just to kill it." He looks at me this time, and I get this strange feeling he's not talking about the fox anymore.

Before I can ask him about that, understanding dawns in me. "Is that why it looks so terrible? It's wild-caught?" I glance back at the cage, but all I can see are two glinting, beady eyes.

"Yep. I heard Chesaning telling one of the guys how

someone from Laurel trapped it. The boss paid about half as much as they would for a captive bred one, on account of it being so rough-looking. I guess they're just going to let the dogs have it after they kill it. It's not like the pelt's worth anything."

"But... but that's against the law."

Tanner raises an eyebrow, a sardonic grin curving his lips. "Really, Mir? This is nothing compared to what they're doing to you, and here you are, worried about a stupid fox?"

I turn away so Tanner won't see the way my cheeks turn red with shame. "It's not just a fox, Tan. It's a living, breathing creature. It's not right, and you know it." Already, I can hear my gears turning. The urge to help this creature is so strong I yearn to ask Tan for help. At one point in time, not that long ago, he would have been right by my side. Now, I'm not so sure.

"So I guess that makes you just a girl, then, right?" His breath whispers the words against the back of my neck a second before his fingers trace my arm. Gently, almost as if I'm the wild animal, he takes my shoulder and turns me around, taking me in his arms. "I'm sorry, Mir, really. I don't have any right to snap at you. None of this is your fault."

I look up at him just as his lips gently touch mine. "Tanner," I whisper, and freeze—the same kind of motionlessness that overcomes a deer when I startle one at the edge of the fields or in the playground. I press my body against his, anxious to feel something, anything but this fear I've felt since being chosen. But there's nothing except the warmth of his lips on mine and a sudden chill when he steps away.

"What have you gotten yourself into?" he murmurs, his lips a breath apart from mine.

I pull away and look down at the dirt smearing my clothes from the barn. "It's just dirt. It'll wash off."

Tanner sighs and looks away, past me, maybe at something he sees, maybe at something in his head. But by the time his eyes meet mine again, I know he's not talking about the dirt on my clothes. He's talking about something else, something bigger. A cool breeze picks up, and one of the horses in the barn rustles in his stall. I shiver. Maybe he's right. Maybe it's not safe even here in the barn, in the middle of the farm. But if I'm not safe here, where else could I possibly be safe?

"We shouldn't be doing this." I bite my bottom lip, and Tanner watches me carefully before shaking his head as my words sink in.

"That's right, you're better than us now. You're Absolved." The anger rages in his voice even though he outwardly doesn't show it except for jerking back a step, as if eager to get some space between us.

"What? No!" *How could things go so wrong so quickly?* "Tanner, that's not it at all!" I reach for him. He looks at my hand, but refuses to take it. I drop it, crushed, and scrub at my eyes with the back of my hand.

"What else could it be? I came by your house yesterday. You were there, Max told me, but you didn't want to see me. Why?"

"I... I..." *How do you tell the person you're supposed to love that you're leaving them forever?* "I... I couldn't."

"This is me, Mira. Tanner. Remember? We've been together forever. I thought you loved me." He shakes his head, and I can see his pain in the sharp movements, the angry squint of his eyes, his mouth, the muscle twitching in his cheek. A body whose signals are almost as familiar to me as my own.

That's it. I can't take it anymore. I rush forward and grab his hands. "I'm sorry, Tanner. I... I just couldn't see anyone. It wasn't you, honest."

"But it *is* me." His voice is low, agonized, and the pain in his eyes make mine close. After his words sink in, he sighs. "Were you even there?"

I bite my lip and look away. "No, I snuck out."

Understanding dawns on his face, relaxes the crease between his eyes. "Rosie?"

I nod.

"I'm sorry, Mira. I had no idea." Sympathy colors his voice.

"It's okay, I just... I had to be alone for a while." Not sure what to say next, I spread my hands on Tanner's chest, smoothing out the wrinkles in his coverall. The urge to hold him, to wipe that painful grimace off of his face, has me moving onto my tiptoes, ready to touch my lips with his.

Tanner shakes his head and steps back, gently setting me away from him. "I'm sorry, Mira. I shouldn't have been so upset. But after the mail came yesterday, I didn't know what to think."

"I know. I know. I should have told you myself but—" I pause as the rest of his words sink in. "Wait. What do you mean about after the mail came?" What could have possibly made him mad in the mail?

"Don't act like you don't know. You got the same letter I did."

"I didn't get anything. My mom would have told me. Yesterday..." *Oh yeah, yesterday.*

I feel the blood drain from my face as Tanner pulls an official, white envelope, well-creased and stained around the edges from his pocket. He stares at it for a few seconds before shaking his head, tossing the envelope on the ground between us, and turning away, stalking toward Tomas's stall. The large bay draft gelding leans his head out, nickering softly.

No. It can't be. After all this time. Oh God, Tanner, what have I done? Taking my eyes from his retreating form, I pick up the envelope and open it, sliding out a single piece of paper. Across the top of the page, fancy lettering reads "Official Marriage Authorization."

"Tanner, wait!" Fingers numb, I drop the paper and run toward him. "I didn't know. Honest." He stops, but doesn't turn around. I dodge in front of him. He closes his eyes and shakes his head.

I grab his hands. "I swear I didn't get anything like this," I plead, my voice rising to a whine.

"Come on, Mira. Everyone knows how Authorizations work. We both get letters on the same day. It's always been done like that." He shakes his head, steps around me, and walks over to Tomas's stall, leaving me behind. Undoing the latch on the door, he clips the lead to the big bay's halter and leads him out. He stops in front of me, his face solid and sure, a faint twinge of sarcasm in his voice. "But I guess it doesn't matter anymore, does it? You're Absolved. You don't need people like me holding you back." He passes me, leads Tomas to a post near the tack room, and ties him to a ring in the wall. He grabs a fresh harness and sets it on the horse's back.

A sob catches in my throat, and I jam my fist into my mouth and bite down. An eerie cry echoes throughout the almost empty barn. I jump and spin around.

"Relax, it's just the fox," Tanner calls. "Poor thing probably knows it's reached the end of the line."

"I still think that's terrible." I turn to the stall as the animal's cry rises to an almost impossible pitch.

"Yeah, well, it's not as if they bought it as a pet. Besides, they've done this dozens of times. It didn't seem to bother you much then."

"Yes, but... this is wrong. It's different this time."

"How?" He seems to have forgotten his earlier anger. "They've all died. What's different now?"

A shiver races up my spine. I know he's talking about the fox, but there's something that tells me it's more than that. "This fox knew freedom, and now she's a prisoner."

"Like you?" He unclips Tomas's lead rope and walks back in my direction, toward the door. I close my eyes and take a deep, steadying breath.

The electronic bell at the manor house rings three times, a deep tone you can hear even from the edge of the fields closest to the house.

"That isn't true. I'm not a prisoner," I cry, but he ignores me.

Tanner's words follow me as I take the long way to the manor, trying to compose myself. *What is he talking about? This isn't a battle, and I'm no prize to be won or lost. What exactly is he fighting for?* Gerald ushers me in and leads me to the tearoom. Lush carpeting muffles our footsteps.

Mr. Flannigan huffs to his feet as I enter the room. "Good morning, Mira. How are you today?" He sits back down, face slightly red.

I plaster a fake smile on my face, trying not to think about Tanner. *I'm not a prisoner, really. I could have said no, right?* "Just great. How about you?"

"Can't complain, my girl. I spoke with Socrates last night."

That wakes me up. I try to mimic his calm and cock an eyebrow at his mysterious response. "Oh? How is he? He didn't look so good when he was here."

"Well, he is almost ninety, so that's to be expected. He was interested in learning how our first day together went." Mr. Flannigan straightens his shoulders and sits back. The wicker creaks and bends under his weight.

"What did he say about the vaccines?" When he nods at the other chair, I gingerly take the seat and turn so I can see his eyes.

Mr. Flannigan hesitates, words perched on the tip of his tongue. "He said it might take some doing to get that amount of medicine here, but he doesn't think there'll be too much of a problem."

"Much of a problem? Does he really think of this as a *problem*?" I tilt my head, the anger in my voice clear even to me.

Mr. Flannigan raises his eyebrows as if I'm the crazy

one. "Well, it is a highly unusual request. Most Seconds don't ask for anything. It is a privilege to be chosen, after all."

"Yeah, you said that before. Still don't see it as much of a *privilege* to me." The anger comes to the surface, and I can't hold it in. "I don't think you get it, Mr. Flannigan. Yes, there's a disease. Yes, kids die. But they don't even let us bury them. They don't even let us say good-bye."

He frowns. "I didn't know that."

"When we die, these people called cleaners come. They wrap us up in white plastic sheets, and take us away to who-knows-where." I look out the big window and can almost see the shiny silver hovercrafts landing gently, doors sliding open, ladders descending, and spilling green-clothed doctors. Fully masked from their heads to the soles of their feet, they follow Mr. Chesaning to whatever house has had a loss and depart with a white wrapped bundle. Oftentimes, it's a small bundle that's handled more like a package than a human being. My fists tighten at my sides.

"I'm sorry," Mr. Flannigan says, and I spin around, jarred from my thoughts. I almost believe him, but he doesn't understand. He doesn't realize what it's like to live the way we do, completely governed by other people. "Unfortunately, we don't have time to discuss this further, but I will certainly relay your concerns to Socrates."

"Don't bother," I snarl, disgust dripping from my words. "If getting one farm's fill of cures is *that* difficult, then vaccinating the whole world would be impossible."

"As. I. Said." He narrows his eyes. "We don't have much time left at the farm, so today we're going to discuss the necessary table manners you will need for the Acceptance banquet."

I raise an eyebrow. "And that's more important than saving lives?"

He picks up his thin tablet from the table between us, taps on it for a few seconds, and speaks without looking at me. "Yes. I understand yours are a bit... lacking."

I shrug, trying not to let his attitude bug me. "We have more important things to worry about here, like growing the crops you people eat."

He shakes his head. "While your manners don't matter under normal circumstances, you're Socrates's Second now, and if you come to the Smith with a farmer's etiquette, well... you're a disaster waiting to happen."

"How hard can it be? We're not animals."

"Do you honestly believe your new role will be easy? Because I can assure you—"

"No, of course not," I snap, then grimace. Maybe my temper needs as much work as my manners. "I'm sorry, Mr. Flannigan. I don't mean to be rude. I guess it's still hard for me to accept that this is happening to me. I've never been off the farm before, and I'll be leaving forever." I get up and walk over to the window, trying to escape my vulnerability.

"You know, your First is an incredible man."

I look at him. "Why? They don't teach us much about them at school. Just enough to do the visits."

"He's actually putting forth a bill called the Free America Act. It will free your people."

"Really?" Surprise and hope kindle inside me. Maybe this isn't so bad after all. "He wants to free us?" Mr. Flannigan nods. "But what'll happen to me?"

"You'll still be his Second, if that's what you're afraid of. He won't send you back."

"Good." I nod and look back out over the courtyard. "I don't think I could bear being sent back."

The dirt-packed courtyard is empty. In the distant fields, men and women work the earth in an ancient dance of life, death, and rebirth. Where would I be if I weren't chosen? Following Tanner to the fields? Tending Spartacus? Watching Max? It already feels like another life.

Mr. Flannigan walks up behind me, surprisingly quiet for someone so large. "Why not? There's something beautiful about life on a farm. So peaceful and innocent since the Climate Act. A simpler time, without technology coming in and complicating the hell out of everything."

I glance at him out of the corner of my eye. "It's not that great," I grumble before going back to my seat. *Get away from there. Don't look any closer. You've taken so much from me, are you going to take this, too?*

"Because we have to do everything by hand, we're so tired by the end of the day we can barely find our own beds, let alone anything dangerous like plot any kind of revolution." Sarcasm etches a familiar tone in my voice. For a moment, I think he's going to yell at me, but he doesn't.

"You think this is the perfect life?" I shake my head and stand up to face him, gesturing with my hands. Another bad habit. "Every morning, I get up before dawn to feed and care for the Chesanings' hunting hounds. Then, I take care of the horses and whatever animals are in the medical barn. After that, I watch the younger kids or work out in the fields, tending the crops or making sure the irrigation system works. I'm stuck doing whatever's needed until I get my permanent work assignment." What would it have been? Would I have been assigned to the barn permanently? I liked animals well enough, I suppose, though smelling like manure does have its disadvantages. Or maybe they'd make me a teacher, though I think I'd rather muck stalls all day than chase a roomful of kids like Max around. I guess I'll never know.

Mr. Flannigan doesn't say anything to that, just measures me with his eyes, and after a few minutes, he walks back to his chair and sits down. Lines crease between his squinty eyes, and his mouth turns down in a pensive frown. He nods at the other chair. I sigh and reluctantly take it. "It appears we are at different levels of understanding with regard to your life on the farm." His voice has a low, gravelly tone. "And I can't do anything about that. There's so much about the world you don't understand, that you'll never be able to understand." My mouth drops open to probably say something stupid, but he holds his hand up, stopping me. "At any rate, we need to focus on the skills you're going to need when you arrive in Washington. On the farm, you're allowed to get away with certain... coarseness, but in D.C., they'll have your head, or more specifically, Socrates's, for the same mistakes."

"Yeah, you said that already." I shake my head. I hear something heavy being rolled down the hall and throw my hands up when Gerald lugs in an antique wooden folding table and sets it up between us. "This is ridiculous!" I exclaim. Both men ignore me, and Gerald brings in a large tray with plates, two covered dishes, and silverware wrapped in cloth napkins. I smile wryly. I've never used a cloth napkin in my life.

"Sit down," Mr. Flannigan commands. Mouth opening and closing like a fish, I shake my head and follow his command. "You may not believe this to be important, Mira, but it is. More than you can ever know."

"Fine." I plop down in my seat.

He nods once, acknowledging his victory. "Good. Now, if you'll take a look at the place setting in front of you, you'll see there are two forks, two spoons, a normal knife, and a smaller one."

"I know what a fork looks like."

"I never said you didn't." A faint smile twitches his mustache.

"Why are we doing all this? Aren't there more important things for me to learn?"

"I'm only here to instruct you on the basics. Socrates himself will teach you the more important facets of your new life." Why does he grimace when he says that? Is there something he's not telling me? "I've worked with many Firsts, but most of the time my instruction begins and ends at the Smith. Rarely do I ever come to the farms, though I find the experience most... enlightening. Socrates is one of only a handful who believes in giving their Seconds time to wrap up loose ends at home before leaving."

"Why would he do that? I know when Adrian left, he went right away."

He takes a sip of tea. "Socrates values the power of saying good-bye."

"What if I don't want to go?"

"Why wouldn't you?" He gestures out the window. "Granted, your farm is a beautiful place, but it's certainly nothing compared to what your new life will be like. Not even that boy I've been told you spend time with..." He gets a sour look on his face. "After your Release, you won't even think about coming back. It'll be as if this part of your life never existed."

Does he know anything? Anger makes me blush. *Okay, so I don't really know what Tanner and I are, anymore, but he's not just a boy like Mr. Flannigan said.* "Tanner and I were supposed to be married," I say, quietly, before looking out the window again.

When I finally look back at my teacher, there's such an intense look of pity on his face that I can't decide whether to get mad again or to cry.

"I'm sorry." He takes a deep breath. "But it can't be helped. Not anymore."

By the time we finish our lesson, the early evening summer sun bakes the brown, hard-packed ground. I lift my face, savoring the heat, and close my eyes. Behind the manor, everything is quiet. I scrunch my eyes shut; making starbursts of red, orange, and yellow appear behind my closed lids. I feel a familiar pull from the forest and turn toward its lush, cool canopy. Going home can wait. *What does he mean I won't want to come back? Why wouldn't I?*

When I enter the apartment, I see my mother sitting at the worn, yellowed table, which only seats four but takes up nearly the entire dining niche.

I slam the door, and the cup wobbles in her hand,

reminding me of my first meeting with Mr. Flannigan. Steadying herself, she takes a sip of coffee. After a long, uncomfortable pause, she smiles at me and asks, "Did you have a good day?"

Are you kidding me, Mom? That's what you're going to ask me? "Umm, yeah. It was... great."

"Good." She looks down at her cup. Her hand clenches a paper napkin, as if strangling it.

"I talked to Tanner," I blurt. "He showed me the Marriage Authorization." She opens her mouth to speak, but my words come out in a rush. "Why didn't you tell me it came?"

She stands up, slams her cup into the cleaning slot, and turns to face me, her face red-splotched. "Does it matter? It can't be changed now. You couldn't marry Tanner even if you wanted to."

"What do you mean? Of course I want to! He's my... my..." Tears burn my eyes. "He's..."

"Your best friend." She sadly shakes her head. "I know you didn't really want to marry him. You don't love the boy, but given time, I'm sure you'd have developed feelings." *But I do*, I want to shout, but something stops me. *I do have those feelings, right?* "However, you were picked by Socrates, so now you don't have to worry about that."

"But Mom—"

"I'm sorry, Mira." She walks over and takes me carefully in her arms, as if she's uncertain how to hold me. Why? She hugs Max all the time. She hugged me after I was chosen. What's different now? Is it me? Is there something wrong with me?

I try to pull away from her, but she holds on. "But Mom, I deserved to know. It's my life. You can't just keep something like that from someone."

She lets go of me, and I stumble back against the thin apartment wall. "I thought knowing would only hurt you, especially since there's nothing you can do about it." Her

76

voice cracks on the last part, as if she genuinely cares about what happens to me, even though something still feels off. "Besides, it doesn't matter," she says, matter-of-factly. "The sooner you get that through your head, the better. None of this matters anymore. The most important thing in your life, in all of our lives, is that you're Absolved."

"But what if Socrates hadn't picked me? What, then? Would you still hide it? Rip it up and send me to another farm? I know you don't like Tanner much, but he's a good man, Mom. He loves me."

She purses her lips. "I wish you'd just let it go, please." I start to say no, but she talks over me. "If you must know the truth, it's those men he hangs out with. Disappearing at all hours of the night. I bet they're making moonshine in the forest and selling it or something. Sarai even smelled smoke on a couple of them one time, and you know smoking is illegal."

"Tanner's not like that," I protest. "He's never done any of those things."

She shakes her head. "Maybe you don't see it, but I do. Breaking the law is nothing but trouble, and he'll find it fast at the rate he's going. Everything happens for a reason, and I think this is your chance to get out and away from this life. You deserve better."

"But what if I don't want to leave?" I narrow my eyes at her. What would she say to that? She's always going on about doing our duty. What would she say if I wanted to quit?

"Stop acting like a child! It doesn't matter anyway. You have to go. It's for the best." She runs her hand down my cheek and over my hair, as if memorizing the look and feel of me. "You'll see."

"I could come back some day."

My mother's caring expression turns sadder, older. "No, you can't. Seconds never do."

After a silent dinner with my mother and Max, someone knocks on our door. Glancing at me, Mom puts her hands on the table, as if to stand, but I shake my head. "No, I got it."

"Are you sure?"

"What are you afraid of, Mom? That someone's going to come in and attack us or something? I can answer the door. I've done it, like, a thousand times before." I roll my eyes as Max snickers.

Mom sighs and sits back down. "Of course I know you can answer the door, dear. It's just... well..." The rest of her words drift away as I swing the thin-paneled door open and see Tanner leaning against my door, blocking it. He pulls me into his arms, and his lips crush mine, contradicting his earlier anger. He runs his hands through my short, spiky hair, and I find myself leaning into his kiss. Maybe it's the passion, maybe the anger that seems to lurk just under the surface, giving my calm, solid—friend? brother?—a sense of danger, but whatever it is, I'm sucked right into it. The musky smell of sweat and horses fills my nose, a heady scent, one that always reminds me distinctly of Tanner. I feel like I'm swimming to the surface, waking up, and I shove against his chest. Tanner doesn't want to let me go at first, so I push harder. Eventually, he releases me, and I quickly step back.

"Mira Marie!" Mom exclaims. Tanner ducks his head, and a blush creeps up his neck. I roll my eyes and kick the door shut so we can have some privacy.

"Tanner, what are you doing?" I search his eyes, but he refuses to meet my gaze.

"Sorry," he says, ignoring my question. "That's not what I planned on doing, but dammit, Mir, I couldn't resist." He runs his hand through his hair and cracks a lopsided grin. "Do you want me to apologize?"

I feel my face flush, remembering how I almost gave in, almost gave back. "No, of course not." I look away.

"Look, I have to get home, but will you meet me later?" His fingertips gently graze my chin, and he lifts my head up so he can peer into my eyes.

"Tonight?" I whisper.

"Yeah, at the edge of the field by the playground." He lets my chin go and pulls me loosely into his arms again, the way we used to when we were playing at being in love. *What do kids know?*

"Sure." His breath grazes the top of my head, then his lips meet mine gently, in a kiss. "When?"

"Midnight." He caresses my cheek and walks away, vanishing around the corner.

THE RIGHT DECISION

socrates

"**S**OCRATES, ARE YOU AWAKE?" MAGGIE'S voice winds its way into my painkiller-induced haze. How many had I taken? Two? Three. Ellie would kill me if she knew, but sometimes, the pain is just so bad, I can't take it anymore. How am I supposed to last six months like this?

"Maggie?" I scrub the weariness from my eyes and roll forward in my chair. Even though it's dulled, the pain hovers in the back of my mind, waiting for me to lower my guard. Ben lifts his head from his pillow on the floor but drops it when he realizes it's only our housekeeper.

In the doorway to my study, Maggie shifts from side to side, her blue robe tied crookedly and her feet tucked into worn slippers.

"What is it?"

"You have a visitor." She looks nervous, and that never happens. Maggie is as unflappable as the red mountains surrounding my home.

I glance at the antique grandfather clock on the wall. 10:42 p.m. "At this hour?" She shrugs. "Who is it?"

Maggie straightens her robe and combs her fingers through her hair. "The President."

"Here? What in the world for?" I push myself to my feet,

knees creaking, back protesting, and I wince. "I haven't seen Andrew in ages."

"Sir, he's waiting," she pleads. I roll my neck to crack it, grab my cane, pull myself to my feet, and limp toward her. Ben pulls himself to his feet, stretches, and joins me.

"What does he want?"

Maggie shrugs. "I don't know. He wouldn't say."

"Well, where is he, woman?" I look around my study. "Is he coming here?"

She shakes her head. "No, he's waiting in the library." She holds the door open for me and I hobble down the hall.

The formerly towheaded boy with a gap-toothed smile and a love of soccer who turned into the President of the United States sips a brandy as he gazes out my floor-to-ceiling windows into the clear Santa Fe night sky. When he turns around, I see that the crooked smile is still the same, as are his father's nose, his wide brown eyes, and thick, calloused hands. Lines bracket his mouth and eyes, and he pinches the bridge of his nose.

"Socrates, my friend. I'm sorry to be calling on you so late. I hope you don't mind, but I helped myself to a drink." Tossing back the rest of his drink, he pulls me into a strong embrace.

I wince at the sudden pain, and Ben growls. The President of the United States releases me and looks down at my dog. "Sorry about that, buddy." He digs in his pocket, pulls out what looks like an ancient strip of beef jerky, and tosses it to Ben.

Having found a new best friend, Ben accepts his treat and hops on the couch to chew on it in peace. I shake my head. "Some guard dog you are," I grumble and head over to the bar. Andrew follows me and sets his glass on the table. I grab the bottle of brandy and pour myself a snifter before tipping the bottle toward his. He nods, and I refill his glass. After resealing the bottle, I settle myself on one of the old brown leather recliners and take a sip.

"To what do I owe the pleasure of your visit?" I raise my eyebrows at Andrew's wrinkled gray pinstriped suit, loosened tie, and mussed up hair.

"You always did get right to the point." He chuckles and takes another mouthful of brandy, swishing it around his mouth before swallowing. "It's this damn bill."

"The Free America Act?"

He laughs, a harsh, hollow sound. Ben raises his head from the couch and lets out a low woof. "What else?"

"I thought you supported it?"

He stares into his glass, swirling the amber liquid. "I do. But I think you and I are the only ones." He clenches his fingers around the glass, then forces himself to release it and lays his palm flat on the dark wood bar. The lines around his eyes deepen, and his eyes lose their focus.

"You know that's not true." My lips twist into a faint smile. "At least half the country is on our side."

He barks out a laugh. "Yes, but they don't get to vote."

"Is that what this is about? Your reelection?" Disgust fills me. This isn't the Andrew I know. His father, Anthony, would never have stood for a son who kowtows.

His eyes shoot up to meet mine, and an alcohol-induced flush colors his neck. "I can't deny that, though I hope you know I'd do the right thing, regardless of whether or not it cost me the presidency."

I try to tamp down the censure rising in my voice. "Of course you would. I completely support you. Your father taught you well."

He throws back the rest of his drink and nods at the bottle for another. "If only he were here. He'd do a damn better job of this than I am."

I put my hand on his and squeeze it. "But he's not, and I think you're doing just fine."

Andrew shakes his head. "Veronica threatened to leave me." Ahh, the real reason for his discontent.

"I'm so sorry." Sympathy fills my voice. I know that kind of heartbreak all too well.

"Yeah." He sighs. "Me, too. And it's because of this bill, Socrates. That's why she's leaving me. She doesn't think it should pass or that the Texans should be freed."

"That wasn't her platform when you were both elected. I thought you both supported it."

"Apparently she changed her mind."

"Huh. Well, I guess, as the vice-president, her personal views really don't come into play unless something tragic happens to her presidential husband." I down the rest of my drink. "Are you backing out?"

"No!" He stands up, knocking the stool back. It crashes against the floor with a dull thud. He quickly rights it and sits down again. "It's something my father always supported. I told him that, if it was the last thing I do as president, I'd get this damn bill passed." His eyes glow, and he bangs his fist on the bar, rattling our glasses. Even now, through the low lights and brandy-infused heat, he even looks like his father. And here I thought the passion had been tempered in the generation since the former president was assassinated on his way to a speech on human rights. No one had been blamed, but the Lifers had taken credit.

I can see Andrew is thinking about his father, too, because his eyes take on a faraway look. He takes a deep breath and holds it. Then, in a quieter, younger-sounding voice, he says, "This is the right decision, isn't it Socrates? I mean, things are pretty bad the way they are. We really shouldn't keep on the same course we've been on for the last two hundred years, right?"

Agonized, he seems to beg me for reassurance, for support. Should I tell him about my own indecisions? That it was the love of a good woman, Eliot, that drove me to support this bill? That it wasn't my own idea, my own passion, but hers? Hers and his father's? No, Andrew needs to believe I want this with the same fire as he does.

"Of course it is, Andrew. Your father would be proud."

DEAD GIRL

mira

MY BAG OF CLOTHING SITS open on the bed. It's only halfway filled, a sad reminder of how few possessions I own. Mr. Flannigan told me I would be getting all new clothing, that I don't have to bring anything, but I want *my* things, the pieces of me that Socrates doesn't own, doesn't control. It's almost like I'm being erased, that as soon as I leave this room, this apartment, this farm, it'll be as though I never existed in the first place.

Tears burn my eyes, and I shut them, squeezing them tight. It won't do me any good to cry. I have to meet Tan, and I don't want him to see me like this. I want to be the strong, laughing girl he grew up with, the girl he petitioned the Chesanings to marry, not the one who's already got her bag packed.

The moon glows huge and low in the sky as I cross the courtyard. In the distance, crickets and frogs sing a melody to which only they know the lyrics. In the forest, something howls, a lonely drawn-out sound that raises the hairs on my arms and the back of my neck. My footsteps clap against the hard-packed earth, and I try to keep to the shadows on the off chance someone else is outside. I need to meet Tanner, but there's something else I need to do first.

In the barn, the steel walls shut out most of the nighttime noises. What remains barely filters through the cracked barn door. I can't leave it open any more or turn on the lights. Someone would definitely notice that.

The horses shuffle in their stalls, then relax when they realize it's me. Tinker nickers softly and pokes her velvety nose over the stall door, her white blaze glowing in the darkness. I ignore her and make my way over to the stall at the end. I may not be able to change my fate, but I can change someone else's.

It's much darker at this end of the barn. The pale sliver of light from the moon doesn't reach nearly far enough, so when I reach the stall, I have to feel my way along the heavy, wooden door. My hand bumps against the latch, and I fumble around as I open it, trying to keep the old iron from clanging too heavily. Once that's done and the door swings open, I slip inside, letting the darkness swallow me. It takes more time than I'd like for my eyes to adjust, but once they do, I can make out the long rectangular shape of the cage in the corner. Walking slowly over to it, I whisper, "Hey girl, pretty girl. It's all right. I'm going to help you. No one's going to hurt you anymore."

Is it even a girl? Oh well, it's not as though the fox really understands what I'm saying, anyway. I crouch down. The metal bars are rusted, probably with sharp edges just waiting to rip into my fingers. There are no handles or ropes, and the crate looks about as old as Mr. Socrates. The last fox came in a plastic carrier with a nice, padded handle on top. Then again, that fox was raised by humans, docile and even wagging its tail for attention. It had no idea the horror that awaited it. This one hisses at me, angry and afraid. I don't blame her. I'm sure I'd be just like that if I were in her position.

Here we go. I reach forward and grab each side of the crate. The hiss changes into a rumbling growl that crescendos into a cat-like yowl. The cage is heavier than

85

I'd expected, so it must be metal. The fox herself can't weigh more than ten or fifteen pounds. I heft it up a few more inches, trying to get a closer look at her. *Maybe she'll recognize me and calm down.* The fox yowls even louder. *Yeah, fat chance, Mira. She's not a dog. She's a wild animal.*

"Shhh." She doesn't listen. *Come on, Mir, it's not like she can understand you.* "I'm trying to save your life here." I lug the cage out the back door and toward the edge of the forest as fast as I can. When the natural path shifts toward the playground, I hesitate. *No, her best shot is the forest.*

As if sensing my plan, or maybe the scents of the forest, the fox quiets. "Just hold on," I whisper, envisioning her dainty paws struggling to balance on the painfully sharp wire bottom. I move faster, panting, taking advantage of her quiet.

By the time we make it to the edge of the forest, I'm sweating enough for the hounds to track me instead of the fox. Breathing heavily, I set the cage down and brace my hands on the top of it so I can catch my breath. Startled by the sudden movement, the terrified creature screeches and leaps forward, nipping at my hand through the bars.

"Hey." I jerk back from the sudden pain. When I tilt my hand toward the moonlight, the pale glow illuminates a rivulet of blood from where one of her teeth grazed me. *Great, that's all I need.* With my luck, I'll contract some sort of wild fox disease.

After wiping my hand on my pants, I glance around to make sure I'm still alone. All clear, but kind of creepy. The forest stretches above and beyond on either side, its once welcoming branches forbidding and sinister, definitely not a place I would want to go, but perfect for the razor-toothed little beast in the cage.

"Now don't you bite me again." I reach around for the latch in the shadowed light. I flip it, allowing the little metal door to swing open. For a few seconds, the fox crouches in the back corner. Her nose twitches, a delicate little movement. The breath I didn't realize I was holding catches in my throat, and in one leap, she's out and zipping through the grass. Then she's gone, just another shadow hidden in the trees.

"Good luck," I whisper. What would it be like to be that fox? To have freedom within your grasp when you thought everything was lost? Would I run? Free in a forest that wasn't my own? Or would I stay, cowering in the corner, afraid to step one foot into the unknown?

Looking down at the cage, I decide to leave it there. I don't have time to take it back to the barn before I meet Tanner anyway. I'll just grab it on my way back.

The playground at night is still full of light, though it's the ghostly kind that makes me think the little kids who are gone might still be around. One of the old, cracked wooden swings clanks against another, a light wind twisting the metal chains. I blink, and in that split second, I hear my sister laughing, that head-thrown-back, open-mouthed laugh only the young have, the one they let out before they realize even something as simple as a laugh should be toned down to a more socially acceptable silence. Within minutes, I weave my way to Rosie's little cross. It's even more forlorn in the moonlight. The wind picks up, tickling the hairs at the back of my neck. It almost feels as if I'm not alone out here. But that's crazy, I tell myself.

I'm about to turn right back around when the brush rustles at the edge of the forest, and a human-shaped figure steps out. Whoever it is hesitates then heads toward me.

"Mira," Tanner whispers as he pulls me into his arms. I feel myself stiffen. Something's not right. "I'm so glad you came. I thought I'd lost you." His words are laced in his breath, desperate, as if he can't waste another second, even to breathe, without telling me how he feels. His passion overwhelms me. I should feel the same way, do the same things. I should be holding on to him with all my might, right? He rests his head on mine. "I just can't."

Unease makes me want to pull away, to ask him what he'll do once I'm gone, but I'm afraid of the answer. "I don't want to lose you, either," I say, but the words almost feel hollow, like it's expected that I say something like this. He presses his lips to mine, but even now, right before I leave, I can't return it.

"No, you don't understand. I *can't* lose you."

"I know. I love you, too." I search his eyes.

"Do you really, Mir? What if this is it? What if this is the end for you, for *us*? I don't know what I'd do without you. I wish I could make you understand how I feel."

I can't take it any longer. I'm sick of everyone treating me like a child, of Tan telling me I don't understand, of my mom acting as though it's so great that I'm going, that it's such an honor. I'm tired of Mr. Flannigan treating me as if I don't know how to tie my shoes or go to the bathroom by myself.

"Stop it, Tanner. Just stop it. I'm not a kid." I push away from him and take a deep breath. "You think I don't know that when I leave, we're done?" My voice echoes in the sudden silence. Even the crickets are too frightened to keep chirping. Tears sting my eyes. "I know that. Why do you keep reminding me?" I bite my lower lip as a ripping pain wrenches my heart apart. Life without Tanner, my best friend... my almost husband... I can't... I can't deal with it right now... I turn away from him and stop. What should I do? Stay here, listen to how much he loves me? Or leave, go home and face those empty walls, the memories crammed into a half-full bag of old, worn-out hand-me-downs.

He grabs my arm and spins me around. "Wait, I'm sorry. Please, I have to talk to you." He takes a deep breath. "I... I met someone."

I look up at him in shock. He met someone? Already? A new girl? Someone prettier, nicer, less prone to getting in trouble? Someone safe? "I can't believe this! It's only been two days, and you're already moving on to someone new? Who is it? Rasina? Cassity? Shauna?"

Anger chases away the concern on his features. "You have got to be kidding me. Do you really think I'd do that?" He shakes his head. "You and I belong together, even the Chesanings know that." He takes me by the shoulders and stares into my eyes. "I don't want anyone else. Not now, not ever." He gives me that sweet, heartbreaking smile that melts all the other girls. "Silly girl, you're the only one for me."

"Who did you meet, then?"

"A man." He lifts my chin so I'm looking into his eyes. "Someone from outside the farm, a Lifer."

"Tanner, no! You're going to get yourself killed!"

He drops his hold on me and shakes his head. "That doesn't matter. I'm trying to save you."

"Save me from what? Leaving the farm? I couldn't bear it if they killed you for talking to a rebel."

"You don't know what you're talking about." He takes my hands in his and squeezes them, as if that might make me listen to him. "Listen to me! These men, your teacher and your First, they want to kill you."

"That's ridiculous."

"It's true. You've got to believe me." I shake my head, trying to pull my hands from his, but he won't let go. "Dammit, Mira. This man, the one who came to the farm, he told me the truth."

"What truth is that?" I finally jerk my hands free and put them on my hips, glaring up at him. "Seems like everyone has their own version of reality, and no one's telling me anything or letting me think for myself. Tell me, Tanner, just like everyone else is quick to do: what should I believe?"

"You've known me your whole life. Why would you trust these people you've only known for a couple of days over me?"

"Wait a second. You say I shouldn't believe Mr. Socrates or Mr. Flannigan because I've only known them for a couple days, but you believe this rebel guy you just met today?"

Tanner looks away, a muscle jumping in his set jaw. Finally he turns back to me. "I didn't just meet him today. He came here before the First showed up."

"How did they know Mr. Socrates would pick me? It doesn't make any sense. Our farm is a good day's travel from anywhere else."

"My guess is they have people near all the farms, waiting for a First to name an Absolved."

"So... what is he supposed to do?" Tanner is involved with these people? These Lifers? That's not the Tanner I know. The man who always follows the rules, does his job, even if he hates it. I look around me, feeling naked and vulnerable, as if the world has dropped out from under me.

"He wants to meet you, of course."

"What if I don't want to meet him?"

Tanner rolls his eyes. "Stop being immature."

"Fine." I huff, almost stamping my feet like Max in a tantrum. "What's his name?"

Tanner runs his hand through his hair and looks to both sides of us, as if making sure we're alone. "Henri Lee."

I shake my head. "I've never heard of him."

Tanner raises his eyebrows. "Of course you haven't. It's not like we can watch the news here or see the protests, or even read about what's going on around the rest of the world."

"Shhh, keep your voice down." Okay, now he's making me paranoid.

"No one's going to hear us, Mir. We're alone out here."

But Tan's earlier warning runs through my head. "Please, just... keep your voice down."

"Fine, whatever. As I was saying..." He lowers his voice. "Henri Lee is a Lifer, one of the largest groups of people rebelling against the government."

"What are they rebelling against?"

Tanner lets out a hollow laugh. "Sometimes I forget how little you know. Unlike some of the other, smaller groups, the Lifers mostly protest Project ReGenesis."

"Really? Why would they object to me being freed?"

"Umm, maybe because you're still not going to be free?"

I tilt my head and narrow my eyes at him. What is he talking about? "But I'm Absolved."

Tanner just shakes his head. "That's just a different name for the same thing, Mira. And if what the rebels tell me is true..." He clamps his mouth shut, his eyes widening, like he almost caught himself saying something he shouldn't.

"What? If what is true? Please tell me! What does this guy want from me?" Tanner looks like he's swallowed something sour, but he doesn't say anything.

"Fine, if you're not going to tell me, I'm going back. I... I need to get some sleep." I turn on my heels but only take a couple steps before Tanner's hand wraps around my arm, stopping me. As I spin around, he pulls me against his chest with a soft "oompf."

"Wait, please. I'm sorry." Listening to the heavy thump of his heartbeat, I feel myself slowly fall into that comfortable contentment I always experience around him.

Shaking the foggy feeling from my head, I pull away, but he doesn't let me go and keeps me cradled in his embrace. "I can't do this, Tanner. Not right now."

"Please wait." Desperation fills his tone. "This man, Henri Lee, said he could help you escape. He'll help us go where no one can find us. Not the Chesanings, not the government, not your precious First. No one. We'll be safe. That's what Lifers do. They try to rescue Seconds and help them make new lives for themselves."

"Who told you this? Was it that Henri person?" Is he serious? Does he really want me to back out?

He shakes his head. "I can't say. It's hard enough

getting messages into or out of the farms. I don't know all the details myself. It's safer that way."

"Safer for whom?"

"Everyone. If I was captured or tortured, I wouldn't be able to reveal my contacts, just the place the contact takes place." He cracks a smile. "The others would be safe."

"But why? I thought this was such a good thing."

Tanner looks off into the distance, as if trying figure out what he should tell me. "You know I'd never hurt you, right?" His hands tighten on my shoulders, and his eyes search mine.

"Of course," I answer quickly. "But you're kind of scaring me."

"Don't be afraid. Fight this with me. Talk to Henri Lee. He can help us. The Lifers can get us out. We'll run away, be safe. You don't have to be a Second, Mira."

A cold shaft of air shoots right through me as I think about running away, the disgraced look on my mother's face, the embarrassment, and the shunning. And Max, standing in a line, all because I was weak. I couldn't do that to them.

But what if I did escape with Tanner, and we took Max with us? We could live in the wilderness, off the land. It couldn't be too hard, right? We could live right in a little cabin nestled in a clearing surrounded by tall pine trees. Made with our own hands. A home where we don't have to look over our shoulders all the time. Someplace safe.

You can have that, a voice whispers seductively in the back of my head. *You can be with him. You can have a future you want, not something someone else chose for you.* But then I see Max standing there next to me, clutching his newly tattooed arm to his chest. "Tanner, I can't."

He closes his eyes, letting out the heavy, disappointed breath he'd been holding. "Just talk to him, please?"

I bite my lip. "Okay, but it's just talk. I'm not running away."

Hope sparks in his eyes, and his lips quirk at the corners. "Fine, just listen to him. That's all I'm asking."

"When do you want me to meet him?"

Tanner opens his mouth just as the shadows behind him move, and a dark shape, larger than either of us, steps forward.

I shriek and stumble back, eyes wide. "Tanner? Look behind you!"

My would-be knight in shining armor jumps in front me as the stranger steps into the little graveyard, carefully tiptoeing around the tiny crosses. His face is liberally coated with black paint, and the whites of his eyes are almost blinding in the moonlight.

"Tanner." The man nods, shortly. Tanner relaxes and steps aside.

"It's okay, Mir. It's Henri Lee."

The man smiles and extends his hand to me. I slowly place mine in his, and he squeezes quickly before letting it go. "It's a pleasure to meet you, Mira. Your friend sent a message after you were chosen, and I came as soon as I could."

Friend? My mind stutters to a stop. That's all we are? *Friends? Wait, I guess I deserve that.* Friends is what I claimed we are to Mr. Flannigan, as well. I glance at Tanner, but he looks away.

Henri Lee doesn't seem to notice. "He told me you'd like to get out of this mess."

"No!" The little cabin in my dream disappears, and all I'm left with is echoing laughter that sounds eerily like my dead little sister. No, my fate is different. I have to keep Max safe. The two men share a look. "I'm not leaving."

Henri Lee looks surprised. "You want to die?"

"Of course not!" What is he talking about? Alessa singsongs in my head "You're a dead girl. You're a dead girl." I shiver, and it has nothing to do with the wind.

"That's what's going to happen to you if you don't come with me."

"What are you talking about?"

Henri Lee takes a step forward. His smile morphs into a sneer, and his eyes narrow. "They treat ReGenesis like it is all some wonderful thing, tell everyone that the Seconds will be making a difference in the world, have an important destiny." Which is exactly what Mr. Flannigan said. "They're lying. Your *great destiny* is death. But if you ask them, they'll say it's worth it to have peace, to have prosperity, that it's better for the whole. What's one servant girl when millions benefit from her death?"

I back up until I feel a tiny bump from the arms of a cross against the back of my legs. "No," I whisper. "That's crazy. They wouldn't dare..."

His arm snakes forward, and he grabs my elbow. "You're more of an idiot than they are if you believe they'd let a Texan be free."

I try to jerk away, but he holds me tightly. "Tanner?" My eyes dart to him, and I can see that he's tense. I guess this isn't part of the deal.

Tanner steps forward. "It's all right, Henri. Let go of her, she's not going to do anything stupid," he growls but entreats me with his eyes, begging *me* not to do said stupid thing.

Henri Lee makes a low grumble in return, but he unclenches his grip.

I finally pull away, rubbing my wrist.

Tanner clears his throat. "This... isn't going well. Please, just listen to him, Mira. He's telling the truth."

"He can't be. That isn't possible. They wouldn't... wouldn't... they wouldn't just *kill* kids like that."

"Why not?" Henri asks, his voice sarcastic, like he's making fun of me, but I don't know the joke. "Do you think the government cares about a few, insignificant brats when Firsts are so popular? Think, girl. They don't give a damn about you. You're just an object to them, worth less than a cow or a horse. Your ancestors fought in the Immigration War. You wouldn't even be alive if the government didn't allow it. They get more use out of the chickens in the hen house than you. You're nothing to them unless you're chosen."

"Please stop," I whimper, looking to Tanner for support.

He's frowning. Is this the person he thought would convince me to run away? He's doing a terrible job; that's for sure.

Henri reaches for me again, and I shake my head. He must read how ready I am to bolt because he stops. "Mira." He glances at Tanner, who shakes his head. He takes a deep breath and tries to calm his voice. "I'm sorry if I'm scaring you, and 1 wish I could explain it better, but I can't. We have to take advantage of this opportunity because it won't happen again. You're lucky it's Socrates who chose you. Most of the other Firsts take their Seconds right away." Like my cousin, Adrian.

I turn to Tanner. "How can you trust this guy?" I quickly look back at Henri, who just stands there, waiting.

"Do you see any other way? This is our best chance to be together." But is that what I want? I shake my head. Wait, but if what this guy says is true? No, it can't be.

I look back at Tanner again. "How can you know that? Do you even know who he is for sure?"

Tanner clenches his jaw. "I trust him. Isn't that enough?" His tone is accusing. He asked me to trust him before, like it should be a given because of our past, because of how much he cares for me. But nothing is the same any more. Do I even know who Tanner really is?

"You expect me to just go with this guy, who I've never met before, to wherever it is he wants to take me? I can't."

"Please." Tanner reaches out for me.

I shake my head and step back again, feeling another cross tilt behind me. I bend to straighten it, and the world explodes.

The playground floods with light. About a dozen men

in black surround us, shouting at us to get down. My mind freezes, and lowering my eyes to avoid the glare, I see heavy boots trampling the faded dolls, tipping over the sun-bleached pink tea table, snapping the arms off of any pint-sized crosses in their path. Splinters fly into the silvery grass. What have I done?

The guards shove their way between the three of us, forcing us apart as they wave deadly shiny laser guns. Masks cover their faces, and body armor protects their torsos. They wrench Tanner away, and I can't see him anymore. I fight the arms holding me, but they're like steel bands.

My legs give out, and I'm only being held up by the armed men on either side of me. Some of the guards carry huge laser guns, but others have sticks with buzzing prongs at the end. I try to scream, but terror has robbed my lungs of air. Two men pull Henri Lee's arms perpendicular to his body while a third searches him.

A fourth guard with the wide face of a bullfrog pulls a small object out of his own pocket and throws it to the ground at Henri's feet. "Sir, I found something."

The guard who was searching Henri stops, pulls his off mask, and wipes the sweat from his brow. His hair, buzzed off to peach fuzz, is almost invisible. He has a strong, athletic build, not very different from the field workers on the farm. He looks at where Bullfrog is pointing, nudges the object with his boot, then looks up at me. "Looks like we saved your life."

"What? No! I saw him—" I point at Bullfrog. "—pull that thing out of his pocket and drop it on the ground."

"Shut up. You don't know what you're talking about." Buzzcut sneers. "It's too dark to see anything clearly. You're imagining things."

"No, I'm not! I know what I saw."

"Shut up! Don't you think you're in enough trouble already without backtalk?"

"I didn't do anything wrong!"

Bullfrog raises his hand to slap me, but Buzzcut grabs his wrist. "No, it's not worth it. Where she's going, she'll get far worse anyway." He nods at the two goons holding my arms, and they pull me backward.

"What? Where are you taking me?"

A thin silver band strapped to Buzzcut's wrist beeps. He puts his ear to it, then shouts, "The transport's ready. Let's go."

In the space of a few heartbeats, the throng of bodies clears enough for me to see Tanner strung between two of the other guards. When he sees me, he wrenches one arm loose and reaches out for me. One of his guards punches him in the gut, and Tanner collapses to the ground with an "Oomph."

Buzzcut calls out, "Avery." When Bullfrog turns, Buzzcut slices his hand across his throat, then jerks his head toward Tanner and Henri Lee.

"No!" I scream and fight, kicking and punching at my captors, but it's no use. Compared to them, I'm no stronger than a newborn colt. They spin me around, so I can't see anything.

Behind me, something pops, a muffled sound unlike anything I've ever heard before. Then there's another, and another, then silence. "Tanner?" Nothing.

"Shut up!" one of my guards yells. "Stupid Texan." He wrenches on my arm so hard I gasp. I start to wobble, my legs give out, and I sag to the ground, held up only by the iron fingers around my upper arms. "Tanner!" I scream again. There still isn't an answer. "No!"

"Mira?" His voice is strained, gasping.

I sob in relief. "Are you okay?" I wrench my head around and see him, bloodied and bruised. When he sees my face he struggles harder.

"Mira!"

"Let me go!" I throw myself forward, backward, kick

out with my legs, anything to get free. But it's no use. They might as well have tied me between two trees for all the leverage I get.

The guard on my left tightens his bruising grip on my arm. "Let's go." Behind me, I hear more muffled noises, ompfs, thumps, and grunts.

"Tanner?" Silence.

No, please, not him. Not Tanner. Please not Tanner.

The men jerk to a halt when we get to the edge of the lawn. Buzzcut instructs two of the other guards to break off and search the area before we move forward again. Numb, I hang between them, so much dead weight.

After the two scouts give an all clear, we cross the lawn and enter the courtyard, which is lit up like midday. People stand in their doorways and look out their windows. My mom's there and so are Tanner's parents. I can't tell for sure, but I think my mother's crying, probably because she's horrified by the scene I've caused. *Sorry for making your life miserable, Mom.* I try to dig in my heels, turn my head, anything at all to see if Tanner's behind me, to see if he's okay, but the men drag me to the manor before I can do more than squeak.

We stop in front of the manor as the Chesanings come out and talk to Buzzcut. I take a second to catch my breath and gasp, "Where are you taking me?"

"Your new home," he growls, and a couple of the others laugh.

A sick, cold feeling roots itself in the pit of my stomach.

I dig in my heels, and Bullfrog nudges me toward the back door by the kitchen. "Move it," he snarls.

Two more guards frame the doorway, guns ready, while Buzzcut and Bullfrog shove me into the huge, stainless steel and tile kitchen. They hurry me through doors on the right to a small room where an egg-shaped tarnished silver pod sits in the corner, amid bins of flour, jars of vegetables, and cans of preserves. I peer around them, trying to look out the door, but all I can see is the darkened kitchen.

"Get in," Bullfrog snaps and pushes me into the pod. A second later he joins me, clenching my arm tightly in his. The door whooshes shut, and there's a bright flashing that blinds me. A sudden shifting of the ground flattens me to the back wall, and I can't move. Bullfrog doesn't seem to notice.

"What's going on?" I shout over a loud rushing sound, like air around my ears, moving faster than I've ever travelled before.

"Will you just shut up!" He snarls and cuffs me on the back of the head. I reach up to touch the spot, and the sound is gone. My feet touch the ground again, and my stomach stops roiling. I close my eyes. All I can think of is the look of anguish on Tanner's face. The soft pop. Heaving, wracking sobs shake my entire body.

"Get over yourself, princess." Buzzcut smirks. The door slides open, and armed guards glare at me over poised weapons. The walls are a cold stone gray, bleak and foreboding. In front of me, Mr. Flannigan is being forced down a long hall, arms wrenched tightly behind him in painfully thin metal cuffs. He cranes his head around and fear widens his tiny eyes. Sweat beads his forehead, his mustache quivers, his red hair is mussed, and he sets his lips into a firm, thin line. Wherever I am, I'm not going to like it.

After they force him around the corner, they lead me down another hall. Through barred doors on either side of me, silent eyes witness my trek. We turn toward another hall, opposite the one Flannigan went down and pass more doors with no windows. From these, I hear muffled moans. Cries of pain and despair rival those of the little mangy fox I freed back at the farm. Ahead of us, an unsmiling man wearing a black uniform and a silver visor holds a door open. When we reach it, the men nod at each other, and then Buzzcut shoves me inside.

I stumble almost to my knees, terrified but glad to be free of them. Maybe they don't think I'm much of a threat. I spin around, somewhat wobbly, looking around at my new surroundings. With no windows, the only light comes from the doorway. An old-fashioned toilet crouches in one corner, but that's it. No bed, no chair. Nothing.

The door starts to close, and I rush toward it. "Wait! You can't leave me here!"

Bullfrog chuckles. "Don't worry, you're not alone. There are plenty like you in these halls." The door closes a little more and my heart leaps into my throat.

"Don't! Please don't leave me here!"

A wide grin slices his face in half. "I'm the least of your problems, princess. Welcome to your new life." The door slams shut. Darkness.

PEOPLE LIKE YOU

socrates

WHEN THE PHONE RINGS IN the middle of the night, I roll over and feel around for the old handset that rests on the nightstand next to my bed. Gnarled hands twisted and shaking, I fumble until I hit the correct button to answer it. "Hello?" *Maybe I should get one of those damn implants that are so popular these days.*

"Socrates?" I don't recognize the high-pitched, nasally voice. Definitely female, definitely annoying enough to start a headache throbbing behind my temples.

I groan, and with my free hand, rub the old scars, my own peculiar crown permanently etched into my head. "Who the hell is this?"

"It's Edith Antinov, secretary to—to Mr. Edward Flannigan."

I jerk upright, old bones protesting. *Oh hell, this must be bad for that mouse of a woman to call me.* "What's wrong?"

"He's... he's been arrested." Her voice breaks into a sob at the end, and my hand clenches around the handset.

I pull it away from my ear for a second and look at it. "Edward's been arrested?"

"Y—yes." She sniffles, and in the background, she blows her nose, a deep honking sound.

"For what?" *The man practically lives in Washington. He*

knows when to talk and when to shut the hell up. Whatever pain pills the doctors gave me make my stomach roil and ache, and I feel bile rising in my throat.

"They're saying that—that he's one of them." She sniffles again on the other end of the line. I've only met the woman once. She's petite, with pinkish red hair, a hawkish nose she never bothered to get fixed, and an icy demeanor. It must be bad if she's falling apart.

"One of whom? You're not making any sense." *Good Lord, Edward, what have you done?*

"A... rebel, sir. A Lifer."

I pull the handset away from my ear and stare at it, the words sinking in. He can't be. No, Edward wouldn't be that stupid. I've known him for what? Forty years now? He'd never make a mistake like that. "That's ridiculous. I've known Edward almost his entire life. He'd never do anything like that. Where is he now?"

"Fullbright Detention Center. And... and that's not all, sir. Your Second..."

A cold, icy feeling replaces the ache. "By the love of God, woman, what happened to her?"

"She's with him, sir. She tried to escape with some rebels. They arrested her, too."

"Shit." An old juvenile detention center, Fullbright is made of cold metal lines, gray cement walls, cameras, and various military officials who specialize in "re-education." Not a pleasant place.

"Thanks for letting me know, Edith. I'll place a phone call as soon as we hang up to see if I can help. Edward is a good man. I'll see what I can do."

"Thank you, sir. I know that if anyone can help, it's you." She hangs up. The cold emptiness on the other end of the line chills me.

After gathering my thoughts, I pull myself upright and leave the bedroom, walking down the long, darkened hall. Ben sighs, gets to his feet, and follows me, his nails clicking on the smooth red tile. On my left is a series of portraits of me in my various incarnations. First, I was Adam with my dark hair and his mother's eyes. He may have been the oldest of them—twenty when he was in the accident—but he was still merely a babe. Second was Alyxander with his wavy blond hair, an eighteen-year-old who suffered leukemia before there was a cure, then Rachel with bright red curls, green eyes, and freckles on her upturned nose. She attempted suicide and when she survived, volunteered rather than seek treatment. She got her wish, and I got to live seventy-four more years in her body. My fourth Second was the youngest I'd ever taken and the first since the Immigration War—Donovan, an eleven-year-old. After Donovan was Milissa, whose dark brown eyes and hair reminded me of fondue chocolate. I stop in front of the last painting. Curly gold hair springs from the youth's head, and his eyes, tilted at the corners, hint at a wisdom belying his age. His smile is that of Hercules, handsome and self-assured in his own body. When I chose Stephen, he was nervous and never smiled. But I can still see his chest puff up with pride when he spoke the words, and he never looked back. He truly understood the process to be a better destiny, a worthy sacrifice. On the day of the Exchange, he faltered a bit, and his hands shook when he pulled himself up onto the hospital bed, but I overlooked that. We are all allowed our moments of fear, especially at the end.

My eyes move automatically to the empty space next to Stephen's portrait. A light has already been installed for an image of me as Mira, which will be commissioned after I've recovered from the procedure. Ben whines and leans into my hand. I scratch behind his ears. At least I have one friend I can trust.

RIGHTFUL PROPERTY

mira

"**S**O WHEN DID YOU BECOME involved with the Lifers?" Buzzcut asks me for about the hundredth time, scowling from across a scarred metal table.

"I'm not!" I lean as far forward as the stupid cuffs on my wrists will allow. Do they actually think I'm a real threat, a seventeen-year-old girl who has to be chained up to a chair so she doesn't hurt anyone?

"You were with them. Don't deny it," he snarls, lips twisting as he bares his teeth at me in hatred. "Once your First rejects you, you'll be sentenced to death, just like that other one we arrested last night."

"Who?" A scared, round face blinks back into my mind. "Mr. Flannigan? But he's just a teacher." I lean back in my chair, letting the cold, uncomfortable metal chill me though the thin shirt they made me put on.

"Like you didn't know." Abruptly, Buzzcut slams his hand on the table, and I jump until the metal cuffs give me a sharp warning jolt. "He's no more a teacher than I am. He's a traitor, that's what he is. Know what his code name was? Paul Revere. As if he could really warn anyone of anything, fat bastard that he is." He relaxes, resting his hands on the table, folded up, like we're having a nice little chit-chat.

"Paul Revere?" My voice is quiet, soft like a child's, afraid to ask a question.

"Yeah, hardly original. Claims he's trying to save our nation, our country, from the likes of your First, but if he'd been any sort of teacher, he'd have realized that the real Paul Revere was a traitor, too. A real patriot wouldn't betray his home country. I'll be glad to see him die. Just like I was glad to see that other one kick the bucket."

"Other one?" I squeak.

"Yeah." He makes a dismissive gesture with his hands, as though it isn't worth worrying about. "The one who didn't live at your farm. What was his name?" He snaps his fingers, as if trying to remember.

"Henri Lee?"

Buzzcut's face lights up. "Ha, I knew it! You do know him!"

I shake my head. "No, no. That's just what Tanner called him."

"Ahh, your little boyfriend. It all comes back to him, doesn't it?" He leans over the table, resting his elbows on its scratched and grooved surface. "Did he put you up to this?"

"No, I—"

"Lemme guess. He told you to go meet this guy so you could both run away together. Is that it?" I must have blushed or something because he chortles in some sort of evil glee. "Oh that's rich. Just wait until the guys hear about this one. True love," he snickers.

"No, it's not. He just—"

"Just what? Wanted to keep you safe?" I nod. Fear rises in my gut. "Newsflash, kid, the rebels exist outside the law for a reason. If they're caught, they're killed. They're all traitors. They betrayed our nation. You would have been hunted down for the rest of your life. Do you want that?" I bite my lip, looking down as tears well up in my eyes. "Even if you'd escaped," he says, lowering his voice to a growl, "some wild animal woulda killed you, eaten you, or youda been captured. No, it's better that you're here, even if you won't make it out alive."

"But... but what about Tanner?" There's that squeaky mouse voice again.

Buzzcut shakes his head and chuckles. "Oh, don't you worry, princess. You're not alone. Your little boyfriend is here."

I jump forward a little, excitement making me forget the cuffs. One little jolt reminds me. "You mean he's here? At the prison?" Buzzcut nods. "Can I see him?"

He throws his head back and laughs. "You have got to be kidding me, girl. You're about to be tried for treason, and all you're worried about is your little boy toy?"

I stiffen. "He's a good man, and I love him."

"A good man who was going to feed you to the wolves." He flashes a toothy grin. "Do you have any idea what the rebels would do to you?"

I shake my head.

"They'd kill you, girl. Kill you so your First can't have you. You, his rightful property. Is that what you want?" I shake my head again, denying what he says. The Lifers wouldn't kill me, would they? If they were dangerous, Tanner would never take me to them. "Mira, Mira, Mira. You're an idiot." He hides his bitterness with a smile. "You don't know anything, do you?" I open my mouth to speak, but he cuts me off. "I guess it don't matter anyway. Maybe we should have let the rebels have you. Either way, you're dead." With that, he casts me one last, cold grin, shoves his chair back so hard it hits the wall, and stomps out. His cold chuckle echoes through the room, chilling me far more than anything else.

ONE OF OURS

socrates

"**I**s it a crime to have anything cheery around here?" I grumble as I step out of the pod at Fullbright Detention Center. My hand strays to my side but comes up empty. I sigh. Dammit, I miss my dog, even wish I could have brought him to the prison. Too dangerous, even for me. Only the worst prisoners are kept at Fullbright, which apparently includes my friend and my Second.

"Excuse me, sir? Did you say something?" The young, pasty-faced guard looks nervous as hell, which isn't surprising as he's probably never had to deal with the likes of me before.

"Is a goddamned flowerpot too much to ask?" I cast a glance at him, and he gulps, hand twitching over the Artos holster clipped to his belt. What's he going to do, shoot me?

"A flowerpot, sir?"

I shake my head and gesture out past the thick fences that separate the Transportation Center from the detention center. Because you can't keep the pods near the prison, can you? It would be the perfect prison break, literally disappearing into thin air. "Look at this place." The tall pale gray stone walls of the prison rise above us in austere fashion. Thinly-slotted breaks in the stone settle for windows, and I imagine old-time Robin Hood-esque archers waiting on the other side of the castle's walls for intruders. "It's dreary as hell, Marty."

The young man gulps and opens his mouth, like a fish flopping on dry land, gasping its last few breaths. "My name's Martin, sir."

I shrug, and limp toward the gate. Marty follows at a safe distance until we reach the first of the three actual physical gates that will lead us to Fullbright. I must undergo a body scan again, and the new guard, with a nametag that reads Alistair, looks none too happy about scanning me, but I suppose it's protocol, so I can't blame the chap.

"You're all clear, Martin," Alistair says to Marty as he casts quick, rodent-like glances at me.

"Of course I am." I scowl at him.

Marty gulps, his huge Adam's apple bobbing in his throat. "Thanks, Alistair." He looks at me. "This way, sir."

"Fine," I grumble. "Let's go." I follow him, hobbling, through a series of gates that slide open. The first is an older type of metal wire, stainless steel. The second is a fine mesh emanating an electronic field. The third is invisible except for the posts that delineate its boundaries. The laser force shields are far deadlier than any of the barriers.

On the other side of the gates, a small, black and silver hovering vehicle that looks the way I remember a golf cart bobs gently a couple inches off the ground. Another guard, this one a little older and not looking too thrilled to be serving as my personal taxi, doesn't even acknowledge us.

"Here, let me help you." Marty reaches for my arm.

I shake him off. "No, thank you. I can get up here just fine." Except that I can't. Every time I lift my foot even a few inches, the damn cart seems to get higher and higher off the ground. After the third try, I turn in frustration and glare at Marty. "Can you get him to just set this thing on the ground?"

The poor boy jumps as if jolted by electricity and spins around to look at his stone-faced compatriot. "Jenson, can you turn it off?"

After giving the barest of nods and heaving a superhuman sigh, he flips a switch in the front of the vehicle, and it lowers to the ground. Its slight hum gives way to silence.

"Thank you." I give the boy what must be a fearsome grin because he looks even more nervous now. He watches me like a hawk as I am finally able to board this stupid little aircraft and arrange myself and my cane in the back seat.

Once Marty is on board, Jenson flips the switch again, and the ship lifts off, moving slowly at first before gathering steam and zooming toward the prison proper. It's not a long jaunt, maybe a quarter mile or so, but long enough that I doubt I could have walked it.

Surrounding the front of Fullbright is a set of about twenty cement steps. Thankfully, Jenson takes us to the top of those, so I don't have to fall on my ass trying to ascend them. Once inside the front door, we undergo another round of searches. Even my cane is scanned three times for weapons. Makes me think of how pitifully unprotected I am out in Santa Fe. Not that many brave the deserts to harass me. No, that privilege is reserved for lower level politicians and the President's staff.

"What is your business here, sir?" the dour-faced woman sitting at the polished metal desk asks for about the fortieth time.

"I'd like to see Edward Flannigan and Mira of Chesaning."

She nods, curtly. "Yes, sir. I'll call that in, and let you know when they have secured a room." She speaks into her wrist unit. "I'm sorry, sir, but Mira of Chesaning is unavailable."

This is odd. "Why? I want to speak to her."

She shakes her head. "The girl is in questioning right

now. Unfortunately, she won't be finished for some time, but you may still see Edward Flannigan."

"You mean I can't see my own Second?" I put on my best scowling face.

"She isn't your Second any longer, is she?" She sounds curious.

"Of course she is! I haven't renounced her."

"But sir... she's a traitor. She was working with the Lifers."

"Bah!" I push her words away. "She's just a kid. Kids make mistakes. I'm certain you were young once."

She opens her mouth but snaps it shut before she makes a retort. "I'm sorry, sir. I overstepped my boundaries. Would you like to wait here?"

I take in the cold black and white marble floors, the painfully bare white walls, and agonizingly stiff benches lining the walls. "Yes." I sigh. "I'll just wait here, but I don't suppose it'll take long. Will it?" She pales a bit under her non-tan and taps her wrist com. It turns bright green, and she turns away as she murmurs into it. After what must be a heated conversation, she nods and taps it again, returning it to its fleshy color.

"It'll just be a moment." She turns away from me back to small screens that reflect back in her eyes.

"Fine, fine, it's not like I've got any place better to be." I walk over to the benches before lowering myself, bones creaking, onto one of the cold, metal benches. About ten minutes later, an older guard with severe posture marches through a door adjacent to the receptionist's desk and stands at attention.

"Socrates, sir?" He scans the room before zeroing in on me. After getting to my feet, I follow him down a long hall, past a line of closed doors to one that stands slightly apart from the rest. My guard, who has no nametag, stops abruptly at the door, causing me to stumble to a stop as well, almost falling down. He peeks in the door, looks back at Marty, and nods. "He's in here." *Hmmm, something doesn't feel right.* The man scans a wrist band on his right arm and his tattoo before the door clicks. Do they do this with all the dangerous criminals?

But it's hard to see danger in a man who's shrunken from his former, pompous self, hunched over the table in a thin gray shirt and trousers, black stripes running horizontally across his body. His head rests in his hands, and his long, thin red hair is shaved short, like a common Texan. His glasses are missing, and he squints at me, taking a moment before he recognizes me. Hope fills his pale blue eyes.

"Socrates, you came. They... they told me you wouldn't. They said you wouldn't want to see a traitor like me."

I don't say anything at all as I hobble into the room and over to the table, lean my cane against it, and settle myself in a straight-backed metal chair across from him. Despite his unkempt appearance, he tries to maintain some semblance of calm. His hands and arms, the sweat stains under his arms and around the collar of his shirt, and the vibrant red marks that line what I can see of his forearms all tremble. As I regard him, the light in his eyes dims. I wait another minute more before shaking my head. "Oh Edward, what have you done?"

He drops his head back in his hands and lets out a deep breath. When he looks up again, it's not the hope I saw before, or the resignation I expect. It's a flash of anger, then sadness.

"How many has it been?"

His question takes me aback, and I sit up straighter in my hard, uncompromising seat. "I'm not sure what you're asking, my friend."

"How many kids have you killed?"

I look down, away. His question makes me uncomfortable. "I don't see how that's relevant."

"Do you remember their names? Who they were before you murdered them?"

"Of course I remember their names!" I look him straight in the eyes. He's not going to make me feel guilty for being who I am, not one bit.

"But you don't remember who they were, do you? Their individual personalities, quirks, goals for the future? It's all gone, isn't it?" His expression softens with his words, as if he feels sorry for me.

I raise an eyebrow. "Why are you asking me this? It doesn't matter. I'm not here to discuss my past Seconds. I'm here to talk to you."

Edward lets out a deep breath and leans forward as far as the thin wiry shackles binding his wrists to the chair will allow. I can tell when he stretches too far because he twitches as if a jolt of electricity hits him. "Don't you get it, Socrates? These kids, what's happening to them, it's the most important injustice going on in the world right now. They celebrate you, people like you." His face morphs into a sneer. "Child-murderers, as pseudo-celebrities. And people like me, we have to prepare these lambs for slaughter, assuage their doubts, make them more comfortable, all the while knowing they're going to die. And the others, the ones who can't be chosen, they're either oblivious or criminally negligent for not doing anything about it."

"Now see here—" I start to stand, curling my wrinkled fingers around the arms of the chair.

Edward shakes his head sharply. "Please Socrates, listen to me."

Something in his voice, his desperation, settles me back down. Folding my hands in my lap, I turn all my focus on him. "Go on."

Edward takes a deep breath, his face sets into a serious look, and a slight smile parts his lips. "I am a member of Live Once, or a Lifer as we're called by the rest of society. We exist everywhere, all around the world, and still nowhere any government can find us. We've infiltrated all levels of society except the President, and I imagine one day one of ours will sit in that chair, too." He gives me a satisfied nod.

"What's this got to do with me?"

"Everything, my friend. You're Socrates, the First of them all."

I chuckle. "Some nerve, calling me a friend."

He winces. "I know, accusing you of murder doesn't help, does it? I apologize. I may have come on a bit strong."

I shake my head. "I've been called worse. Just last week at the Smithsonian—"

The guard at the door clears his throat, and Marty glances at Edward. "Sir, you have five minutes, then we have to take the prisoner back to his cell."

"But we're not done—"

He shakes his head. "I'm sorry sir, but those are my orders."

"It appears we don't have much time left."

Edward throws back his head and laughs, freer than I've ever seen him. "That's funny, coming from you, my friend."

"Do you know when the trial is? I'd like to be there."

He looks down at his hands and shakes his head. "No, I think they're planning it for after your Release to minimize the likelihood of turning me into a martyr." I open my mouth to interject, but he holds up his hand, stopping me. "But when this goes to trial, they're going to ask me to admit my part in Live Once, and I will say yes. They will sentence me to death, and even though I imagine I'll be afraid, as I'm sure every person is in their final moments, I'll also be smiling because I'll know that, in death if not in life, my existence will make a difference. My fight, my struggle, which is the struggle of all mankind, to have freedom from oppression, freedom to live my life the way I choose, will not be in vain."

"Why? Is it really worth dying for?"

He smiles, the expression tired as it twitches the corners of his once dashing mustache. "You should ask your Second that question." Edward looks at the guard, nods at him, and sits back in his chair, seemingly at peace. The interview is over.

ANOTHER LIFETIME

mira

"YOU'RE LUCKY, PRINCESS," A GUARD who looks like his nose has been smashed in a few times says as he grabs my arm and escorts me from my cold, dark, drafty prison cell. I'm almost actually glad to see him, even though he was one of the men who brought me here, and smile in spite of my fear as he opens the door. A shaft of light so bright my eyes ache pierces the darkness.

"Lucky? How?" I shade my eyes to protect them from the glare.

"Your First is bailing you out. If it were up to me, you'd die here." He leers at me. His words make me wish he'd just shut the door again so I can curl back up in the corner of my cell, the one farthest away from the toilet, and wish I am anywhere else.

"He's getting me out?"

"Are you deaf? Naw, you're just stupid, like the rest of them. Not a brain spread out among the lot of you."

"Hey!" I stand up. *Oh, that hurts.* My legs are dead, tingling from too much time spent in one position with nothing soft to sit on. "We're not—"

"Look, I don't care. Maybe you're the smartest in your family." He looks me up and down. "It doesn't matter. Your First must have seen *something* in you, since he picked you and all. But to me, you're still a traitor. Just like the rest of the scum here. You just get to walk out of here, free, while your friends rot. It ain't fair."

"Tanner?"

Pugnose, growing impatient, grabs my elbow. "Come on. Let's go."

"Wait!" I dig my heels into the cement, for as much good as that does me, and his grip goes painfully tight around my elbow, pinching the nerves. "Tanner. Where is he?"

Pugnose stops. "The boy? Don't worry." He chuckles. "He's alive. I can say that much for him. Don't know what they're going to do with him yet, but he's sure doing better than the other one."

I try to jerk free from him, but it's as though my arm is tied to one of the plow horses, and I can't hold the reins. Digging my heels again into the hard, unyielding floor, I cause enough trouble that he stops. "I want to see him," I say when he turns around.

"Tough. That ain't gonna happen." He pulls me forward again, and even though I'm fighting it with all my strength, I can't help being dragged forward.

"Why not?"

My question must surprise him because he stops again, while we're in the hallway, in the midst of other doorways like the one that capped my cell. "Just no, all right? My orders are to take you to the transport room and get your precious little behind to the Smith. If you have any more questions, ask your damn First when you see him."

Behind the door immediately to my left, there's a heavy thumping, like someone's hitting it over and over again. Why? To get someone's attention? Pugnose sees my interest and growls. "Let's go, now. You don't need to be looking behind these doors."

"Why not?" A cold thought grips me. "Is Tanner here?"

"What do you want me to say, girl? This is Fullbright,

116

the only detention center in America where we keep the rebels. Of course that teacher from Washington and your boyfriend are here." His words drip with disgust, but I can't tell if it's meant for me because, well, I'm supposedly a rebel or because I'm an idiot. I guess it doesn't really matter. "Either way, you're never going to see either of them again. Is that what you wanted to hear?"

Tears threaten, and my mind goes blank, so I don't resist as he leads the rest of the way to the transport room where he scans his tattoo on a small lighted bar next to the door. He forces my hand up and does the same with my tattoo.

"Wait! What are you doing?" I struggle to wrench my wrist from his grip, but he's too strong. He forces it to the thin blue-lit bar anyway, which flashes and my wrist feels hot for a second. When it's done, he lets me drop my hands to my sides, and I rub my wrists, casting a glance at the doorway. Could I escape through there? Where would I go? Then I look at the pods. Could I just jump in one of those? Maybe I could program it from the inside?

"Don't even think about it." He doesn't even look at me as he stiffly marches over to what looks like a central control panel. He scans his wrist again, and the machine blinks. "You've been scanned through, and if you try to leave, the whole damn place will go into lockdown. You do not want that to happen."

"What was that for?"

"To check you in. All your information has been stored in your bar code, and that was registered with Washington the instant you were chosen. If you even think about trying to run..." He smirks. "There's nowhere you could go where you'd be safe. Now, get over here. I have to scan you in to enter your destination."

"Why all the scanning?" I walk over to him. No use fighting this, I guess. At least I'm getting out of here.

"To make sure it's you who goes in the pod. There's

another scanner in there, though you don't have to scan your wrist, and if it's not you, let's just say it won't transport you anywhere you want to go, that's for sure." He scans my wrist again, and the second transport from the door lights up, humming softly. "Let's go." He grabs my wrist again, just as feeling was returning to it, and leads me over to it. When the door slides open, he shoves me inside, jumps in behind me, and shuts the door. I barely catch my fall before the air around me starts thrumming, and once again the ground tosses up from under me, and I'm helpless to keep my feet right side down.

When the door slides open, I shakily push myself away from the back of the pod and step into a long, white room, filled with silver pods on both sides. Several silver-suited attendants with the same sort of handheld tablets Flannigan had wait by the machines. None of them look our way, at least, not officially, but I catch more than a couple of them casting quick glances under their straight-laced expressions. Bullfrog, following me, leans over to growl in my ear. "This is your last chance. You screw up, and I'd love to throw you back in that cell forever."

Buzzcut comes up to us and nods before eyeing me shrewdly. Bullfrog stands next to him, looking bored. "The prisoner made it here safely, I take it?"

"Of course, sir." He clicks his heels together, stands up straight, and salutes. "As requested."

"Good."

"What's going on? Where are we?" I look at both men. Buzzcut just shakes his head. Bullfrog smirks.

"You don't recognize your nation's capital?"

I shake my head. *No, this isn't possible. I'm not supposed to be here. I'm supposed to be... where? What happens after you're chosen but then been captured as a rebel? Has this ever happened before?* When I don't move, Buzzcut shoves me ahead of him, swearing under his breath. "This way." He jerks his head toward the door at the end of the

118

room. Pugnose waits at the pod until we reach the door, before climbing back inside and leaving.

As we reach it, a tanned young man with short dark hair, which is apparently the style reserved for us at the farm and military guys like Buzzcut and Bullfrog, steps forward. My jaw just about drops. This guy is handsome. Not that I should be noticing or anything. His face is pleasantly broad with expressive deep brown, almost black eyes and a wide, smiling mouth. He opens the door and bows. He's older than I am, but not by much. His gaze flits up to my face, and I freeze. Captured by his eyes, I can't breathe. I can't speak. I can't do anything but stand there like an idiot until he looks away. Except that he doesn't. His eyes probe mine, and in those chocolaty depths, I see surprise, a jolt, as if he feels something, too, but he quickly covers it with a smooth transition to boredom as he finally looks at my captors. He nods at them, and they nod back. What are they doing, trading me from one jail to another?

"Welcome to the Smithsonian Institution. My name is William, but you may call me Will." His voice is low, deep, and once again, I feel trapped in its depths. I shake my head quickly. *Stop it, Mira. You're not some innocent schoolgirl. This is ridiculous.* He holds the door open, and the guards lead me inside. "This entrance is mostly reserved for delivery and basic service, but they wanted to keep your arrival as quiet as possible, so they brought you in early."

For the first time, I notice how rumpled his blue uniform is, as if he just got out of bed. Was he not expecting me? "Did we wake you up? I'm sorry."

He stops abruptly and turns around to face me, quirking a dark eyebrow as if I've surprised him. "You have nothing to apologize for, ma'am. My job is to help Seconds." His voice is rich, like honey out of the beehives at the far edge of the fields. I shake my head again as he starts walking. Bullfrog pushes me, none too gently, after him.

"This way, please." He leads the way down a narrow corridor with lights that flash on as we near them. Ornate burgundy carpeting, worn and faded, muffles our footsteps. I can see pictures on the walls—not screens like in the manor house, they're actual pictures—but I can't make out any details because we're walking quickly, and the light is pretty dim.

The guards seem more relaxed, like they know they don't have anything to worry about here. Like we're safe. People dart in and out of narrow white doors. None of them stop or stare, and all of them wear dark blue servant tunics and pants like Will's.

"This is the Castle," Will says as we leave the hall and approach an octagonal desk at the center of a large, open room. "I need to check you in, and then we can go to your room."

We? As in both of us? Is he staying with me? I... I can't. It's not right. I open my mouth to speak, but Will is already walking away.

A pudgy, washed out-looking man perches on a small stool in the middle of the eight-sided desk. His thin arms and legs jut out from his body like tiny sticks out of one of the mud pies Rosie and I used to make when we were younger. And, well, when she was still alive.

"Good evening, Alfred." Will smiles. "How'd you end up working the late shift?"

"Drew the short end of the stick, I'm afraid." Alfred shakes his head. "That, and the boss thinks I have a personality problem. Can you believe it?" He huffs out a breath, puffing his cheeks. "He said I have no people skills, so I'm stuck here until I learn some because he said he can't have me pissing off the Firsts. Bunch of pansies, the lot of them."

Will leans over the desk, letting Alfred get a good look at me. "Well, at least it's quieter," he says.

Alfred pales and takes a deep breath. "Don't mind me, Ma'am, I'm just a complainer. I didn't mean nothing by it."

"Don't worry about it," I say, and both men look surprised.

Alfred studies me, as if taking in every detail so he can describe me later to his friends. Then he shakes himself, some semblance of business coming back to his mannerisms. "I'm sorry, sirs. My clock's still all messed up. You want her room number?"

"Yes, if you don't mind."

"Three-twelve is open."

Will nods, thanks him, and we walk away from the desk, turning right, down another long corridor before stopping in front of a pair of metal doors. "We'll take the elevator to the museum."

"Okay." I must look a bit queasy because he smiles reassuringly at me.

"It's okay. They're perfectly safe. Much safer than a pod, in fact."

"Much safer? But they can... they can fall, or what if they get stuck or..."

He chuckles. "You've never ridden in one before, have you?"

I shake my head. "We don't have them at the farm, just stairs. All I know is what I've heard from the Chesanings from when they've come here."

"Well, let me assure you, they're quite safe."

"But they're... they're... a thousand years old?"

"Not quite," he smiles again, a brief flash of white teeth. "After the war, they were refurbished to run both vertically and horizontally, enabling us to reach any destination at the Smith complex in one trip. They're routinely updated and inspected, so honestly, you have nothing to worry about. Besides, if you've ridden in a pod, you have nothing to fear."

He quickly scans his wrist tattoo, and the door clicks, sliding open. Would that work for me? If I were to scan my code, would it get me out of here?

We walk through the doors, and the guards follow like faithful dogs. After the doors close behind us, Will uses a silver recessed numberless keypad and types in the number to my room.

"The Castle might be the central hub of the Smith, but it's not where you're going. You'll be staying in the American History Museum," Will says, trying to take my mind off the queasy feeling in the pit of my stomach as the elevator moves down.

"I'm staying in a museum?" I squeak, tightening my hands in the pockets of my pants.

Will glances over to me, as if to check to see if I'm okay. He studies me for a moment before speaking. "Well, yes. All government business has been conducted in these buildings since the Immigration War."

"I knew that." Darnit. I *did* know that. *Good job, Mira, way to look even more stupid.*

The elevator speeds downward, then stops and moves at a 90-degree angle. When the door slides open, Will leads us down another hallway, this one lit by bright lights even more glaring than the noon day sun when I'm out in the field helping Tanner work the plow horses. The carpet is thick and dark blue under my feet, so plush that we make no sounds as we pass room after room. The plain wooden doors are decorated with numbers starting at 302.

Will stops in front of the door with 312 engraved on a bronze plaque next to it. He opens the door and gestures for me to precede him inside. Before I take a single step, Buzzcut grabs my arm while Bullfrog slides into the room ahead of us.

"Wait, we gotta check it out, first."

"For what?" I back away from him, and he doesn't try to stop me.

"More of those rebel scum." He sneers.

"You think they'd try to attack us, even here?"

"They're everywhere, girl." He looks down the hall, then

back into the room. I turn to Will, but he's looking straight ahead, as if he doesn't hear our conversation or is trying really hard to make it look that way.

After a moment, Bullfrog comes back and says, "All clear, boss."

"Excellent." Buzzcut glances at me. "After that mess at Chesaning, we must remember not to underestimate our enemy."

Does he mean me? I shiver. Both of the guards step back, and Will gestures for me to go into the room. Once I get past the doorway, however, I stop and look around.

The room is much nicer than anything I've seen in the manor house and about a gillion times better than the four white walls I had at home. It's got velvety blue curtains and thick cream colored carpet. The bathroom is on the left, and past that is the huge bed, which must be more than twice the size of mine at home. There are more fluffy pillows on that bed than I've ever seen in my life. A small metal nightstand and dresser rest on either side of the bed. Against the wall, a huge video screen is mounted next to a small dark wooden desk with a chair tucked inside.

I gawk at the screen, then turn back to Will. "Are you sure this is the right room?"

Will arches his eyebrow at me. "Of course. Why would you ask? Is this room not suitable?"

I feel my face flush. *Think, Mira. This is normal for him.* I grab onto the first thought that comes to my mind. "Well, umm, we don't use screens at the farm. They're illegal."

"Oh, right." He looks relieved. "It's okay, here, to watch videos and use computers. You're Absolved. It's not illegal anymore."

"Are you sure? My brother got in trouble for it back at the farm."

"Trust me, it's completely normal here. Do you want me to show you how to use it?"

123

"Umm, maybe later."

"Okay, if there's anything you need, let me know." He nods at the screen. "Do you see that red button? That's how you contact me. If you push that button, it'll ring me on my wrist monitor." He points at the black band around his wrist. "You can contact me wherever I am, and if I'm unavailable, I'll make sure to send someone you can trust." Will's eyes pierce mine, holding me there. It feels as if there's something more to his words, like there's a deeper meaning. Is he trying to tell me something?

"Thank you," I whisper, finally breaking his gaze.

"Do you need any further assistance?" I shake my head. "Well, I'll leave you to get settled and rest up. Please call me if you need anything." He backs out of the room.

"We'll be right outside the door, princess," Buzzcut says gruffly from the doorway. "Don't worry your pretty little head about anything."

"Yeah," Bullfrog cackles. "We'll keep you safe from those rebels." *Oh, great. Babysitters.* "Just don't even think about going anywhere."

"So am I a prisoner here, too? Might as well have left me at the prison," I yell through the doorway.

He laughs. "It's like our supervisor told your First: it's for your own safety. Can't let anything happen to Socrates's newest pet." He slams the door before I can think up some snarky comment. Jerks.

Feeling cold, I rub my hands up and down my arms. Through the walls, I hear a deep-throated chuckle followed by a low murmur of voices, and then someone laughs. After a brief pause, two sets of footsteps echo down the hall, leaving one to babysit. Who is it? Pugnose? Buzzcut?

Suddenly exhausted, I strip out of my clothes and into a pale blue tunic from the dresser. The cloth smells different, of flowers and freshness. Feeling tears sting my eyes again, I chuck the dirty, smelly clothes that remind me of the prison and curl up on my side on the bed. Tanner's face flashes through my head. His eyes twinkling, then the pop of the Artos. The terror. I'll never see him again. I didn't even get to say good-bye. *What if he's...?* A sob catches in my throat. *No, he can't be. They wouldn't kill him for that.*

------&>◇<&------

I'm awakened by a knock on the door. I swing my legs over the side of the bed and pad over to answer it.

Bullfrog stands to one side of the door while Will brings in a tray of food.

"I thought you might be hungry, so I brought you a bite to eat. If you don't want it, let me know, and I can take it away." He sets the tray on the desk by the bed. "Is there anything I can get for you?"

I run my hand through my messy hair and then try to straighten the crinkles out of my tunic. Seriously, they should warn me before they just waltz in here so I have time to look at least somewhat presentable. I shake my head. "What time is it?"

"Just after noon."

"Really? How long was I asleep?"

"Just a few hours."

"Oh, well, thank you. I don't think I need anything else."

He nods, his lips barely betraying a hint of a smile.

"Fine," I say, "so you woke me up, all right? I had a rough night."

His eyes soften in sympathy. "Of course, ma'am. My apologies. After you eat, your physician, Jessiah, will come to give you an exam, if that's all right."

"That's fine, Will. And please, call me Mira. All this ma'am stuff isn't me."

He flashes a quick smile. "Of course, Mira. As you wish." He turns and leaves me with my food, which is rather like what we have at the farm, only the composite here has some kind of sweet, buttery sauce on it, and I've never had that luxury before.

After I finish eating, I contemplate messing around with the screen on the wall just as it blinks, and an older woman in pale green scrubs smiles at me from the screen, as if she hasn't a care in the world, like the ground hasn't just been pulled out from under her. I swallow and take a deep breath before switching my attention to the video screen. A petite woman, about the same age as my mom, smiles back at me, faint lines framing her eyes and threads of gray shining in her thick black hair.

"Hello Mira. My name is Jessiah Matthews, and we have you scheduled for a physical this afternoon."

"Now?"

"Well, yes. We like to get you checked out as quickly as possible after your arrival at the Smith. Does right now work for you?"

"I guess so." As if I have any say in the matter, anyway.

"Excellent, I'll be down to get you shortly." When she comes to collect me, I realize Jessiah is just as pleasant in person as she is on the com unit. She smiles a lot and promises, "This won't hurt a bit." *Yeah, I think I've heard that before.*

She leads me through a set of double doors marked Infirmary, past a small, comfortable-looking waiting room, to a small sterile room with a padded examination table in the center. A chair sits right next to it, along with a scrubbed-clean counter with drawers that I'm sure hold a bunch of really painful medical instruments. "Please take off your clothes, and put this on." She hands me a paper-thin white gown with ties in the back, then leaves me alone.

I change quickly and just have time to fold my clothes, put them on the floor, and hop up on the table before there's a soft knock on the door. Jessiah enters, slipping her tablet into one of the big pockets on her jacket. "Welcome to the Smith, Mira. I'll be performing your exam." She pats me on the knee. "This is standard for Seconds, so you

126

don't have anything to worry about. We'll just check you over, then do blood and DNA tests."

"What's the DNA test for?"

She shrugs. "It's nothing to worry about. It's just to check your lineage for any genetic abnormalities."

"My lineage? What does that mean?"

"It's to make sure you're Mira of Chesaning Farms, of course, and not a plant by the Lifers."

"That's stupid. Why would I be here if I wasn't myself?"

She lifts her slender shoulders, then drops them. "You never know. Maybe to disrupt the Release ceremony, kill Socrates, bomb the Smith, who knows? It's been tried before. Besides, it's nothing personal, just a precautionary measure. There's nothing to be afraid of."

From one of the large, deep pockets on her jacket, she pulls a small, handheld scanner. "Hand me your right index finger." She extends her hand. When I hesitate, she wiggles her fingers impatiently. "Come now, Mira, it's just a simple DNA test. It'll only take a fraction of a second."

When I finally place my hand in hers, she efficiently jams my finger in the device. It clicks, and I try to remove my finger, but it's stuck. Then there's a stinging pain which makes me hiss, and Jessiah smiles. "There, all done. See? That wasn't so bad, was it?" Her bland smile is meant to make me feel better, but I just sit there, swinging my legs off the side of the table, watching the blinking lights on the little machine flash between red and green. Glancing up at Jessiah, I see that she's watching it, too. Eventually, the little machine slows down. It spends more time on red then green, and I catch my breath. *What if I fail? How is that even possible? Red must be bad, right?*

I close my eyes until there is a high-pitched beep. When I finally look, I breathe a sigh of relief. It's green. "Good," is all she says. She sets that device on the counter, and then from a drawer underneath, she pulls another device, small and black with two long thin things coming off the top, kind of like the antennae on a bug.

"What's that?" I bite my lip, folding my hands in my lap in front of me. My pointer finger still stings.

"Just another scanner. This one looks at all your internal organs and joints to make sure everything is functioning within an acceptable range."

"Will it hurt?" I eye the machine skeptically.

She shakes her head. "No, you won't feel a thing." And I don't. She scans every part of my body she can reach, then has me stand up and turn around so she can scan the other half. When she's done, she sets that on the counter as well. "There, that wasn't so bad now, was it?"

"No, I guess not." I boost myself back up onto the table. "What's next?"

"Your vaccination, of course. I'll be right back." After patting me on my knee, she leaves and returns after a couple of minutes with what looks like a tiny silver gun. The tip is pink rubber, and in the middle, I can see the tip of a sharp needle. "You won't even feel a thing."

"That's what you said about the DNA thingy." I pull my arm away as she lifts the device toward me.

She chuckles and presses the gun to my upper arm and pulls the trigger. There's a cooling sensation, then heat, then a tingly feeling. Then, nothing. She pulls the gun away and presses a cotton pad to the site. "There, now you're really all finished."

She pats me again on the knee and tosses the cotton pad into a hole in the wall. "You're all set, so why don't you get dressed, and I'll have someone take you back to your room."

I hop off the table as she reaches the door. "You don't have to do that. I'm sure I can find my own way."

"Nonsense." She pauses. "I'll be right back."

By the time I finish dressing, she knocks again. "I have one of your guards out here waiting for you whenever you're ready."

"Where's Will?"

"Who?"

"The guy... I mean my servant."

She shrugs, as if she doesn't care. "I don't know, probably off on his other duties." She opens the door and leads me out, to the waiting room where Bullfrog leans back in his chair, legs spread out, hands folded on his stomach like he's about to take a nap.

"It's about time, princess," he grumbles, slowly stretching and getting to his feet. Jessiah frowns at him. "Is she good to go?" he asks her.

"Yes, she's done here."

He nods. "Good. Let's go."

I follow him back to my room, where I start pacing. *What should I do now?* I hate being cooped up. If I were at the farm, I'd have my chores, or be watching Max, maybe taking him swimming in the stream or just relaxing with Tanner. I stop, my thoughts going back to Tanner and Mr. Flannigan. The walls start closing in on me. What at first felt beautiful and opulent now feels more like the box where I was punished for sitting with my little brother, whose only crime was watching the news. *I have to get out of this room.* I glance at the red button Will told me to push if I needed anything. Does this count?

Making up my mind, I press the button. The screen immediately changes, and Will's face fills it. He smiles pleasantly and maybe a little bit surprised. "Good afternoon, Mira. How may I help you?"

"I-I'm sorry to bother you, but is there anywhere I can go to get out of here for a little bit? I'm not used to being inside this much." I twist my hands behind me, feeling the sweat slick my palms. I definitely have to get out of here.

He narrows his eyes at me. "You can't leave the Smith, you know."

I shake my head. "Oh, I know that. I just want to get out, go somewhere, maybe somewhere outdoors. Is that possible?"

Will pauses, then his face lights up. "I'm sure the gardens can be made available to you if you wish. Would you like me to take you there? If not, I'm sure your guard can escort you."

I gulp, replaying the image of Buzzcut leering at me, calling me princess, implying that Tanner had been beaten. No, I'd rather stay in my room than go anywhere with that monster. "Can you take me? If you don't mind, and you're not busy, that is."

"Of course. When would you like to go?"

"Oh, whenever." I take a deep, centering breath. "I'm ready when you are."

"Okay, just give me a few minutes to make the arrangements, and I'll come by to pick you up." I nod, and he leans forward. He must push a button similar to mine because the screen goes blank.

After a couple of minutes, I hear a quiet knock on the door. When I answer it, Will stands in the harsh light of the hall, wearing his customary blue servant's uniform. He smiles, his teeth white against his bronze skin. "Are you ready?"

I nod. Outside the room, we stop in front of Bullfrog, who grudgingly rises from a chair next to my door and scowls. *Or maybe that's his happy face.* "The Second's supposed to stay in her room."

Will inclines his head toward the guard. "I understand that, but Mira is not a prisoner here. Your duty is merely to provide for her safety, not her confinement."

"My boss ain't going to like this."

"My apologies, sir. But my orders are to see to the comfort of the Second to whom I'm assigned."

Bullfrog puffs up his chest and glowers at him.

Will shrugs. "You are, of course, welcome to accompany us to the garden if you wish."

He grimaces. "You'll bring her right back?"

"Of course." Will nods. "You have my word."

"Good." Bullfrog settles himself in the chair again, stretches out his legs, and closes his eyes.

Walking down the hall, Will starts in on the tour guide routine again. "Like I said before, this was the Smithsonian Institution, a world-renowned collection of museums, but by the time of the Immigration War, many of the buildings were in disrepair and unused, due in part to people's reliance on Firsts to hold much of history's memories. Computers mostly took care of the art, with high resolution and more accessibility to common people. I'm sure even you were able to see pictures of some of the art that was housed here."

Even me? "What's that supposed to mean?"

"I'm sorry?"

"We do go to school, you know. I'm not a complete idiot."

"My apologies. I didn't mean to imply anything."

I shake my head. "It doesn't matter. Is Socrates coming here, too?"

"Of course. He'll be here later today."

We reach the end of the long tunnel and come to a plain metal door. "The gardens were an original feature of the Smithsonian called the Enid A. Haupt Garden. They're located centrally to most of the rest of the buildings, except this one. We'll take another elevator to the main entrance." Will scans his wrist, and the door opens.

I follow him into the elevator.

When the doors open, I see a small ivory antechamber with dark green padded benches on both sides. A bronze plaque with the engraving, "Enid A. Haupt Garden" crowns the pressure-locked doorway.

When we step through the thick glass doors, spritzers descend from the ceiling and cover us in a mist so fine it dries instantly, not even dampening our clothing.

I wipe a bitter taste from my mouth and blink it from my eyes. "What was that stuff?"

"Disinfectant. It'll kill any foreign bacteria on our

bodies. The gardens contain a variety of animals and plants long extinct in the wild, and they need to be protected." He grabs the door handle. "Please don't touch anything. Some of the plants and animals are poisonous."

"Why?"

"The President's wife favors them."

"Do you grow any crops here?" I look around, stretching my head in either direction to look for familiar fields—long stretches of grain or corn, marching into the horizon—but there's nothing but the dense green vegetation, wet with humidity and new life. The path we're on looks like old, broken stones, and little weeds and grass grow in the cracks. If I look hard enough through the thick glass of the dome, I can see the outline of tall towers in the distance, a faint reminder that there is a world outside this paradise.

Will laughs. "Of course not. This is all for show."

"Oh, yeah. Your food comes from farms, doesn't it?"

He shakes his head, a sardonic smile quirking the corners of his mouth. "Not *our* food. Only the wealthy can afford food without any chemicals or genetic modification. For servants like me, food comes from places like South Africa and China. Places without a lot of regulation."

"Isn't that dangerous?"

"Who's going to care? If I get sick, there are a dozen people training to take my place."

He twists the handle, the door whooshes open, and humidity engulfs me. I forget to breathe, the heady scent of flowers on a hot summer day, damp earth, and growing things overwhelming me. Vibrant green presses in on all sides from leafy trees stretching straight toward the garden's ceiling to smaller, darker bushes and ferns. Flowers explode with orange, red, and sunny yellow blooms. The petals feel like the soft velvet of a cow's nose as I run my fingers gently over them.

"Be careful," Will reminds me. "It might be poisonous."

I jerk my hand back. "Sorry." Overhead, birds flit across the glass-domed sky. The birds' songs are music to my nature-starved ears. The garden is beautiful, but still, just another cage. "Amazing, I've never seen anything like this." I step out onto a worn dirt path. My toes twitch in their soft-soled shoes, and I almost give in to the urge to set them free. Back at the farm, I wouldn't have hesitated.

"I thought your farm was on the edge of the wilderness?" He looks curious as he says this, and although he's not looking at me, I can tell I have his total concentration. It's almost as if he actually wants to know more about me.

A strange tingling starts in the pit of my stomach, but rather than think about that, I answer his question. "It was, but we still didn't have anything like this. All the trees, plants, everything we had was naturally there. We didn't plant anything except crops, and flowers in the playground." Immediately, tiny little crosses, trampled by thick, heavy, unforgiving boots, the snapping of their little arms, echoes in my head. I gulp.

"Are you okay?" Will leans toward me, concern beetling his brow. "Is something wrong?"

On the tip of my tongue perches the truth. Should I tell him what happened? Would he understand?

"It's all right, Mira. You can trust me. Anything you say will be held in the strictest of confidence."

I look sharply up at him. "Do you know what happened to me before I came here?"

Will shakes his head, looking around uneasily, as if he's afraid someone might be listening. "No, just that your departure from your farm was... abrupt."

I chuckle, a hollow sound that immediately silences the birds. "I guess you could say that. We were attacked."

"What?" Real alarm crosses his features. "By whom?"

"The guards. The military. Whatever you call them."

"Why would they do that?"

I roll my eyes to hide my discomfort and turn away,

jamming my hands deep in my pockets. "They thought I was a rebel."

"You?" the disbelief in his voice turns me around.

"What, you don't think I'm capable of anything like that?" I gesture wide with my arms.

"No, of course not. I'm sure they were just trying to save you." He frowns.

"By coming after us in the middle of the night, arresting me, my... my friend, and my teacher, Mr. Flannigan, and throwing us in prison?"

His frown deepens. "They must have thought you were a Lifer."

"No," I whisper. "But I wasn't... they asked me to go, but I wouldn't." The *pop* from the guards' weapons echo in my head. I close my eyes.

"Who?"

"The one guy's name was Henri Lee and the other was..." I pause again. "... Tanner."

He looks closely at me. "Did you know them well?"

I glance at the ground. *Can I trust him?* "Tanner. He was my... friend." Will raises an eyebrow at me. "Tanner wanted me to talk to Henri. That's all. Yes, they wanted me to run away, but I swear I wasn't going to. And then Bullfrog planted evidence beside Henri while they were searching him and—"

"Who's Bullfrog? What do you mean by planted evidence? Are you sure?" I wince. *Think, Mira. Think before you open your mouth.*

The heat rushes up my neck, and I'm sure it turns my face a brilliant shade of red. "Umm, yeah. That's what I call one of the guards. The other two are Buzzcut and Pugnose."

"Should I be afraid to ask why?" His eyes twinkle, and the corners of his mouth twitch. Is he making fun of me?

"It's what they look like, kinda. Bullfrog is squat and short like a toad. Buzzcut has really short hair, and Pugnose, well..."

Will's chest shakes with laughter, though he doesn't make a sound.

"Look, just forget about it." I huff and turn away.

Will moves to stand in front of me, all seriousness. He quickly touches my arm to stop me from walking away. I look down, and he jerks his hand away. "Have you told anyone else about what the guards did?"

"No. Who would I tell? Who would listen?"

"You'd be surprised. If I may, I recommend keeping this information to yourself."

"Why?"

"You already have one strike against you by associating with rebels. That alone has probably already put you on the military's radar. If you were to publicly accuse one of their own of falsifying evidence, there would be an investigation, which would also call into question everything that happened. Including anything the guards might want to keep quiet. They might be under the President's command, but the military fervently protects their own."

"Do you think they'd do something?" The cold gray walls of my cell close in on me again. I gulp.

Will shrugs. "Of course not, but accidents happen, even at the Smith. Even with our advanced technology, people still get sick, injured, and die despite extensive treatment."

"Thanks for warning me. I don't have any friends here, and well, I think I need all the help I can get."

A flash of surprise appears, then vanishes on his face, replaced by a faint blush. "You're most certainly welcome, Mira." I like the way he says my name, softly rolling the "r."

I shiver. His voice runs like fingers stroking along my spine. From Will's lips, my name flirts, exotic and unfamiliar. I rush to change the subject. "We have a stream like this in the forest near the farm." I turn away from him to watch the water tumble over the smooth stones. "It was one of my favorite places."

"You must miss it terribly."

I crouch down at the edge of the bank, trailing my fingers in the cool stream. "Yes, but then, you're from a farm, right?" He pulls back the sleeve of his shirt, showing me his tattoo.

"Yes, though my farm was in South Dakota. It's not like free citizens would do this kind of job?"

I stumble back a step at the venom in his voice. "Huh, I've never thought about it that way before."

"The farms have a steady supply of workers, so if no one else wants the jobs, they bring us in."

"How old were you?"

"Six. I was very studious and well-behaved for my age, so I was a logical choice." He clenches his hands at his sides. What would that have been like? Getting ripped from your family at such a young age? Rosie's smile dances through my mind. *I guess it's not that unusual after all.*

I touch his arm, but he jerks away from me.

"I'm sorry." I pull my hand back to my side, embarrassed.

"It wasn't your fault." Will shakes his head and leads me to a bench with the words "In God We Trust," engraved in the stone.

"Still..." I run my fingers over the deep grooves etched to look weather-beaten and aged. "It's not fair." I look away as the tears return, blinking them back. *This is stupid, Mira. Get a hold of yourself. Stop being so weak.* I sit down, and Will follows suit.

When I look back, Will raises his hand toward my face, but then lowers it. "I know." He puts his hands in his lap, as if not sure what to do with them.

"I didn't want to be a Second. I was supposed to have a nice, safe life on the farm, marry Tanner, raise a family, just like my parents. Maybe even fall in love." My lips curve in a faint smile. I glance up at him. "I'm sorry for bringing all this up. I'm sure listening to me whine isn't in your job description."

"Don't worry about it. My mother once told me that I'm a good listener."

136

"Can I ask you something?" I hate the wistful, desperate lilt in my voice.

"Of course."

"What's your job when you're not taking care of people like me?"

Will smiles. "When there isn't a Second in residence I work in the gardens. Four years ago, they offered me this position, and I jumped at the opportunity."

"You wanted to help Seconds?"

"Well, yes. It seemed logical to me at the time. Most Seconds are younger than you, and if you think about it, they're not that much different from seedlings in the greenhouses. Both need special care, nurturing, and someone to remember they're alive."

His wrist unit beeps. Will glances down at it, stands up, and walks a few steps. I can hear someone talking, but I can't make out the words.

He lowers his arm. "We have to go back to your room. My presence is being requested elsewhere. I'll have someone fetch your dinner, but if you'd like to come back, I'm sure your friend Bullfrog can escort you." His eyes twinkle with humor.

My face flushes again. "No, thanks."

He chuckles and holds out his hand. I take it, and his grip, firm and warm, makes me feel safe. He pulls me to my feet, and Tanner's face flashes through my mind. *I felt safe with him, too, and look where that got me. Be careful, Mira, you can't afford to trust anyone right now.*

We get to the elevator without saying anything else, and I watch Will again as he types in the code to get us back to my hallway. The little box rumbles to a start and goes down, over, and up, before coming to a stop. Neither of us even sway at the sharp turns. *Heck, I'll be a pro at this by the time I leave.*

When the doors open, Will holds me back with his hand and steps out ahead of me, looking in both directions. Unease trails down my spine. *What is he looking for?*

"All clear?" I ask.

He jumps. "Yes. One can never be too safe."

"I didn't think there was anything to worry about here."

"There isn't," he answers, contradicting his actions.

He gestures, and I follow him down the hall. We turn the corner to my room, and I see Bullfrog slouching in his chair, snoring loud enough to wake the dead.

"Ahh, yes, I can see it now. Definitely toad-like." Will grins.

I flush. "Cut it out. You'll wake him up."

When we come to the door, Bullfrog doesn't even twitch. "You're right. He's obviously a light sleeper."

I sigh and shake my head. "Fine, whatever."

With a reminder to call him if I need anything, Will backs out, shutting the door behind him.

Another servant brings dinner, a real chicken breast with lightly seasoned steamed vegetables. I pick up a roll and take a bite, then put it back down. *All this food, did it come from a farm like mine? What if Tanner harvested the wheat used to make this roll? What if I fed the chickens?* I put it back on the plate, not hungry anymore.

After eating, I use the touchpad on the bottom of the screen to scan through the various channels on the video screen, avoiding the news and finally settling on one about the wilderness. A wide panning shot shows deep-green forests and mountain ranges, then the scene changes to a small clearing, focusing on a man in khaki pants and a button-down shirt. He wears a ridiculous round hat, like an old-fashioned helmet.

"The forest is home to a wide variety of predators." He gestures at the trees. The scene cuts away to show pictures of mountain lions, bears, wolves, and some sort of spotted cat—all suitably snarling, growling, and looking terrifying. "These creatures slaughter humans and are prolific since the Immigration War. Even though the border between the United States and the wilderness is heavily monitored, it is still fraught with dangers." Border? The boundary between my farm and the wilderness is a bubbling stream. Its narrow outline of rocks is the only fence I've ever known.

"Many a child has been lost to this forbidding landscape, devoured by fearsome predators and killed by unforgiving elements." *Okay. I'm done.* I raise the remote. "And even worse..." I pause mid-click. "... are the rogue humans living in this horrible place. Desperate for any sort of food and water, they abduct those who venture too far into the forest. Those unfortunate souls are never seen again."

I click off the screen and fall backward on the bed. If this is what people choose to see, maybe it's not such a bad thing we're forbidden to watch it. I fall asleep, fully clothed.

THE GREATER ADVERSARY

socrates

"**V**ERONICA." I CAN'T HIDE THE surprise in my voice. Her pleasure in that is unmistakable. "I wasn't expecting you." I motion for the servant boy at my side to drop my bags by the large four poster bed. He does, bows, and after I turn my full attention to the viperess in front of me, he darts out of the room.

The President's wife, our nation's Vice President, wearing a long black dress with her hair coiffed to show off her pale, slender neck, arranges a tall bouquet of electric blue and violet flowers in an etched glass vase. The flowers boast viciously pointed spikes partially hidden behind feathery green leaves. Poisonous, just like the woman positioning the blooms.

"Socrates," she purrs, turning to fix me with a fake red-lipped smile as she strips white gloves off of her hands. "I didn't know you were arriving so soon." Right. Veronica knows everything. She keeps her red-tipped fingernails in every aspect of the government. She flicks her fingers at the bouquet. "I just wanted to beautify the place up some. You know, these rooms can get a bit... monotonous... for an esteemed celebrity such as yourself."

"Hoping I'll prick my finger and fall asleep?"

She gives me the barest of nods. With her pale skin and

deep brown hair, she could pass for Snow White herself. If Snow White had been the villainess. "It's not my fault the most beautiful blooms are also the most deadly."

"By your design, no doubt." She had, after all, been a famous botanist before she married and entered politics.

Veronica lifts one elegant shoulder and drops it. "At your age, a man should know to look before touching."

I lower myself onto the edge of the bed, and she leans against the wall across from me. "To what do I owe the somewhat... dubious... pleasure?" Ben sits warily at my feet, eyeing our guest.

"Oh, nothing really. Just welcoming an old friend."

I eye the flowers again. "What's the real reason you're here?"

She lets out a huff. "Fine, you've never been one for pleasantries or small talk. I hear my husband visited you last night."

"He fancied a brandy."

"I'm sure." Her icy voice drips with the same venom tipping the roses' thorns. "You know, I almost had him turned around. He very nearly agreed to drop this stupid bill and concentrate on more important matters."

"Oh?"

"Until he visited you, of course. Now he's full of this preconceived notion that he has to follow his father's footsteps and free the Texans." She shakes her head. Not a hair dares to drift out of place.

"Preconceived? Madam Vice President, I thought you supported him?"

"Of course. He is my husband."

I crack a smile. "For better or for worse, right?"

Her lips thin into a firm line, and she turns and crosses the room, her steps so smooth, so effortless, she could be floating. When she reaches the window, she pulls open the curtains, and peers out. I don't know how she does it. The brightness blinds me. "Some might argue that those vows are as antiquated as some esteemed members of society."

I chuckle. "You might be right on the second part, but like those vows, many people also believe that the oldest of us still has some purpose in this world."

She barely inclines her head toward me. "Yes, they're quite useful. They serve to remind us of harsher, more brutal times. Times better left forgotten."

I raise my eyebrows. "If you're so against us, Madam Vice President, then why do you oppose the bill to free the Texans? It will effectively limit the number of available Seconds. You know as well as I do that the younger the Second, the more effective the transfer process." She nods again. "Why would you try to stop it? How many people under the age of eighteen would volunteer for something like this?"

Veronica turns toward me, a faint smile stretching across her lips. "When you put it that way, it almost makes sense. Perhaps I'm merely a creature of tradition, set to follow the same patterns over and over again."

I open my mouth to speak, but she raises her hand to stop me, her dark fingertips glistening. "My motives, my dear Socrates, are very simple." She slinks past me toward the door. Her hand hovers over the knob. "Assess the threats and determine which is more dangerous. For our society, for our people, for our way of life, the Texans are the greater adversary, if by nothing else but numbers alone. You, my friend, are merely a dinosaur. A creature of historic significance but little political impact." She grasps the handle and turns it. "My goal is to neutralize the bigger threat to our country, with or without my husband's support, and I shall let nothing stand in my way."

WHAT I WANTED

mira

aLOUD BEEPING FROM THE COM unit wakes me up. Scrubbing away the sleep gumming my eyelids and pressing a button, I see Will's smiling face on the screen.

"Good morning?" I grumble.

"I thought you farmers rose before dawn?"

I mumble something my mother would smack me for. "What time is it?"

He chuckles. "It's nearly noon. You must have been exhausted." *On overload is more like it.* "Lunch will be ready shortly, then one of our assistants will come to get you ready for your interview."

I sit up quickly and swing my legs over the side of the bed. "Do I have to?"

He chuckles. "It isn't what you think it is. Trust me. I'm sure you'll find the experience... enlightening." The screen goes black.

After a quick, sharp knock, the door opens, and a young blonde hurries in, carrying a tray of food. Right on her heels is a tiny bald man carrying a silver-topped platter and a black bag slung over his shoulder. He brushes past her, and she backs away after putting the tray of food on the end of the table. He shoves the tray aside with his dome-topped one.

"My name is Theodore Reynard, but you may call me Mr. Reynard." He smiles widely as if I should recognize his name, and his face falls when I don't.

He sighs, opens the black bag, pulls out a pale cream-colored tunic and slacks, and throws them on the bed. "Here, change."

"What's wrong with what I'm wearing?" I look down at myself.

"It's wrinkled. Change. You need to look perfect for your interview."

"Whatever." I snatch the clothes off the bed and stalk to the bathroom where I quickly climb into the new clothes. When I come out, Mr. Reynard insists on tying a white sash around my waist, just as I did for Max. The memory flashes behind my eyes, and I tear up.

"None of that, now," Mr. Reynard snaps. "It'll be impossible to do your makeup if you have puffy, red eyes." He pulls out a silver and gold etched box and opens it. Inside are needles and bottles of color, from creams to browns, reds to blues, white to black. Some kind of handheld device, similar to the silver gun used for the vaccine, sits in a special slot.

"What are those for?" I ask, eyeing them skeptically.

"It's your makeup, of course. It's only temporary, and the effects will only last a couple weeks, maybe a month at best. You young ones always seem to heal faster, dispersing the pigments." Studying me for a moment, he picks up the gun, snaps in a needle, and runs his fingers over the bottles, before selecting a dark brown. "This will go nicely for your eyes."

I stand up, quicker than I've ever stood up in my life. "You're going to inject me with that?" I shake my head in disbelief.

"This?" He looks down at the gun and snaps the bottle into the back. "Why, yes. How else would I get the pigment into your skin? You can hardly expect me to just paint it on, can you?"

Backing away from him, I continue shaking my head. "You are not sticking that stuff in me."

"But you have to," he sputters. "Everyone does it. It's expected of you."

"No. Not going to happen." I back up until I hit the door and fumble behind me until I find the handle. Twisting it open behind me, I practically fall into the hallway.

Bullfrog lurches to his feet. "What's going on here?"

I spin toward him, an ugly angel in black fatigues with a laser gun strapped to his hip. "He... he's trying to torture me!"

"It's makeup!" Mr. Reynard exclaims, waving the black device around. "Tell her it's harmless. Tell her she has to get it done."

Bullfrog shrugs. "If she wants to look like crap on national television, let her. Don't matter to me one way or the other. Why don't you ask her First?"

Mr. Reynard pales. "I... I can't bother him about something like this. He has more important things to do!"

"So..." Bullfrog pulls his chair to the other side of the hall and straddles it. "It's not a big deal, then, is it? I don't care what you do, but I say, let the girl look like an idiot." With that, he pushes me back into the room, shoves Mr. Reynard after me, and shuts the door, chuckling all the while.

"Fine, have it your way," Mr. Reynard snarls, ejecting the dye and slamming the gun back into its case before snapping the lid shut. "If you refuse to wear makeup, at least wear this." He lifts the top of the tray with a flourish. "At least with this, you won't look too terrible." A brownish-blond hairy lump stares back at me, perched on a round metal ball.

"You brought me a dead cat?"

He wrinkles his nose, and mutters "idiot" under his breath. "Of course not."

I reach out to poke the thing. Silky soft strands of hair

run through my fingers like a dark golden rain. "Is that a wig?" *Seriously? He wants me to wear that?*

"Of course." He looks wounded. "It's the perfect solution to..." He flicks his hand, still holding the domed silver top, at my head. "That."

I touch my soft, short curly-ish, mostly unruly hair. "What's wrong with my hair?"

"Look at it! This wig is made from the finest, most magnificent hair in the entire country." When I still don't immediately agree, he sighs. "It's from the farms, girl. The best place to find pure, untreated hair." Bile rises, sour and bitter in my throat. I think I'm going to be sick. *That could have been my sister's hair if they'd cut it before she died. It could have been my hair.* My stomach roils, and I breathe, in and out, in and out, until the urge to hurl disappears. "I can't wear that."

"Why not? It's perfectly safe. Thoroughly cleaned and disinfected."

"But it's... it's *human* hair. What if it belonged to someone I know?"

"I highly doubt that. You're far too old for any acquaintance of yours to have hair this beautiful."

He sets the platter and lid on the desk and taps the top of the chair. "Sit, sit."

In shock and still slightly nauseous, I do what he says. He gently picks up the wig and sets it on my head. With a wire brush from his pocket, he fluffs the strands, making them fall around my face in tousled curls.

"See? Much better." He smiles. "With some makeup, you'll almost pass for a free citizen."

I glare at him, and gazing in the mirror, I reach up to touch the hot, heavy mass. "I still think it looks like I'm wearing a dead animal on my head."

"Hmph!" He sniffs and bats my hand away. "It's a million times better than the butcher job they did on your own head. I usually prefer to work with a person's own locks. But in your case..."

"My hair's not that bad."

"No, of course it isn't." He smiles and pats me on the shoulder, as though I'm a young child who needs reassurance.

"Wow," I whisper, reaching up to touch the hair.

"Don't you dare! This is a masterpiece. I don't have time to fix anything you destroy."

I jerk my hand back into my lap.

He packs his supplies and leaves me gawking at my reflection.

"Mira?" Will's voice is hushed as he approaches me from behind. He reaches out and fingers the long silky strands. "What happened to you?"

I laugh. "Yeah, I hate it, too." I turn around and raise my hands to the wig. "It's not me. It's awful."

He grabs my hands before I can do any damage. "You're right. It's not you, but you have to leave it alone."

"It's *human* hair."

"So?" He quirks an eyebrow in confusion.

"It's from one of the farms."

"Where did you think it'd come from?"

"I don't know." I glare at him, frustrated. "It's disgusting. I mean, look at it. It was some little kid's hair before they entered the program."

He shrugs. "I think it's beautiful, but..." He grins. "I think I like your hair better."

My stomach flip flops, and I bite my lip. Is that his way of calling me attractive? *Stop it, Mira. You don't have time for this, either. Focus on what's important.* I turn away from him, grumbling, "It's not funny." Will slides in front of me so I face him again.

"I'm sorry." His voice is lower, more serious. "You're right. It's not funny at all. Sometimes I forget that you're not from this world. Here, you're expected to look a certain way, dress in the latest fashions, and adhere to approved social norms."

I blow out a breath, making the hair in front of my eyes puff out. "But I'm not like the free citizens who come here all the time. I don't want to be."

"I know you don't." He puts a finger under my chin, lifting my face until I fall into his deep, dark eyes. "You're nothing like them, and that's what makes you amazing."

I bite my lip as he lowers his head toward mine. Is he going to kiss me? *What am I doing? What would Tanner think?* I push the chair back and rise to my feet. "I... I think we should go."

Will closes his eyes, and when he opens them, that mask of impassivity rests firmly on his face. "You're right." He walks toward the door. "We'd better go."

This is what I wanted, right? Frustration makes me grit my teeth. *Yes, exactly what I wanted.*

Will leads me down the hall to the elevator, where we ride down one measly floor and stop at one of the plain wooden doors, Will scans his wrist, and the lock clicks as it unlocks. The room we walk into next is tiny, only about half the size of the room I'm staying in upstairs, and it's nearly completely bright green with a plain wooden stool in the middle of it. Two men are there, one wearing a brown shirt, the other red, both in black pants. The one in red glances up as Will guides me toward the stool. Brownshirt stands in front of a screen that stretches the entire wall behind me while Red meddles with a tiny box perched on a thin tripod.

"Where are we?" I ask Will.

"This is the interview room."

I turn to face him. "Umm, no it's not. I've seen interviews in school for other Seconds, and none of them have been in rooms like this."

He smiles thinly, the skin around his eyes tightening. "Remember what I said about appearances?"

Before I can respond, Red motions for me to sit on the stool, saying, "Right this way, miss." After I'm seated, he positions my knees, asking me to shift to the left and then to the right. "Perfect." He finally backs away. "I'm Mark, by the way, and the guy in the brown shirt is Nero." He holds out his hand, and I shake it. His easy smile immediately makes me feel comfortable.

"I'm Mira."

"Great. Now don't take this the wrong way, but can you read?"

"Of course I can read. I'm not an idiot."

"Sorry, you never know. Some Seconds can barely recite their names. Since you can, this'll go a lot easier." He turns to his partner. "Hey, Nero, are we good?"

Nero gives Mark a thumbs-up.

Mark gestures at the screen. "Now, you'll see a series of sentences. I want you to read each one, smile as if you're happy to be here, and pause at the end. When I motion with my hand like this—" He waves his hand. "—another prompt is going to flash on the screen, so you'll have to be ready. Got it?"

"What's this for?"

"They're your interview answers."

"But who's going to ask the questions?"

He shakes his head. "Don't worry about it. Those will all be added in later. Trust me. You won't even recognize yourself. Now, are you ready?"

"Um..." I glance at Will, who nods. "Okay, I guess."

"Great." Mark backs away and hits a switch. The back wall dims to black, and words appear. "Ready in five... four... three... two... one."

"Hi, I'm Mira," I mumble, then remember I should be smiling. *This is ridiculous.*

"Cut." Mark stands up and walks over to crouch down in front of me. "I know this is strange, and you've never done anything like it before, but all you have to do is read the lines and smile. Okay? Do you think you can do that?" I nod. "Let's start from the top again, all right?"

149

I take a deep breath. "I'm ready."

"Five... four... three... two... one."

"Hi, I'm Mira." This time my voice is louder, clearer, and I'm smiling even though it still feels wrong. Like I'm a fake and I'm lying to the whole universe. *Is this what Adrian did? Did he have to go through this for his interview?*

I pause before smiling at the box. "No." *That's it?*

Mark nods and gives me a thumbs up.

The screen flashes. "Just lovely." Smile, pause. "Chesaning Farms." Smile, pause. "Yes." Smile, pause. "Before I was chosen, I worked with animals on the farm."

"Yes, they're thrilled." *Who's thrilled?*

"I felt very excited and lucky!" *Is that really what the screen says?*

"I want to make my family proud of me. I want to repay the debt of my people and show that I'm not like the Texans who rebelled two hundred years ago." *Oh, geez! I sound so stupid and ridiculous.*

"I feel betrayed and hurt. I can't believe I trusted him." *Wait, what? Are they talking about Tanner?* I glance at Will, but he's standing by the door, arms behind his back, more like the bodyguard Bullfrog claimed him to be than a servant.

"I never want to see him again." I feel a horrible sinking feeling. I don't smile, but I guess it's all right because Mark doesn't stop me.

"Thank you."

SOMEONE TO TALK TO

socrates

aRRIVING IN WASHINGTON ONLY GARNERS Ellie the barest of receptions. I wait with a handful of servants in the central transport room, the one reserved for dignitaries and Firsts. Very few people are privileged enough to see the inside of one of these pods. The rest take airbuses, sitting in boxes separated from shipments of grain meant for the Smith, or clothing or precious metals that can't be transported by pod. Some choose to pay extra at a transport station to take one of the older, less comfortable mass transport pods. Honestly, I prefer the buses, less worrying about whether or not the pod is going to malfunction. They don't anymore, but I remember the old days. At least you have a chance at surviving if your airbus crashes.

When the door slides open, she smiles, and I extend my arm to help her from the pod. Only using me for the barest of leverage, she steps out. "Thank you." The ache in my joints and in my stomach is worse today, and I can barely smile without grimacing.

"Of course. I'm glad I got out of my meeting in time to meet you here. I've been worrying about you." She pats my arm and releases it. "Unfortunately, I'll have to leave momentarily for a physics conference, but I wanted to be here when you arrived."

"Then shouldn't you have arrived before me?"

She shakes her head and reaches down to scratch Ben behind the ears.

A tall, young dark-eyed boy smiles and bows. "Welcome, sir. It is an honor to greet you. My name is Will, and it will be an honor to serve you."

Ellie clasps his outstretched hand. "Thank you. It is an honor to be here."

Will shakes hers gently but briskly, before releasing it and gesturing toward the wide-open exit about thirty yards ahead of us. "If you're ready to go, I will show you to your room." Ellie nods, and we set off. It is a testament to his intelligence and training that the boy doesn't ask me if I want any help. Ellie isn't so discreet and follows half a step behind, watching my every slow, labored step.

When I catch her reaching out a hand to help me, I murmur, "Stop shadowing me, woman. I can walk just fine."

She makes a tsk tsking noise. "You can't fool me, Socrates. I know you. I can tell when you're in pain." When I look back at her again, I see concern etching grooves next to her deep brown eyes. Her deep blue suit coat and cream top are impeccable, as always, but she clenches her fists and jams one in her pocket when she sees me noticing.

The walk to our room from the transport room is so long that my knees ache in protest. Maybe I should have had those replaced. It's an easy enough procedure nowadays, in and out in the same day, not like it was during my first life.

A couple guards stroll through the halls, not stopping to look at anyone, merely making their presence known. That's enough, usually, to quell most rebellions. When we reach our room, two attendants are already inside, unloading her clothes into the bureau on the opposite wall. The vase, Veronica's gift, sits untouched on top. "Where's your Second staying?" Ellie asks.

I shrug, and she glances at Will. A myriad of emotions

flash behind the boy's eyes, quickly masked by that calm indifference, and never reach the rest of his face. "She's in three-twelve, sir. Would you like to see her?"

"Yes. After everything that's happened, I would like to make sure for myself that she is all right."

"Didn't you see her at the prison?"

I narrow my eyes at him. "No. She was being questioned. Who told you she was at Fullbright?"

He shifts from side to side, uncomfortable. "No one, sir. Just rumors." He flashes me a panicked smile. "You know how those are."

"Hmph. What else did you hear?"

"Ahhh." He struggles to find the right words. "Not much, just that she was arrested trying to escape her farm."

I shrug. "Do you blame her? Given the circumstances and the propaganda the Lifers have been feeding her, I'd likely do the same, if I were in her shoes."

Looking shocked, the boy lets his mouth hang open. "Ummm, sir?"

I shuffle over to the chair next to the desk and, groaning, lower myself into it. Ben follows me and sits obediently at my side. I rub the scruff of his neck. Something about his unease piques my interest. "Did she mention anything about it to you?"

He shakes his head. "No, not a word." He's lying. I can feel it. But why? Does he think he's protecting her? "She seemed shaken up, but I figured that might be from her experiences and getting sent to prison."

I stop petting Ben, and he looks up at me, a low whine in the base of his throat. "My thoughts exactly," I murmur. Will looks at me, confused. I wave him off. "Don't worry about it, boy. If you don't mind, though, I would rather not have any further rumors spread about my Second. Is that understood?"

"Yes, sir." He spins around and leaves quickly, before I can change my mind.

153

"Well, my love." Eliot takes my arm, and I face her. "I know I just got here, but I need to leave, as well."

"Where are you going?" I beetle my eyebrows into furry caterpillars. *Did she tell me?*

"The physics conference, remember?"

"Oh." The haze covering my mind clears a bit. "Right. Is it at the Smith?"

She nods. "The Air and Space Museum. You know—" She looks me up and down. "I don't have to go. I'm sure they'd understand..."

"Nonsense." I shake her off. "You're probably the guest speaker. Am I right?" She doesn't answer, which is answer enough. "Then that settles it. You have to go."

"If you're sure..." Her voice trails off. I can tell she doesn't want to leave me, which I find ridiculous.

"Come now, Ellie. I'm not dead yet."

She rolls her eyes. A low chuckle escapes from her lips. "Very true. And even then I'm sure you'd still stick around to give me hell."

After Ellie leaves, I decide to take a quick nap, and as I climb onto the bed, Ben hops up after me, curling in a tight ball at my feet. A couple minutes later, his quiet snoring makes my own eyes feel heavy, and I drift off.

In my dream, I'm standing in a large open stadium with seating all around me. I'm looking up at a stage, and Edward stands in front of me. He wears the same style of uniform Mira wore for her choosing, and he points at me.

"It's your fault," he shouts. His face contorts in rage and disgust. "You're more of a traitor than I ever was. It's you who should be up here, not me."

"What are you talking about?" I scream up at him, but he doesn't act as if he hears my voice. "I didn't do anything wrong."

"You killed them," he continues, as if I haven't spoken at all. "You killed all of them."

He jabs his finger behind me, and when I turn around,

I see a sea of children of various ages, all standing, stiff as boards, pale, and wearing their Second uniforms. Their eyes are blank, and even from this far away, I can tell they're dead. "Oh God!" I turn back to him, but he's not there anymore.

Now Mira takes the stage, and she has the saddest look I've ever seen in my life on her face. *She feels sorry for you. She pities you.* "Mira?"

She shakes her head. "No, I'm Alyxander and Milissa, Stephen and Donovan, Rachel and Adam. I'm all of them, and we're all dead because of you."

"No," I whisper, backing up. Then I remember the dead children behind me, spin around, and wake up, heart pounding.

Sitting up, I notice a blue glossy quarter-sized sheet of paper, folded in half so it can stand like a little tent. On it, ornate hand-stamped lettering reads:

> *Are you feeling lost? Alone? Unsure of your place in the world? Do you need someone to talk to? Our counselors are available 24 hours a day. Just dial 599 on your in room com unit and ask for Dr. James Scoffield.*

GET OUT

mira

WITH NOTHING ELSE TO DO, I decide to figure out the screen on my wall. Running my fingers along each side, I can't find any buttons and am about ready to give up when a pleasant female voice booms from somewhere in my room. "I see you are having difficulty working your screen. All you have to do is say the word, and I will do as you wish."

I crane my neck from side to side. "Who are you? Where are you?"

The soothing voice continues. "I'm your all-in-one entertainment advisor. I come pre-programmed with a list of appropriate channels for," there's a pause, "Mira of Chesaning Farms. If this is correct, say yes. My voice analyzer system will process your unique vocal signature to determine its authenticity. If you are, in fact," pause again, "Mira of Chesaning, a list of predetermined shows will be displayed for your viewing pleasure. If you are not, my security program will alert security to the presence of an intruder and appropriate actions will be taken. Please proceed when ready." Her pleasant monotone sends chills up and down my spine. Is she for real? What if I don't say anything?

"But I'm Mira. I've never programmed this stupid machine. I just got here and—"

"System processing," she interrupts me. I twist the top blanket on the bed in my hands. Would they throw me back in prison? Torture me? Kill me? I bite my bottom lip. Then from wherever the voice comes from now comes a low beep and she says, "Welcome, Mira of Chesaning. My name is Auto Voice Activated System, but you can call me AVAS. If you would like to proceed and view the designated broadcasts, please say 'Proceed.'"

What the heck? "Umm, proceed."

"Good. What are you interested in viewing today?"

I sit back on the bed and relax. Looks like I'm not going to get tortured today. "Umm, I don't know. I've never watched anything before except in school. It was illegal where I came from." Even now, faint twinges of unease, almost like I'm doing something wrong, make me look around, afraid to get caught.

"Might I suggest a news broadcast to start you out?"

I shrug. "Uhh, sure."

The screen flashes to a pleasing forested background with a petite woman in a red suit and bleached blond hair standing in the front. She has a scary bright smile that never quite reaches her sky-blue eyes and a face that obviously let her make-up artist do what he wanted.

"Good evening, everyone. This is Ariel Rose with the DC Chronicle. Earlier today, I interviewed our nation's most recent Second, Socrates's chosen, Mira from Chesaning Farms. This is the same farm that not long ago hosted another Second, Adrian, selected by Thoreau." Pictures flash of my cousin, a man who must be Thoreau, then Socrates, myself, and the farm. Next are the Chesanings sitting in what I recognize as their dining room.

"We are just so pleased." Mrs. Chesaning clasps her hands together. "Mira is like one of our own children. She used to play dress-up and hide-and-go-seek with my daughters." *What world is she living in? I've never played with those wretched brats in my life.* "We feel honored that

Socrates picked his next Second from our farm and hope that he's as happy with her quality as we were raising her."

Quality, as in a piece of meat cooked to order? Nice, thanks, Mrs. Chesaning.

The camera shifts back to the reporter. Her fake smile fades into what she must think of as her serious face. "Two days ago, Mira was threatened by a vicious member of the Live Once movement, the rebel leader Edward Flannigan. Luckily, military personnel were able to save her, and as I'm sure you'll see, she is still quite shaken by her ordeal."

The image changes to the lush green of the gardens. I'm perched on one of the stone benches, and Ariel Rose is on another one, facing me.

"Good morning. Do you mind if I call you Mira?"

My image says, "No," and smiles brightly. Coldness spreads upward from my stomach.

"Excellent. How are you today?"

"Just lovely." I smile at the camera.

"Great. So, Mira..." Ariel leans closer to her captive. "... tell us a little bit about yourself." She smiles at the camera. "I'm sure there have to be a few of our viewers, somewhere out there, who aren't familiar with your story." She lets out a fake giggle. "Where are you from?"

"Chesaning Farms." I watch myself stare blankly at the camera before smiling yet again. I look so stupid.

"Isn't that the same farm where, only two years ago, your cousin was picked by Thoreau as a Second?"

"Yes."

Ariel smiles brightly at the camera. "What was your job at the farm?"

"Before I was chosen, I worked with animals on the farm."

After a pause, she continues. "How does your family feel about you being chosen?"

"Yes, they're thrilled." My interview-self stares blankly at the camera. I watch Ariel take a deep breath and smile, as if she's actually talking to me.

"How did you feel? It's such an honor."

"I felt very excited and lucky!" *Wow*. I shake my head. Seeing it from this end, how could I ever think it was real?

"Why do you want to be Absolved?"

"I want to make my family proud of me. I want to repay the debt of my people and show that I'm not like the Texans who rebelled two hundred years ago."

Ariel leans in closer, as if we're best friends. "Now, everyone wants to know. How are you holding up after finding out about Mr. Flannigan's betrayal? He was your mentor and teacher at the farm. It must have been extremely traumatizing." She smiles at interview Mira, glances at the camera, then back at me.

My interview-self says nothing.

I can't believe this. Will *knew*. He knew they were going to do this and didn't tell me. "It's all about appearances," he'd said. *Thanks for the help, Will.* I don't even try to quell the bitterness rising from my stomach.

She shakes her head. "You poor dear. You don't have to protect him any longer. The free citizens know the truth. Those rebels aren't going to hurt you anymore. You don't have to be afraid. Mr. Flannigan has been sentenced to death."

My interview-self smiles yet again, as if her words actually comfort me. "I feel betrayed and hurt. I can't believe I trusted him." *Is Tanner watching this? Does he know it's fake?* They showed us Adrian's interview. Surely, they'll show mine as well.

"I never want to see him again." At least I don't smile this time. Pain wrenches through me. Please let Tanner see the truth and understand that this isn't me.

"It's all right, Mira. We know the rebels threatened your family and were prepared to kill you if you didn't go with them. You're such a brave young woman to be strong throughout this experience."

Do people buy this? I think back to Adrian's interview:

how happy he looked and how pleased that made his parents. I even thought he was better off, so yes, they do buy it. My family probably will, too.

"Thank you."

"Denial, fear, terror: these are the legacies left over from her rebel attack. However, Mira has shown herself to be extremely strong, and I'm sure Socrates is very proud of her. You've heard it first from the DC Chronicle. We'll bring you more as events unfold. This is Ariel Rose. Keep safe, everyone, and please report any suspicious activity. You never know who might be a rebel." A dark blue and white Capital News emblem flashes on a backdrop of the American flag.

My mind whirls. How dare they? That wasn't a real interview. I flit back to what Will said about how I wouldn't even recognize myself. Was this was he meant? Did he know this was going to happen? I stand up, enraged. I have to get out of here. I can't—

"Would you like to watch anything else, ma'am?" AVAS asks, her voice just as pleasant as before.

"No," I snap. "Just turn it off."

"As you wish." The screen goes blank.

The need to punch something, hit something, scream, and shout rushes to the surface. What can I do? I can't leave. I can't just go to the playground or relax by the stream in the woods by the farm, and I'm sure it'd get out if I trashed my room. Mr. Flannigan's voice echoes in my head, telling me that his goal is to prepare me so I don't embarrass Socrates. Right. They should have picked someone else.

I finally settle for picking up one of the gold pillows on the bed, scrunching it up in my fists, and throwing it across the room. *Some dangerous rebel you are, right, Mira?* I have to get out of here. The walls are closing in, and I can't breathe. Should I call Will? No. The thought of seeing him fills me with the same anger I felt watching the news and seeing the lies they made me speak. He's the last person I want to talk to right now. Frustrated, I walk to the door and try the handle, half expecting it to be locked, but it clicks open, and I step cautiously into the hall. Bullfrog's chair is empty. Where is he? Taking a break? Might as well take advantage of it while I can, right?

Three other doors are at this end of the hall, one on my side, one on the other, and an exit at the end. In the other direction, I can see the darting shadows of people bustling at the other end of the hallway and turn away. I don't really feel like company right now, so I follow the hallway until I find the service elevator.

I put my hand up to the pad, which glows white as it senses my presence. I scan my wrist. The pad blinks, then turns red. Shoot, what am I supposed to do now? All Will did was scan his wrist, right? I try it again. It flashes red again, and I remember the AVAS system in my room telling me that if I wasn't who I was supposed to be, she would contact security. Would this do the same thing? If I scan my wrist again, will guards suddenly come pouring out of the locked doors, weapons drawn, ordering me to get down or they'll shoot, like they did at the farm? I hesitate before lifting my wrist to the scanner again. Maybe I just don't have the right angle. Maybe my hand has to be exactly straight to—

A broad hand lands hard on my shoulder, and another wraps around my mouth, jolting me out of my reverie and pulling me back away from the scanner. Terrified, I crane my head around to look into Will's stormy eyes, now black with anger, which terrifies me, and I gouge at his hand with mine, but it's no use. I'd have about as much luck moving the manor house with my bare hands. I stop struggling, and after a moment, he lets me go. Jumping back, I start to speak but he interrupts.

"What are you doing out here?" he growls.

"I-I-I just w-wanted to get out of my r-room," I stammer. It sounds weak, even to me.

"You should have called me. What were you thinking? Do you have any idea what could happen to you? Where's your guard?"

"I don't know. He wasn't there." I glower at him. "I'm fine, obviously. No reason to be so mad at me."

He takes a deep breath. "Please forgive me, Mira. But you don't understand. This Smith isn't like your little farm, where you can go off in the woods whenever you want. People are dangerous here." Fear chases the anger away on his face. *What is he afraid of?*

I step back, folding my arms in front of me. "You might have forgotten," I reply, feeling snarky, "but there were some pretty dangerous people at my *little* farm, too."

He lets out another deep breath, as if I'm taxing him somehow. "Look, I admit, that was a poor choice of words, but you can't risk your life like this. Walking around unguarded is very treacherous. All those safeguards to make sure you are who you are, the guards at your door, having me at your beck and call, it's all for a reason. Rebels have tried infiltrating the Smith before, and who knows," he pauses for effect, "they might be in here already. Plotting something." His words make me shiver. *Maybe he's right? Maybe the guards and all the security is for my safety.*

"But regardless of that," he continues, "protecting Seconds is my job, and I'm pretty good at it."

"I'm sorry for sneaking off." I search his eyes, looking for some of our earlier connection, but now there is only the blank façade he's polished from years of serving others. "I just had to get away." I tell him about the interview and grow furious all over again.

"I understand. It can be quite a shock coming here for the first time." He cracks a smile that only tilts one corner of his mouth. "Look, I'm on my way to get some lunch, would you like me to pick some up for you?"

I see myself alone in my room, the walls closing in.

"Can I eat with you?" I blurt, heat rushing to my face. "I mean, not if you're busy, but..."

Will raises his eyebrows. Curiosity sparks in his eyes, and they seem to glow in the dim light. "Of course. That would be fine with me, if that's what you wish."

"Never mind, it's all right. I'm just..." I blurt out the truth, "I've been alone too much." *Are you serious, Mira? You don't even really know this guy. Why did you say that?* I dip my head, blinking away frustrated tears. I hate feeling weak, needy like this.

Will steps closer to me, and his fingers graze the bottom of my chin, tilting up my head. The warmth, the shock of his touch, make me catch my breath. His voice lowers into a whisper. "I thought you liked the solitude?" I can feel the heat of his body standing so close to mine, and he smells like the minty green you'd find picking certain herbs in the forest.

"M-mostly, yes," I whisper and try to catch my breath. His fingers linger on my skin then he releases me and steps back. I feel the loss immediately and shiver. "It's just that... I'm not used to eating alone. At the farm, there are people everywhere, and I used to go to the forest or the playground to escape in the evenings sometimes, but we always ate together."

"If you'd like to eat with us, I'm sure it'll be all right. We have a specific cafeteria for our use. We just need to inform your guard, if he's there, about our plans." *Is he giving me a chance to back out? Should I?*

"Okay." *What am I getting myself into?*

Will offers me his elbow, which I take, tentatively, not because I need the support, but because a part of me, an evil selfish part, wants to feel his touch again. And a different part pipes up. *Why didn't you feel the same with Tanner? What's wrong with you?*

As we turn the corner to my room, I see Bullfrog speaking rapidly into his wrist band. When he hears our footsteps, he whirls around, weapon drawn.

163

"Where the hell have you been?" he shouts, glaring at us before holstering his Artos.

"Mira wants to go to lunch. When we left, you were not at your post." Will leaves the accusation that Bullfrog was neglecting his duty unspoken.

He gets it, though. His face turns red, and he clenches his fists. "I had to go the bathroom." He turns his attention to me. "Can't you stay put for one goddamn minute?"

I start to shrink until I feel Will's fingers thread with mine. He squeezes my hand. Stiffening my shoulders, I look straight into my guard's eyes. "It's not my job to protect me, is it? Seems to me you should have been here."

His hand tightens on his weapon once again. "Get the hell back in your room. I can't protect you if you go wandering all over kingdom come."

I shake my head. "No. I want to go with Will for lunch."

"I said"—his voice lowers into a bear-like grumble— "get. Back. In. Your. Room."

I take a deep breath. "No." I turn and walk away, pulling a shocked Will behind me.

"You get me fired, girl, and I'll kill you myself!" Bullfrog shouts from behind us, and his words chill me, but I can't stop moving. Can't stop walking or I might collapse. I might stop going and never get up again.

Will and I stop at one of the service elevators. "Are you sure you want to do this?"

I nod. "What did he mean when he said he'd kill me first?"

Will blinks, his long lashes covering his eyes before opening them again after a heavy minute. "Nothing." He pauses. "I think he was just being a jerk." He's hiding something. I know it. "Would you like to file a report?"

The thought of actually getting Bullfrog in trouble almost makes it worth it. "No, it's not that important." Will looks like he's going to say something more, but then shakes his head, minutely, and decides against it. "Let's just go." He raises his eyebrows. "If that's all right with you, I mean."

Will scans his wrist tattoo, and we wait for the door to slide open. "Of course." His normally blank expression softens, and he smiles, crinkling the corners of his eyes.

I flush and look away.

"But just so you know, it may get a little strained down here."

"How so?" I glance up at him in alarm.

"The people down there aren't like you. Or rather, you're not like them. They're not the family you lost. Your friends. Your Tanner. You're Absolved now, not a servant like us." His words are cruel, even though he says them as kindly as possible, and they cut me. But he's right.

"Maybe we should go back."

"Is that what you want? I wouldn't blame you if you did." Is he trying to get me to change my mind?

I shake my head, thinking of the walls in my room, the loneliness. *Anything has to be better than that.* "No. Let's go."

"I'm sure it'll be fine." The door slides open, and we enter. "The cafeteria is down two floors. The service elevator will get us there faster."

"They have an elevator just for the servants?"

"Of course." He looks surprised. "You expect the President to ride in the same car as the person who cleans his toilet?"

"No, I guess not."

We get into the elevator, which is smaller than the other one, and with a couple of shakes, it starts down. It stops on a floor where the bright white lights glow harshly, making everything look dingy and old.

We pass several doors and come to a large double set propped open to reveal an enormous open area with rows of tables. The place is filled with people. *Just like home.*

He stops abruptly, and I run into him. "Sorry," I mumble.

165

He turns to me, gently taking my elbow. "Are you sure you want to do this? It's okay if you change your mind."

"I'm okay." I take a deep breath and look around. "It kind of reminds me of home."

"But it's not." I shake my head, recognizing that fact. "Look, before we go in, I want to warn—"

"Will?" A shapely brunette who looks about six months pregnant walks up to us. "What are you doing down here? Who is this?" She touches his arm with a familiarity that makes jealousy course through me. Then shame. Who is she to him? His wife, judging by the baby bump? His girlfriend? Maybe they don't have strict rules here regarding abstinence and boy-girl relations the way we do at the farm.

He jerks out from under her touch and looks at me, then back at her. "Evie, this is Mira."

The people at the nearest table stop talking and stare at us. Like a wave it spreads, until I'm sure just about everyone is watching.

"The Second?"

"Yes."

She curls her lip a little, as if smelling a dead animal rotted and bloated in the sun. "Why'd you bring *her* down here?"

My face grows hot, and I feel my shoulders stiffen.

"She wants to eat with us."

"Why? She's not one of us. She's one of *them*. She needs to stay up there with her own kind." She looks me up and down, taking in my choppy mouse-brown hair and wrinkled clothes. I can almost imagine she sees inside my head. *Why did I think this was a good idea again?*

Will shrugs. "She's different."

"So what?" She gets close to him, jabbing her finger in his chest. "You're just going to bring her down here? *Flaunt* her in front of everyone?"

What is she talking about? I'm not a prize or anything.

Will pushes her finger away. A guilty look flashes across his face. "Stop it, Evie. Don't make a scene. You know this is my job."

"Yes, and you're *so* good at it, too," she sneers.

I push myself in front of him. "What's your problem? We just came down here to eat."

"Stay out of it, dead girl," Evie snarls, leaning toward me.

I clench my fists. "Get out of my face."

She shoots a sharp glance from Will to me. Her face is red, and her muscles tense as if she's going to hit me. *Bring it.* Then, she seems to remember where she is and tosses her thick shiny hair over her shoulder and rests one hand on her protruding belly.

"You know what? You're not worth it." She smirks. "You're just a job to him. At night, he comes home to—"

"Evie, please," Will interrupts, his face going pale. "We'll talk about this later."

She huffs. "Fine. But I can't believe you brought her down here." She stalks out of the cafeteria.

After taking a deep breath, Will turns to me and touches my arm in apology. "I'm sorry. I should have known she'd be down here."

"Is she your wife?" He shakes his head. "Girlfriend?"

"No, just... a friend." *Like Tanner was* just *my friend?* "Look, just ignore her. It's nothing personal, honest. After she found out she was pregnant and left her husband, she's been looking for someone to help raise her kid." Will guides me toward the long line that stretches up to the people serving food.

"So she picked you?"

He lifts his shoulders and drops them, casually, as if it doesn't bother him. "I suppose that's one way to put it. It doesn't matter, though. None of it affects you."

As we reach the end of the line, talk resumes around us.

"I'm nothing like those people, the Firsts, or anyone else for that matter."

Will holds up his hands. "Don't get mad at me. I agree with you. It's just that *I* might be the only one who sees you that way."

I nibble on my bottom lip and look down. "Maybe you were right. I shouldn't have come."

"Don't be ridiculous. I think it's amazing you wanted to eat with us. I've never seen anything like it. The last time someone from up there came down here was to buy a few extra servants for the vice president's mansion. It was awful, kind of like your lineup. They checked our teeth, asked us questions, had us do jumping jacks and pushups, and even looked at our grades in school." He grimaces.

"That's terrible."

"No Second has ever come down to eat with us. Of course, they're going to be shocked."

"Well, what should we do?"

Will smiles, a quick, bold flash of white teeth. "I say we eat." The line starts moving, and in a few minutes, we're at the front.

Will hands me a tray with a chipped white bowl, some silverware, a cup, and a napkin. The cook slops a brownish-gray scoop of something into the bowl without even looking at me. Little multicolored chunks slowly rise to the surface.

"Is that supposed to be soup?" I ask, sloshing the brownish liquid around its bowl. My stomach rumbles, but I don't know if I could even take a bite. We had better food at the farms. This stuff looks just awful.

He grins. "I warned you, remember? Only the finest cuisine here at the Smith."

We find an empty table near the back, and Will smiles at a few people as we pass. I pick through my food. *Maybe this was a mistake. I should never have come down here.* In my mind, I keep seeing Evie's hand on Will's arm, her possessiveness, her obvious familiarity. *What did she mean when she said that at night he comes home... to her?*

If he hadn't interrupted her, what would she have said? Should I trust him? Maybe he's telling the truth, that they're nothing, and she's only trying to get him to help look after her baby when it's born. Will's been straight with me so far, right? I look up at him and catch him watching me.

He takes my trembling hand in his across the table. "It's okay, Mira. It's all right."

I chew on my bottom lip.

At the table next to us, conversation picks up as a plump man with sweat-slicked black hair sits down. "Finally finished the expansion to the President's library," he says as he spoons a bite of soup into his mouth. "Though I don't see why they didn't just add another level to the top. He didn't have to take away our quarters."

An older, thin white-haired man pats him on the back. "You know how it is. Why add to the top when they can take room away from us? Not like we need it, right?"

The other three men at the table grumble in agreement, then start gossiping about who's working hard and what they're doing, who's pulled one over on his supervisor, and who's getting a little extra on the side. Honestly, they're worse than the older women at the farm, complaining like a bunch of chickens.

As we finish eating, a burly man, clearly agitated, stomps over to us. "Evie told me you brought her down here." He growls at Will, pointing at me.

A hush falls over the cafeteria.

Will leans back and looks up at the man. "Nice to see you, too, Gregory."

"I didn't believe her. I said even *you* wouldn't be that stupid." His feet are spread wide apart, and his hands are in rock-hard fists at his sides.

"It's not against the law. She can go wherever she wants."

"I don't care. She don't belong here. What if *he* sent her? Ever think of that?" He points at the ceiling.

"Who?"

"The Firsts, the President. I don't know. Does it matter?"

"Stop being an idiot. No one sent her. She wanted to come down here herself." Once again, the voices around us quiet.

"Don't we have any place that's free of *them*?" He leans menacingly forward.

Will jumps to his feet. "Back off. Mira's not one of them. She was ripped out of her home, away from her family and everything she knows, just to be some old windbag's next attempt at immortality." *What's he talking about?* "Cut her some slack."

"Just how close are you two?" Gregory's beady eyes scrutinize me, taking me apart inch by inch. "She's kind of scrawny, but some guys like them like that." My eyes widen, and I take a sharp breath. Did he really just say that?

"Leave her alone," Will growls, his eyes narrowing.

"So that's how it is." He looks around at the audience the conversation has drawn. "Providing for her *every* need, eh?" He wiggles his bushy eyebrows.

Anger smolders to life, but I squash it down. This is no place to get into an argument. I jump to my feet. If Will and the others think I'm just going to sit back for this, they're the idiots.

"Mira," Will says in a warning tone as I step forward. "He's not worth it."

Thanks, Will. Thanks for your help. You're a champ.

He touches my arm, stopping me. He's right, as much as I hate to admit it. I can't do this here. For some reason I think my punishment for misbehaving here would be far worse than a metal box with only three holes in the bottom for air and weak shafts of light. I take a deep breath and look Gregory up and down. "No, you're right." I shake my head. "He's not worth it."

"Not worth it? You spoiled brat! I'll show you…" Gregory reaches out to grab my shoulder, but Will whirls between us, blocks Gregory's arm, snakes out his leg, and hooks Gregory's, kicking his foot out from under him. The larger man crashes to the floor.

"Don't touch her," he snarls. Then Will piles his tray on top of mine, picks up both of them, takes me firmly by the elbow, and leads me to a large window where people collect them. "We should go back to your room." Will flashes me a sardonic smile after depositing our trays.

I nod, feeling kind of numb. In my mind, I keep seeing Will drop Gregory to the ground. That's not how a part-time gardener should act. Who would he need to use those moves on, the plants?

At the elevator, Will turns to me. "Mira, I'm so sorry, I didn't know any of that would happen. Gregory, he's just... he's got a short fuse, that's all." He runs his hand over his short-cropped hair.

"It's not your fault. Why do they hate me? I didn't do anything to them." My anger rapidly fades away to sadness and exhaustion.

"They don't hate *you*, as a person. It's because you're Absolved. You're above us all, and they're afraid that they might slip up, say something, and get reported. You're about as close to free as any of us could ever get." His gaze flits away, and I get the feeling there's something he's not telling me.

"It doesn't feel like freedom. I'm just as much a prisoner now as I've always been, maybe more." I clench my fists at my sides.

"All it is," Will explains as he takes me back to my room, "is a way to say you're not like us anymore. But then again, you're not like them either." He shakes his head.

"That's stupid. It's not like I'm doing anything important. I'm not Socrates."

He frowns and glances away from me. *Is there something more he's not telling me?* The elevator slows to a stop, and the doors glide open. We walk out and down the long hall by my room. Will is wearing a pensive look, as if he's trying to figure out something that doesn't make sense.

"Unfortunately," he says, finally breaking the silence, "that's the way it is, and nothing you or I do will change how other people think and act."

We pause at my door.

Bullfrog leans against the wall and glares at us over the top of his handheld screen. "Have a good dinner, princess?"

I scowl, and he grunts out a laugh. "Not such hot stuff as you thought you were, eh? I knew it. I just knew it. Gonna hide back in your room now? Well, you better hope your bodyguard is good enough to protect you now. I'm outta here." He gets to his feet and stretches, as if enjoying this.

A momentary twinge of panic hits me, but I don't let it show, rolling my eyes at him instead, as if I don't care. "Yeah, right. You're leaving?"

"You don't have to sound so happy about it. Yeah, I got the orders an hour ago. I been promoted to the President's own detail." His chest puffs up.

I imagine he'll let out a croak any minute. "That's... wow. Congratulations."

"Big pay raise, that's for sure. No more grunt work for this soldier. I'll be living the high life in the President's ritzy mansions, babysitting his annoying little rug rats, drinking champagne. No more of this sitting outside doorways waiting for cowards to try something. Gotta go where the action is, that's for sure."

"Why are you still here, then?"

"Hadta wait 'til you got back." He tucks his handheld in his pocket, gives us a mock salute, and says, "I'd like to say I'll see ya later..." He sneers at me. "But we all know that ain't gonna happen."

After watching Bullfrog swagger down the hall, chuckling to himself, I look at Will. "What's he talking about? That's the second time he's mentioned something like that."

He grimaces. "I have no idea what he's talking about. He's an idiot. Just ignore him."

Something cold roots itself in my stomach. "Will..."

Will tries to laugh it off. "Well, he's not going to be drinking any champagne, if that's what you're asking."

"Will..."

"I'm sorry, Mira, but I really can't stay to talk about this right now. We've had enough unpleasantness." *What does he mean unpleasantness? Is there something else? Something he's not telling me? What is he hiding?*

After checking my room, he holds the door open for me, but at the last second puts his hand on my arm to stop me as I pass him. "Oh, I almost forgot, Socrates wishes to meet with you."

Looking up at him, I realize we're standing very close, and the hairs on my arms stand up. Too close. Electricity buzzes along my nerves, and I can almost hear his heartbeat. "Is he mad at me?"

"I don't think so, but this is pretty unusual. Firsts generally try not to get too attached to their Absolved, given the circumstances. Usually they don't see them until the Release banquet."

"What circumstances?" A chill races down my spine. "Why wouldn't Socrates want to get attached to me?"

Will looks at me peculiarly, but says nothing.

"You're scaring me. Is it really that bad?"

He grimaces. "I wish I could tell you, but I'm afraid I can't. It's one of the topics I'm not allowed to discuss without permission."

"Why not?"

He shakes his head. "I'm sorry, Mira." He looks as though he's fighting with himself, wanting to say more. He frowns. "Let me... let me think about this. I'll talk to your First. He'll be able to get it approved."

"Is it really that much of a secret? I thought being Absolved is a good thing."

"It is. It's great for our country, our history, and the world. It's just... complicated, that's all."

Something's not right here. I grab his arm. "Will, please. Tell me." Panic rises in my voice, but I can't help it.

He shakes his head, shadows chasing the light from his eyes. "I can't." He takes my hands in his and gently squeezes. "I have to talk to Socrates anyway, so I'll ask him about it."

"What if he says no?"

He shakes his head. "I don't know. I'll think of something. I'll let you know what he says, okay? I just... I can't break the law like this. If I told you without permission, well, that's worse than your little jaunt outside today. I could be executed for treason."

"No one will know, Will. I won't tell anyone."

His lips press into a firm line, and he squeezes my hands again, leans down, and whispers, "I'm sorry, Mira, but I can't."

A BIT OF A MESS

socrates

tHE COM UNIT BEEPS, AND a large pale man with thick white hair and a red, bulbous nose fills the screen.

"Socrates?" His voice comes across more nasally on screen than it usually does in person.

"Yes, Kendal." Damn, why couldn't I be sleeping or something? "What can I do for you?"

"About a month after the Release, the President would like to hold a luncheon at a local elementary school. Good PR, you know. He would appreciate it if you would give a short speech to the kids about what life was like back when you were a child the first time and then do a short question and answer session. Do you think you'll have recovered adequately by then?"

Do I have much choice? Kendal speaks for the President, after all, and I would do well not to get on his bad side. But what will I talk about? The advent of the Internet? Learning to ride a bike? Getting married and having kids? I don't remember much more than a snippet or two at best, and I'm sure elementary-aged children would love to hear about that boring nonsense. I'll have them all down for a nap in five minutes. "I'll be ready. It's not a problem."

"Great. President Davidson will be pleased. It's always positive publicity to show the recently Released healthy and contributing to society. It's good for morale. It's also easier for the next generation to relate to Firsts when they've known them as children like themselves." Could that smug bastard be any more self-satisfied? Jesus, I hate people like him.

"Of course, which is why I'm sure he has me speak at *important* events such as this."

Kendal pauses at the other end of the line. "Well, you are one of the most articulate of the Firsts."

I snort. Now he's really reaching. I wouldn't even pick myself as the first choice for any public speaking engagement. I'm gruff, say what I think, hate writing speeches, and some people—Ellie most of all—have even called me rude to a fault. I'll probably scare the little kids half to death. "That's ridiculous and you know it. Ellie is much better spoken than I am. Hell, any of the others would be a better choice."

"But you're *the* First." Ah yes, it always comes back to that, doesn't it?

I scowl at Kendal, and his video visage looks affronted. "That doesn't mean anything, not anymore. Even then, I was a fool trying to kill myself. You know it, I know it, the whole damn world knows it. Just too damn lucky for my own good."

"You know that's not true," Kendal sputters.

"It is, and you know it." I shake my head, and when he starts to speak, I hold my gnarled hand up to stop him. "But it doesn't matter. I'll play in your dog and pony show if that's what Andrew wants, but it doesn't make me *your* puppet, you know. I've known him far longer than you have, and his father before him. Both are good men fighting for a just and honorable cause."

He glowers at me, reaches forward, and clicks off the screen. Great, now I've pissed him off, too. My day's just getting better and better.

No sooner am I settled back in the bed, when I hear a knock on the door. "Who is it?" I yell.

"Will," the boy answers. Grumbling, I limp over to the door, open it, and gesture for him to enter. He does, carrying a silver platter over to the table. Steam curls around the edges, and I smell lamb, my favorite. As if in response, my stomach rumbles, a sound not that much different from my own voice. If he notices, the boy is too well-trained to say anything.

"May I?" he asks with his hand on the top of the silver dome.

"Yes, please." I watch as he reveals a meal of roasted lamb, bread pudding, green beans, and a side salad. Real food. Much better than that synthesized plastic mush the doctors try to shove down my throat. I sit down to eat. "Have you talked to the girl yet?"

"Yes, sir. About that..." The boy takes a deep breath. "Mira doesn't know anything about the Release ceremony."

"Really? I thought Edward was going to tell her."

"No, sir. Perhaps with her sudden departure and his arrest, it was... overlooked?"

"Hmm." I scratch my beard. "That's an interesting way of saying it, but I bet you're right." My old friend's frightened gaze torments me as I close my eyes.

"She has no idea what's going to happen to her. No idea that she's going to die. She still thinks she's moving on to some great adventure as your Second." He clamps a hand to his mouth, clearly shocking himself with his words. I merely arch an eyebrow. Even though what he said amounts to treason, I've heard worse. "I'm s-s-sorry, sir. I misspoke. I wasn't thinking..." His eyes widen with fear.

I frown. The action beetles my brows, so I can see the hairs of the bushy white caterpillars drooping over my eyes. A sudden, painful spear arches between my temples, and waves of dizziness swamp me. I forget where I am or what I'm doing, completely losing track of the conversation. "What did you say?"

"Nothing, sir. I'm... I'm terribly sorry." The boy bows

his head, his trembling hand still holding the lid. One word from me could get him killed.

"It may not seem like it, nor may you believe it, but it *is* a privilege to be chosen as a Second. Very few are strong enough or smart enough to make this sacrifice. Absolved Texans like Mira have a great destiny that goes far beyond their pitiful lives on the farms." I can still see how worried the young man is, so I decide to put him at ease. "I know you think I should tell her what's in store, but now is not the time."

Will grimaces. "You aren't going to tell her?"

"No, we have enough on our plates right now. There will be plenty of time for that when the dust has settled after the Acceptance ceremony."

After he leaves, I pick through the food, barely tasting any of it. When I finally give up, I put the plate on the floor, letting Ben finish it off, a task to which he applies himself wholeheartedly.

I change for bed, slipping off my wrist scanner and putting it on the nightstand next to my pillow.

Lying in bed, I struggle to keep my eyes open, seeing Edward's face every time I close them.

"What would you do, old friend?" I ask no one in particular. Ben lifts his head, licking the last bits of sauce from his nose, but when he realizes I'm not talking to him, he returns to his cleaning duties.

In my mind, I see Edward sitting across the table from me, shackled and bruised with a triumphant look on his face. "Would you tell her?"

The Edward in my head answers. "Of course. I would have told her from the start. I would have treated her like a human being and given her an actual choice." He stares accusingly at me.

"A real choice, eh?" What could it hurt? I suppose if I ever had a Second say no, I would probably have released him from his duties. It's never happened, but it's not out of the realm of possibility, either.

"Personally, I never would have gotten into this mess in the first place." He leans back, folding his hands, restrained as they are, on his stomach. "Everyone deserves a chance to live their own life, don't you think?"

"Seems to me you are in a bit of a mess," I grumble, feeling raw and put out for some reason. Maybe he's right? Maybe I should give her a choice. Probably the first damn decision she's ever had to make in her life.

NO CHOICE

mira

i CAN'T SLEEP. THAT STUPID INTERVIEW, then Evie, then Gregory's words run through my head. What do they mean? What do they know that I don't? What can't Will tell me? What about being Absolved makes him look at me with such pity, like he knows something I don't?

Frustrated, I bunch up my pillow behind my head.

"Having trouble sleeping?" AVAS asks, her voice soothing and calm. I jump anyway. I don't think I'll ever get used to some super-intelligent computer watching my every move and commenting on what I'm doing.

"Yeah, but I'm fine."

"Would you like to view some of the prescribed entertainment? Based on my news schedule, there is a very interesting broadcast on right now. It's being watched by eighty-seven percent of the viewing audience."

"Really? What's it about?" I sit up straight. This might actually be interesting. Might actually take my mind off the way Evie put her hand on Will's arm, the guilty look in his face, the baby she's carrying. Anything would be better than this, right?

"A longtime teacher and rebel supporter, Edward Flannigan, is being charged with treason against the state. If he is found guilty, his sentence will be carried out immediately." AVAS pauses.

"Mr. Flannigan?" I whisper, my mind going numb.

A deep coldness seeps into my bones, but AVAS continues. "How would you like me to proceed?"

What do I say? Something tells me this isn't a normal trial. Treason is the worst crime in our country. This is bad. Really bad. Not even recognizing my own voice, I whisper, "Show the broadcast."

"Yes, Ma'am."

The screen flashes on, then shows a good-looking, dark-haired man with light-green eyes wearing a beige suit standing in front of a towering stone building. The sign in front of the building reads Fullbright Detention Center. Is that where I was? Unease trickles up my spine. Bright, glaring lights shine on the impossibly high walls and more gates and fences than I can count.

"This is Corey Schram with the DC Chronicle. I'm here outside Fullbright Detention Center with breaking news. Absolved Advisor Edward Flannigan has pled guilty to terrorism and awaits sentencing." Wait, there's no trial? I thought he gets a trial? I perch at the edge of the bed, eyes glued to the screen.

The image shifts to show Mr. Flannigan in dull gray prison garb, shrunken and pale, standing in a large outdoor space, hands chained together in front of him. He stares defiantly at a panel of five black-robed men and two women who sit at a long, raised table, almost like a stage.

"Edward Flannigan, you have been charged with four felony counts of terrorism, accessory to a terrorist organization, and plotting to commit a terrorist act against the United States of America. All of these charges carry the death penalty. How do you plead?"

Mr. Flannigan takes a deep breath, straightens his back, and says, "Guilty."

One of the men, a white-haired guy with a thick mustache leans forward and frowns at Mr. Flannigan. "Are you certain that this is your answer? Do you realize that, if you plead guilty, we will have no choice but to sentence you to death?"

"I understand," Flannigan's voice rings out sure and confident. "I'm not afraid to admit that I support the freedom of every person in America."

Another one of the men, taller and bald with wrinkles sagging around his face, sighs and looks at his compatriots, who nod. "Then I believe we are in agreement. Edward Flannigan, based on your guilty plea, you are sentenced to death. As written in the Human Rights Act of 2394, you have the right to choose the method of your execution." The reporter, Corey Schram, comes back on, restates what just happened, and calls those old people the Councilmen. I tune him out.

Death? No. He... he can't. What happened to him in there? Did they torture him? Beat him? The Mr. Flannigan I knew was so crafty, he'd never admit to being a rebel. What did they charge him with again? Terrorism? Terrorism of what? Telling me what fork to use? How to fold my napkin in my lap? The screen shifts back to show the Councilmen, with the bushy white mustached one standing up in front.

"As per the Human Rights Act of 2394, you have the right to choose any form of capital punishment, past or present you desire. Methods include, but are not limited to: hanging, lethal injection, electrocution, firing squad, intercranial injection, laser-destimulation, or neural disentanglement. Which do you choose?"

The other councilmen look bored, that is until Mr. Flannigan smiles slightly and says, "I choose the firing squad." They all jump in their chairs a bit and turn to each other.

"Are you sure?" the head Councilman asks him.

"Yes." He stands up even straighter, as if he isn't on trial, as if he isn't telling them how he'd prefer to die. My chest aches. *This can't be real.* They really wouldn't do this, would they? They can't be...

"As you wish, then." The head Councilman gestures with his hand, and four guards approach Mr. Flannigan, leading him to a wooden pole in the middle of the yard. "Your sentence will be carried out immediately."

What? No! They can't do this! "No!" I gasp, not realizing I spoke out loud until AVAS freezes the frame and asks, "Would you like me to find another program? My systems sense that you are becoming agitated."

"No, no, turn it back on!"

"As you wish." She unfreezes the screen, and I watch the guards march Mr. Flannigan to a pole in the center of the arena and stand him up against it. One of the guards produces a silvery cord to tie him to the pole, but Mr. Flannigan shakes his head, saying no, he'll stand on his own.

Admiration almost takes over the fear and disgust rising in my stomach. The guard looks at the head Councilman, who shrugs. Giving up, the guard pockets the cord. The other guards look confused, talking to each other and glancing at my old teacher, as if nervous. Do they even know what they're doing? Have they ever had to do this before?

While Mr. Flannigan stands solid with a slight smile on his face, the guards turn, walk away, and stand about twenty feet from him. They're joined by another who hands each of the men an old-fashioned gun, the kind that takes actual bullets, before joining them in the lineup.

The image on the screen changes back to the reporter. "Edward Flannigan has chosen the firing squad as his method of execution. This outdated form of capital punishment became popular in the early twentieth century but lost favor when easier and more humane methods, such as lethal injection, became widely used. In this form of capital punishment, all of the gunmen use guns appropriate to those used in the era in which this method was used. All but one of the weapons are loaded with live rounds. This ensures maximum success while still maintaining the mental stability of the volunteers."

The screen switches back to the Councilmen. The leader stares soberly at Mr. Flannigan. Almost as if he knows him from somewhere and really doesn't want to do this. "Do you have any last words?"

Ice runs through my veins. *They're really going to do this, aren't they? They're really going to kill him. I... I can't watch.*

Opening my mouth to tell AVAS to turn off the screen, I stop when Mr. Flannigan appears to look directly at me, and says, "Let my death be a testament to the brutality of a government where one man who disagrees with those in power can be put to death. Where one man who voices his opinion, who tries to make a difference and save the lives of millions of children is immediately shut down and executed. May God have mercy on your souls." He closes his eyes, and a guard marches forward and puts a black cloth bag over his head. After the guard returns to his position at the sidelines, the head Councilman nods, and at once, five guns rise from their vertical positions, point at Mr. Flannigan, and fire. Four red spots burst on my teacher's chest, stark against the pale gray prison uniform. His body jolts with each impact. As the ringing of the shots fades away, Mr. Flannigan's body falls, down to his knees, then face forward on the ground. The dust puffs up around him. Then silence. He doesn't stir.

"Turn it off," I say quietly, and the screen goes black.

"EVERY MAN HAS HIS SECRETS."

socrates

STAND AT THE PODIUM IN front of Congress and the President, dressed in my finest tuxedo, with Ellie standing behind me. Everyone is quiet. All eyes are on me, the first of the Firsts, and for that reason alone, the person dubbed most suited to support this bill. I have, in fact, gone through with the procedure more times than any other living person.

"And that, Mr. President, is why I support the Free America—" There's a loud noise behind me. A dog barking? I spin around, not inconvenienced by the ravages of old age. Ben? What's he doing here? He barks again, and I blink. Oh yes, dreaming again. Figures.

"Ben, shut up." I groggily pull myself into a sitting position, but the sharp knives in my back don't allow me to go any further. Someone's banging on the door. Who the hell would it be this late at night?

"Hold your goddamn horses." The knocking continues. "Who is it?" I pull myself to the edge of the bed and swing my feet over. Seems harder than it was yesterday.

"It's Mira, sir, and Will." The boy's voice calls from the other side of the door. Ben ratchets it up a couple hundred decibels.

"It can't wait until morning?" I push myself to my feet. My mind is still fuzzy, but that's the pain talking. Maybe I should have gotten that stupid implant Ellie told me about. Although, I never did like letting anyone else have control of my body and what goes into it.

"No, sir. I'm sorry, I couldn't stop her." The boy sounds worried. He should be. *Waking me in the middle of the night. Should be outlawed. Against the law. Definitely illegal and punishable by something pretty terrible.* I push my wrinkled feet into slippers after contemplating one last time whether or not I could just roll over and forget about them. Ben's continuous barking rules that out.

"They killed him!" Mira screams from the other side of the door. That stops me cold. Who?

"What in the hell are you talking about?" I hobble over to the door as quickly as I can, my body a throbbing mass of pain. "Who's dead?" I open the door, and Mira, frantic, nearly falls through the doorway. Ben pushes toward the invaders, his hackles rising and a low growling noise coming from his throat. "Down, boy. It's okay." I grip the scruff of his neck, and he quiets, steps aside, and they both enter.

Mira is clearly distraught, her eyes red and puffy. She wrings her hands and bites her lip. She looks as if she's holding on by a thread, as if at any moment something could happen, and she could snap. Will, on the other hand, isn't panicked so much as he is nervous. He knows he's not supposed to be here, not supposed to interrupt me without permission. *If only my Second used the same manners.*

"Mr. Flannigan, he's—he's dead." Another tear tracks down her face, and she scrubs it away.

I feel the blood drain from my face. "What? No... he can't be. They hadn't set the trial date. They said they were going to wait until after the Acceptance." Suddenly dizzy, I wobble on my feet, and Will drops Mira's arm before grabbing mine, leading me to the hard-backed chair by the desk. Like a child, I let him.

"Edward," I whisper. "No, he can't be." My friend's jovial face flashes in my head, his smile, his quick-witted humor, his sarcastic wit. No. He can't be gone. "Are you sure?" I can't even see them clearly, my vision's gone fuzzy, and it's as if I'm underwater, and they're above the surface, trying to talk to me. I can't understand them, but I can see Mira nod tearfully and know she's telling the truth.

"It's true. I just—I just saw it on the news. He—He said he was a Lifer, and he—he was sentenced to..." She can't even say the word.

"Death," Will finishes. Mira closes her eyes. Is she trying to wipe clean the memory of seeing someone die? It doesn't work, I should know.

I glance at the clock. 12:12 a.m. Executions always take place at midnight. All of them are broadcast live. I should have known he wouldn't have wanted me to be there, and he knew I would have insisted. That's what friends do, even if the other is a traitor to his country.

"It—it was awful," Mira cries, finally falling apart. Will folds his arms around her, and she buries her face in his neck. "They—they asked him what kind he wanted, and they—and they listed all the different ways to die. He—he chose the firing squad."

I close my eyes and gulp down the bitter taste of bile in my throat. "No. He wouldn't have." Most people choose neurotoxin, a quick, nearly painless way to die, if not especially interesting. Edward must have wanted to make a statement. But about what?

"They kept playing it over and over again." Will gazes up at me. Even his eyes are haunted.

"You were with her?" I nod toward Mira.

"No, I saw it in my apartment. Once I remembered his connection to Mira, I went to her room to make sure she was all right." He squeezes her tighter, and slowly her sobs give way to hiccups as he rubs circles on her back.

"I had no idea. When I spoke with Edward, they hadn't even set a trial date. It should have taken weeks, months even. I would have had time to appeal, to speak on his behalf." I close my eyes, and I can almost see him standing there, proud as a peacock, accepting the Council's decision. "Why, Edward?" Shaking my head, I open my eyes and find both of the children watching me. Mira's eyes are dry now, and she seems to have pulled herself together.

"I'm sorry you had to see that," I say stiffly. What else does one say in response to this sort of situation? As if becoming aware of her position in Will's embrace, she sees my gaze and steps away, as if realizing this is not an entirely appropriate position for an Absolved and a servant to be in. She flushes bright red. "I didn't know Edward meant that much to you."

She takes a deep breath and wipes at her eyes one last time with the sleeve of her night shirt. "I... he... he was the first person I met after you picked me. And he, he taught me about manners, and silverware." She smiles at the memory. "But I... he was my friend. He was your friend too, wasn't he?"

"Of course, I've known him for nearly thirty years."

"Did you know he was a rebel?"

I shake my head. "I hadn't the slightest idea. I suppose every man has his secrets, but I had no idea Edward would turn out to be a Lifer. I never would have dreamed he had any rebel sympathies."

"Don't you get it, Socrates? These kids, what's happening to them, it's the most important injustice going on in the world right now. They celebrate you, people like you... And people like me, we have to prepare these lambs for slaughter, assuage their doubts, make them more comfortable, all the while knowing they're going to die." Suddenly, I can't stand up any longer, and I stumble back to the bed, sinking onto the mattress. I close my eyes, blinking back my own tears. "Edward. Jesus, I'm so sorry."

Maybe he was right, after all.

BY ANY MEANS NECESSARY

mira

"tHERE'S SOMETHING I WANT YOU to see," Will says, looking nervous as he walks me back to my room. When we get there, he quickly goes in ahead of me and searches it before returning to where I wait. *Just like Bullfrog did when I arrived.* Is it really that dangerous?

"Do you mind if I join you?"

I step aside. "You kind of already have." Neither of us laughs at my attempted joke.

"I was able to locate the video footage of your cousin's Release."

Cold fingers scratch their icy nails down my back, and I shiver. "Socrates okayed it?" He looks away. "Will? I don't want to get you in trouble."

"It's fine. This is important, trust me. I know of a way that... well, they can't trace what you're watching."

"Okay, I guess." I bite my lip. "When do you want me to watch it?"

He swallows, and his hands fiddle with a thin bracelet. The kind the Firsts, like Socrates, wear. "Now." He's got this serious look in his eyes, and I know that whatever he wants me to see, it's important.

I try to lighten the mood anyway. "Sure, it's not like I have any other plans."

Will doesn't smile. Something is definitely wrong.

"Will you stay with me?"

"Yes." He nods and walks past me. "I don't want you to be alone."

Gee, that makes me feel more comfortable.

Will walks over to the wall screen and runs the bracelet over an invisible scanner. The screen comes to life with the words "Welcome, Socrates" in bright white against a dark blue background. Wait, what's he doing? He's not Socrates. Something tells me we could get in a world's worth of trouble for this. I blink and feel the cold, hard floor of Fullbright beneath my feet. No, I can't go back there. I open my mouth, but Will shakes his head and gestures for me to sit down. Something in the sharp way he does it makes me listen. Was this what Tanner was talking about? That the rebels knew things, information, that the rest of us didn't? I feel frozen inside, like I want to run away, but I can't. I'm rooted to this spot.

Will perches next to me on the end of the bed, and the sight of him sitting there, all stiff-backed and serious, makes my stomach tighten.

"Good evening, Sir. What would you prefer to watch tonight?"

Will clears his throat. "Thoreau's last Release procedure."

"Voice activation rejected. Please state your full name or scan your bracelet to proceed. Refusal to follow protocols will result in full lockdown, and security will be notified immediately." The lights flash, and Will jumps up to scan the bracelet again. The lights go back to their normal glow, and Will sits down again, letting out a nervous, shaky laugh. "That was close," he murmurs. Before I can say anything, the screen blinks brightly.

At first, all I see is a broad view of a nearly circular room, empty except for two bare hospital beds with padded straps dangling off the sides. Connecting the two beds is a large machine with cords running to smaller consoles beside each bed. The floor is the pale gray concrete reserved for places where no one cares what the floor looks like. The round portion of the wall is made of mirror-like glass.

Three people dressed in light green walk in from a door set in the glass. One heads to the larger machine in the middle, while the other two go to the consoles by the beds. They check the various machines, cords, and straps. The central machine lights up—red, then yellow, and finally blinks green. The two men by the beds leave and return with metal stands holding clear, liquid-filled bags.

The camera cuts to show another room filled with people sitting in red padded chairs. They look relaxed as they sip from fluted glasses of amber liquid. They look through a large window as they talk and joke. Are they at a party? Laughter and idle chatter fill the room, and I jump.

The chairs face the round glass wall from the hospital room in the previous scene. A sinking feeling fills my stomach. *Maybe I don't want to see this after all.*

On the left of the large window, a reporter stands in front of another camera, smiling widely and speaking in a hushed, but excited tone. "This is Beverly Beaumont from the D.C. Chronicle, and I'm here for Thoreau's sixth Release procedure, which follows closely on the heels of the dramatic attempt on his life just moments ago."

The perspective on the screen shifts to the room where the beds and machinery wait. The door opens, and an ancient man, frail and supported by two orderlies, enters, followed by my cousin, who has an orderly of his own. He looks so scared, not at all like the smiling, laughing boy I remember. The one who worked with me in the barns, was in training to help take care of the animals, and who always made time to spend with my brother, Max.

Adrian's fair hair has been clipped even shorter, and someone has marked purple dots on his forehead and around the back of his skull. He looks dazed, drugged. The tall, impassive orderly at his side guides him by the elbow to the bed on the right, while the other two help the elderly man onto its twin.

The orderly whispers something. Adrian gets on the bed and lies down. Business-like, the man straps my cousin in at the ankles, wrists, around the waist, and across the forehead. He inserts a clear tube into one of his arms and attaches electrodes to his thin, adolescent chest. Adrian's breaths are quick and shallow. He's terrified, and his eyes dart from side to side as if looking for a way to escape. What's going on here? This isn't like anything I've been taught or shown before. Were Henri Lee and Tanner right? As a final act of kindness, the orderly covers him with a white blanket.

Now the screen zooms in on the old man. He's not tied down, but he also has an IV inserted in one arm. His head rests on a small pillow, and he's covered by a blanket.

The scene changes back to the reporter, Beverly Beaumont. "This is likely to be one of the most exciting events of this decade. We're so thrilled that Thoreau has decided to share this memorable moment with all of the citizens in our glorious country. It's truly an honor to be here."

A doctor attaches a metal device to Adrian's head. The helmet-like thing has pink buttons spaced at his temple, behind his ears, and at the base of his skull, right over the purple dots. Long thin needles must be centered behind each dot, and when the doctor pushes one of the buttons, Adrian winces.

I glance at Will. "What are they doing?"

"They're preparing him for the procedure by inserting thin, hollow tubes to create pathways directly to the brain. After the body..." He stops and clears his throat. "... is prepared, Thoreau's mind can enter freely."

I gape at him. "But that's my cousin! He's not just a... a *body*."

"I'm sorry. I don't know how else to explain it."

192

I turn back to the screen. A trickle of blood escapes through one of the holes around Adrian's skull, and tears track down his cheeks. The orderly wipes at them but smears most of the blood. My dinner rises into my throat, and I swallow hard. *This is going to be me.* "Will..."

The camera focuses on Thoreau. Liver spots dot his face, and perspiration trickles down his brow. The probes piercing his head are on top of old scars, just like the ones on... Socrates.

"How many times?" I know Will knows what I'm asking.

"Six. You'll be number seven."

Black spots appear before my eyes, and I shake. Will grabs my hand and squeezes it gently.

The reporter's voice brings my attention back to the screen. "The doctors use hollow probes inserted in the Second's skull to create pathways to his brain. Once both participants are ready, drugs will be given in the Second's IV to stop his heart. Then, the same will occur for Thoreau. As the First's body shuts down, his mind will be uploaded into the central computer." She points at the console in the middle of the room.

"After the Second's vital signs have stopped, new drugs will restart his heart. As soon as a solid rhythm is established, Thoreau's mind will be downloaded into the brain, using the pathway created by the electrodes." The room darkens, and the audience hushes as the camera flashes back to the main chamber.

The orderly beside Adrian flips a switch on the small machine next to his bed. Cloudy liquid inches slowly down the tube. Adrian's eyes squeeze shut as the liquid reaches his body. Then he relaxes. *What's happening to him? Is he okay? Sleeping?* His chest rises and falls. He must be sleeping. I shake my head. Something still doesn't feel right.

I turn to Will. "Does he feel it? Does he know what's happening?"

"Yes, he knew. I was his servant, too." Will's voice is quiet, full of sadness. He looks away, and I sense that he's close to losing it, too. "He was a great kid."

Anger fills me. My fists ball at my sides, and I jump away from him. "What? You're calling him great, but you let this happen to him?"

"Damn it, Mir. You don't understand. I had no choice. Just like now." His eyes, full of agony, are nearly my undoing, so I turn back to the screen.

The screen focuses back on Thoreau. A doctor stands at his side, smiling as they chat. *How can they smile at a time like this?* The liquid starts down the long tube, then stops. The doctor fiddles with the dial, and the fluid flows more quickly. I look back at Adrian, but the camera pulls away, not focusing on either one while I, and the audience, watch them die.

Adrian jolts against his restraints, jerking his hands and kicking under the blanket. I jump, and only Will's quick tug on my hand keeps me in my seat. My cousin thrashes even harder. His pupils dilate, whites showing as his eyes roll back into his head.

The orderlies and a doctor rush to Adrian's side. His head whips back and forth, and his mouth opens in a silent scream. Spit and blood leak out. Bloody rivulets seep from the wounds on his head, down his cheeks, and into his eyes. The orderly tries to wipe some of it away, but only smears the red everywhere. The doctor fiddles with the machine next to the bed, adjusting dials and making the liquid drip even faster.

The camera shoots away to focus on Thoreau, whose face is the picture of serenity as the drugs erase his pain. His eyes close, and his lips tilt up in a smile.

The camera flashes back to my cousin's body, so small on the bed, and his chest rises, falls, rises, falls... then stops. It just stops. I hold my breath, and tears burn my eyes. Is this my future? This will be me. My death will be broadcast around the world.

A final, small spasm shakes Adrian's body, and a whimper escapes from my mouth. I bite my lip, scrunching my eyes tight against the tears. But all I see behind my eyelids is my blond-haired, poetry-loving cousin dying in front of an audience, yet all alone.

Will gently wipes at a tear on my cheek with the pad of his thumb. "I'm so sorry."

The contact makes me shiver, and I pull away, turning my head.

Back in the screening room, the audience is glued to the window. The reporter is quiet, watching the dying boy and man as if they're entertainment. As if it's right. I blink, the pain quickly becoming anger. *This is okay? This is accepted in our world? In our society? This is what it means to be a Second? A lonely death on a hospital bed with the whole world watching?*

The orderly next to Adrian's bed flips the switch on his machine, and the monitor beeps.

Thoreau's orderly reaches for the blanket and covers the old man's face.

At Adrian's table, the orderly uses a cloth to wipe the still-trickling blood. After a bit, the man at the central computer nods and turns to the orderly at Adrian's side, who flips another switch on the machine, stopping the flow of one of the liquids.

One by one, the long, hollow needles are removed from my cousin's head. The orderly cleans his wounds and puts a small round bandage on each injury. Adrian's eyelids flutter, and the orderly loosens his restraints.

On the other side of the room, Thoreau's body is wheeled away. The orderlies return and turn off the various equipment. *Is it over?* I look down at my hands through blurry eyes. They're shaking. "I... I can't believe it. He's dead. He was my cousin and now... they just... just killed him."

Will pulls me back down. "Wait," he says, grimly. "They're not done, yet."

Slowly, carefully, Adrian sits up, flexing his hands as if unused to them. He looks down at his body, then touches his head, but doesn't even grimace at what must be throbbing wounds. An eerily wide grin lights up his face, and he swings his legs easily over the side of the bed and gets to his feet.

With the two orderlies standing on either side of him, my cousin stretches, cracks his shoulders, knuckles, and back, bends down to touch his toes, then arches toward the sky. Grinning again, he glances at both of the orderlies and shakes his head. He obviously doesn't need their help.

A doctor walks up to him. "If you're ready, sir, I have one question for you."

"I'm ready."

"Do you know who you are?"

"Yes." Adrian nods again, his once-familiar face displaying an eerie smile that belongs to someone else. "I am Thoreau."

In the next instant, the camera is back on the audience. The reporter talks hurriedly about how wonderfully smooth the exchange was and how they will run more tests, of course, but that it appears to have been a complete success. The audience claps and smiles, nodding at each other, as if this is their personal celebration. I feel sick as servants pass around more fluted glasses.

"Please, Will, turn it off." I turn my back on the screen.

Will nods. "Screen off."

"Yes, sir," AVAS intones, her electronic voice bland. *Her world hasn't crumbled. Everything she's been told wasn't a lie. Tanner was right. Henri Lee was right. I am going to die.* When the sound is gone, the screen black, the silence final, it's as if Adrian just died again, even more horribly this time, now that I know what's happened to him. A sour taste rises in my throat, and I gulp it back down.

"I don't believe it. I... I... just..."

Will reaches for me as bitterness and anguish contort

his face. "It's not usually that... that bad." He spits out the words. "But sometimes people react to the medications in different ways. It blurs their minds and dulls their reactions, sometimes exaggerating emotions or feelings." How can he sound so detached? So clinical? Does he do this all the time? Show these horrors to every new Second?

"How can they do this?" I whisper, my own voice full of horror. Will doesn't have an answer for me.

"And you." I pull away from him. "How can you do this? Take care of these Seconds, these children, every day, and you're... you're okay with it?"

"No!" Pain rips through his face. "Of course I'm not okay, but... but you've got to understand. I can't do anything to stop it. I'm just a servant. I'm nobody. I can't... I can't *do* anything."

I close my eyes for a long minute. He's right. He's helpless, too. *How horrible it must be for him, getting to know these kids, only to watch them die.* I let out a deep breath, centering myself. "Does everyone here know what really happens?"

He looks away. "Everyone at the Smith, pretty much. They think it's... well, you've heard the lines: it's a great destiny, an honor, and an amazing chance to make a difference."

"If they're televised, how come I've never seen one?"

"Only the free citizens watch. It's illegal to show footage at the farms."

It all makes sense now. Sick, horrible sense. This is why I was chosen: to die. "Would that also be why no First comes back to the same farm after choosing a Second from it?" Like pieces dropping into place, the puzzle starts to make sense, and hatred fills me. For Socrates, for everyone in the audience, for Thoreau, for all of them.

"Yes, that would be... awkward." He tries to take my hands in his, but I pull away.

"So that's it, then? I'm going to die."

Will takes a deep breath, and I swear I can see his eyes shining in the low light. "During the Release procedure, your mind will leave your body, yes, and Socrates's mind will take its place."

"And this is okay? All my life I'd been raised to think this was this great opportunity, this great contribution to society, but I'm just a warm body." *The fairytales were right. The boogey man does exist, and there's no way for the princess to slay him.*

"To them, you're not *physically* dying. Your body is still alive, walking and talking. If you add that to the contributions your First will make to the world..." His lips tighten with words he won't say. "Perhaps most people just don't want to see the reality. They don't come into contact with Texans unless they're wealthy enough to employ them. They firmly believe that you would be honored to be given such a privilege."

"Employ them? Will, they buy and sell us! It's not like we're being promoted to another job. We don't have a choice."

"You're right. I'm sorry. It was an unfortunate choice of words. We have more power here at the Smith than people do on the farms, probably because we're more visible to the public. They have to keep us at least somewhat satisfied because, if we rebelled, the common person might question the way things are, and the government doesn't want that. They like to remind people that the Texans started the fight. Texans killed thousands of soldiers and blew up the White House and the Pentagon. In their eyes, and the eyes of many others who didn't rebel, offering children as Seconds merely rights their ancestors' wrongs."

"But I didn't start that fight. What about you? You're like me. Can you be chosen?"

"No. It's the law. No Texan who works at the Smith or any other public agency can be chosen. We're seen every day, recognized, and some of us form attachments with our benefactors, our dignitaries. It would, for lack of a better way of phrasing it, be too disturbing for them to see us go through the procedure." His eyes slide away from me, as if he feels guilty that he can't face the same fate. He fidgets in his seat. His hands clench at his sides.

"This is insane." I look at the walls, which seem to form a cell more than the nicest room I've ever had in my life. "Then, I guess I don't have a choice. Do I?"

"No," he says quietly. "I suppose not. When you're born and raised on a farm, if you're chosen, that's it."

"Does my mother know?" Would she have sent me to my death if she did? No, we might not have the typical mother/daughter relationship, but even she wouldn't do that. Even if I killed my little sister.

"No. How could she? What parent would allow their child to be in a program where they could die?" He's right. I smile in relief. That makes sense. Not even my mother would do that to me.

"Do you show other Seconds these videos?"

"No. Most of them never find out. Usually I'm a companion and servant, nothing more."

I bite my lip, seeing my cousin's tortured thrashing in my mind. "And here I thought... well, I don't know. I thought I would be trained, travel the world as his servant, his helper, I don't know, maybe take his place when he dies, not that he was going to... to... kill me and take over my body." I shake my head. "This is murder. There have to be some people who oppose this."

"Of course there are. Several groups in fact, but the Lifers are the largest." I meet his gaze, and his eyes hold me.

"Like Mr. Flannigan?"

Will nods. "They believe it's better to die than be a Second. That people should live out their lives as they see fit, where everyone's free."

I raise an eyebrow. "You sound like you know a lot about them."

His eyes widen. "No. Definitely not. I just know what I've heard. People talk around here, and most ignore us servants."

"I just... I can't... I don't get it." I shake my head. "I don't understand."

"Believe it," he says grimly. "Politicians and the government look at this program as a great way to stay in favor with the common people and to keep Texans in line. Most people love the idea of the Texans earning some sort of freedom. And they get to keep around the greatest and most influential people of the world. So what if every year, a few hundred teenagers are chosen as Seconds? What contribution would a normal person make to the world that even comes close to that of John F. Kennedy, Abraham Lincoln, or George Eliot? People die all the time, but the government and the free citizens don't consider this a death. Look at Socrates's companion, George Eliot. Not only was she the first female president, but in her second lifetime, she helped scientists find a cure for autism. In the first three of his lifetimes, Thoreau worked as an ambassador and eventually brokered peace between Pakistan and India. Many people see this as a higher calling."

"So what did Socrates do?"

He is silent for a long moment and looks at me, surprised that I don't know anything about the man who wants to take over my body.

"Well? What makes him so important?"

"He survived," Will says, his voice flat.

"Yeah? So did George Eliot, Thoreau, and the others."

"No, he was the *first* to survive."

"So all the others before him died?"

Will nods.

"Why did he make it while the others before him didn't?"

"He used a younger Second."

I gulp. "Like me?"

"Yes. His son, Adam."

Nausea overpowers me, and I stand up on wobbly legs. I half run, half stumble to the bathroom and throw up in the toilet. Warm hands rub circles on my back. At first, I'm embarrassed to have Will see me this way, but it's so comforting, I give in to the feeling. I rest, waiting for the dizziness and nausea to pass. They don't, but I can't spend the rest of my life leaning over the toilet.

When I feel strong enough, I lift my head, pull myself to my feet, and stagger over to the sink to splash water on my face. I don't recognize the person staring back at me in the mirror. I look older, tired. I close my eyes, and see Adrian's face. Blood runs down his face, his eyes roll back in his head, and his mouth opens in a silent scream.

"His son? What happened?"

"Back then, you understand, things were a lot different than they are now. Adam was riding something called a motorcycle and crashed. He hit his head, and suffered damage to his brain. His body was fine, but his mind, gone. He was only twenty."

I gulp back the bitterness in the back of my throat again. "What kind of monster would do that, though?"

Will stiffly walks over to me and leads me to the bed. At first I don't want to sit down, but I let him take me. For some reason, I don't think I can do anything else. "He was dying already. The Highlander project was big news at that time, though they hadn't had any lasting success. Socrates volunteered. His first wife, Vanessa, convinced him to try using Adam's body. I remember reading that, even though she knew her son was already gone, she hoped that maybe her husband could live on and help the future."

"That's just sick." I shake my head, shivering.

"I don't know if Socrates even thought he'd survive the procedure. He probably hoped he wouldn't, after losing his son like that." Will closes his eyes, as if imagining himself in Socrates's position.

I examine him closely. "How do you know so much?"

He smiles briefly. "It's nothing really. It's part of my job. When I find out a First is coming, I learn as much as I can about them."

"You're not always assigned to Seconds like me?"

"No. Just as often I serve Firsts." He squeezes my hand. "In fact, I wasn't even supposed to be assigned to you. A younger boy named Tomas was, but he's still in training, so they had me do it instead."

Taking a deep breath, I pull my hand from Will's. *I can't do this. Not right now. Not ever. I can't take comfort in him, not after this.* "I think I'm going to go to bed now."

He nods, and I try to smile to convince him that I'm going to be okay, even though all I want to do is fall apart. Or maybe I'm already broken in a million little shards of glass, and nothing can ever bring me back together again.

"Are you going to be all right?" he asks as I walk with him to the door.

No. How could I be? "Yeah, I'm fine. I just need some sleep."

"I'm sorry."

I shake my head. "It's not your fault."

He turns back and wraps me in a hug that is both tender and fierce. I freeze. A strange, hard heat gathers inside me, and I start to feel myself relax. *I can't do this right now.* I push myself away from him. He looks hurt, but I can't feel sorry for him. I just found out I'm going to die, and he knew it, they all knew it, but no one had the decency to tell me.

"Good night, Will."

"Good night." His com unit beeps, and he looks down at it. His face pales even further. "I've been instructed to remind you that the Acceptance Banquet is tomorrow."

"The Acceptance Banquet?" What is he talking about? The Acceptance Banquet? Realization dawns. Oh yeah... "That's what Mr. Flannigan—" A sharp pain pierces my heart. "—was supposed to prepare me for."

Will settles me loosely in his arms. "Don't worry about it. It's just some dinner to introduce you to the rest of the Firsts and other dignitaries. It's not a big deal."

"So they can recognize me after the Release, is that it?" His lips set in a firm line. "I can't just lock myself in my room, right?" I look up into his eyes, drawn into their deep, chocolaty depths.

He shakes his head, a rueful smile on his face. "No, I'm afraid not. But look, seriously, it's not a big deal. All you have to do is sit there, eat, and watch Socrates talk."

I lean in closer to him, drawn by his warmth, his solid chest, his firm arms cradling me. All the horrors of the night seem to slip away like water between my fingers. "After tonight, it couldn't get much worse."

"No," his voice is a low rumble. "In fact, you're expected to do absolutely nothing."

I rear back. "That's because the next time they see me, I'll be dead."

"Mira!" He looks stricken. "That's not what I meant."

I pull away from him and rub my arms in the sudden chill. "It's the truth." I turn away from him, letting my words fill the space between us.

He takes me in his arms once more. "I didn't mean it like that. I—"

"Save it, Will, alright?" His eyes widen, but I continue, so he gets my meaning. "Look, I don't blame you. It's not your fault. It just... stinks, that's all. That's a huge understatement. They have the right to take me from my home, parade me around, and then kill me. That's insane. Maybe Tanner had the right of it, after all." Tears burn my eyes at the unfairness, the wrongness of it. "I'm going to die, Will, and they're having a party."

He closes his eyes and pulls me closer so my head rests against his chest. His heart thumps next to my ear. It feels good here, in his arms, like he understands. He holds me until I grow so comfortable I can't remember where he ends and I begin. Eventually, though, he slowly pulls away, as if he regrets putting space between us.

"I really need to go, Mira. But if you need me..."

"I'll just push the button and ask." I smile waveringly.

His lips quirk at the corners. As he is about to close the door behind him, I put my hand on his arm. The muscles flex beneath my grip.

"Will?"

"Yes?"

"Thanks." Will looks confused, as if he can't figure out why I'm thanking him. "For being here with me. I know it probably wasn't what you wanted, but I really appreciate it."

Will nods, a ghost of a smile skating across his face. "I only hope that it was worth it."

"What do you mean?"

"That finding out the truth was worth the cost," he murmurs, squeezing my hands in his.

My teeth worry my bottom lip. Stupid habit. "It was." At least now I know. And even if I feel like a piece of me has been stripped away, it's for the better, right? *Even after I found out my cousin's dead, and Socrates took his own son's body, and my whole life has been a lie, and I was chosen to die so Socrates could live another lifetime.*

"And to be honest, there's no place I'd rather have been." He turns away, and the darkness of the unlit hall swallows him.

I step back into my room and shut the door, turn off all the lights, lie down on my bed, and curl up in a little ball. A sharp pain pierces my brain behind my eyes, and I rub my temples. I stop. Is that what Adrian felt as they stabbed the needles into his head?

Mr. Flannigan's face flashes behind my eyelids. Was he trying to tell me something? Was he in on Tanner's plan to get me out of there? I should have gone with him. I should have escaped. All he wanted was to save me, and

I wouldn't listen. *You're such an idiot, Mira.* Vomit rises in my throat once more, and I rush to the bathroom again to heave into the toilet.

"LET IT GO."

socrates

"**H**E DID WHAT!" ELLIE MERELY raises her eyebrows at my outburst and sips her coffee. "I can't believe he stole my bracelet and showed her the video. The nerve of that boy!" I shake my head, rage clouding my vision. "How dare he?"

"Calm down, Soc." Ellie's voice is soothing, but it won't work. Not this time.

"That boy has gone too far." I grimace. "I specifically told him not to show the girl her cousin's Release. He did it anyway. Directly went against my orders and showed her anyway."

"Well, at least you can tell he cares for the girl." She crosses her legs at the ankle and watches me fume.

I snort. "Only a little, right?" I think for a moment. "I should report him. Have him arrested."

She leans forward. "Think about it. The boy did what he thought was best for Mira, even going against your command to do so."

"But that doesn't erase the fact he stole from me. That is grounds enough for his immediate arrest and punishment."

"Did he hurt her?"

I narrow my eyes. "No, not specifically, though I'm sure the video was mentally debilitating and painful."

"But he thought he did it for her good. What better protector could you have than one who is willing to defy the rules and do whatever he thinks is right to protect his charge?"

She's right, dammit. My shoulders droop. I hate it when she takes all the wind out of my sails. "I see your point. I still think I should talk to him, though." I plant my hands on the edge of the bed and push myself, wobbling, to my feet.

"Why?" She makes no move to help me, though I think if she thought I was even remotely in danger of falling, she'd be by my side in a flash.

"Because he disobeyed me! Woman, listen to me. I don't want to repeat myself again. The boy stole a piece of property that belonged to me, then acted against my wishes. He could be banished or killed for his transgressions."

"You think he doesn't know this?" She sets her coffee cup on the table next to her, stands up, and stretches. She walks over to my small window and looks out. "He was willing to risk your censure to tell her something he thought she should know. How do you think he'd react if you called him on the carpet for this?"

I sigh. "Defiantly, angrily." I chuckle and limp over to her side. Ben remains in his position on the bed, watching us. When I glance at him, his tail thumps, but he doesn't move. Thanks for your help, dog. "What do you suggest I do, oh wise one?"

She briefly smiles at me before turning back to the window. "Let it go."

I scratch my chin through my beard. "Why on earth would I do that?"

"Because sometimes it's better to pick your battles. You've got a huge battle coming up, Soc, and one lowly servant boy who stole your I.D. bracelet hardly factors in."

I let out a deep breath and close my eyes, trying to envision what would happen if I did turn the boy in. "I hate it when you're right."

She smiles humorlessly. "But I wouldn't forget what he did, either. He's loyal to Mira to a fault, and your enemies might use that."

PART OF MY CHARM

mira

"tONIGHT WILL BE THE MOST extravagant night of your life," Mr. Reynard says with a flourish as he puts the finishing touches on my wig. *That's not saying much,* hangs from my lips, but I pull the words back in time. *This is stupid,* I almost say again, as I refuse to let him inject me with that makeup stuff, but he seems to have expected that and dramatically rolls his eyes at me.

I glance down at the deep blue strapless dress Mr. Reynard has dressed me in. The fabric clings to my body, and the long skirt falls to the floor and pools around my feet. It's beautiful, but I want to rip it off. Tear it to shreds, throw it at him, and yell. Scream. Tell him my cousin's dead, Mr. Flannigan's dead, and I will be too. Does he know this? Are Texans the only ones kept in the dark? Or maybe it doesn't matter because his kids, if he has any, can't be picked. His kids get to grow up because he's not a Texan.

As an afterthought, he hands me a pair of matching gloves that go up to my elbows. "To hide that hideous tattoo." He wiggles his fingers at my wrist.

"It's not like I had a choice." I look at his arm. It's smooth and bare. Of course it is. Why would he have a mark like mine, like Will's, like even the guards?

He puts his hands behind his back. "Of course you didn't, it's just... unattractive. Most Firsts have them removed after the procedure. However, from what I understand, Socrates has always been... different." He hands me a pair of ridiculously pointy silver heels. "Hurry up. Put these on."

"Are you serious? I've never worn heels in my life."

He rolls his eyes at me. "Just try not to fall over and ruin your wig."

I stick my tongue out at him, but he's already folding the empty garment bag. Sighing, I slip on the shoes and stand up, tottering back and forth. My ankles burn already. *Yeah, this'll be fun.*

Someone knocks on the door, and Mr. Reynard calls, "Come in," as he gives one final fluff to the top of my head.

When Will opens the door, his eyes widen as he looks me up and down. "My lady." His eyes fill with surprise. Is he buying into this? I thought he was better than that. "Are you ready to go?"

I stand up and let out a shaky breath. "As ready as I'll ever be, I guess."

Reynard reaches out and moves a strand of someone else's hair back off of my shoulder. "Yes, she's ready. Well, as ready as she'll ever be, I'm afraid." He examines me a final time. "Try to keep your wig on straight, please?"

I roll my eyes at him, and Will snickers. "I'm not that—"

"Let's go." Will holds out his arm for me. I slip mine into it, feeling his muscles bunch and flex under my touch. Delightful shivers find their way into the pit of my stomach.

Will squeezes my hand with his free one and leads me out the door. "You look amazing." I glance down at my dress, the shoes, eye the wisps of hair framing my face, and open my mouth to object. "But I favor you without the rug."

I blush and look away, fighting a grin. Me, too. *What*

210

would Mr. Reynard say if I ripped it off? Changed back into my own clothes and went like that? When the elevator doors open, we turn left and walk through the main lobby. After passing several darkened exhibits, we veer into another short hallway with plush, ornately-patterned carpet. Bright lights illuminate everything, from the landscapes and portraits on the walls to the heavy dark wooden doors where we stop. I hear muffled music inside, and the urge to throw up, run away, or both, fills me. I put my hand to my stomach, as if pressing there will help calm me down. *I can't do this.* Will turns me toward him and squeezes my shoulders, as if sensing my nerves.

"I have to leave you here," Will says. "I'm sorry, but I'm not allowed in there."

Panic fills me. *No, he can't do that!* I shake my head. "Please, I... I can't do this alone."

He pulls me into a fierce hug. "You won't have to," he whispers into my hair. "There will be a seat next to Socrates at the head table for you." He nods to the right as he reaches for the door handles. "Just..." He pauses, searching for the right words. "Be careful."

I'm about to ask him why when he lets go of my hands after giving me a final squeeze, then grabs the polished brass door handles and pulls the doors open. *You can do this, Mira. Remember, your cousin did it. If he could, so can you.*

Enormous multi-tiered glowing glass chandeliers hang throughout the banquet hall. Round tables covered in lily-white tablecloths and napkins are spaced throughout, and for several heartbeats, I stand frozen, hands clenched in front of me, palms growing sweaty. People wearing expensive dresses and suits sit around the tables, chatting like old friends. I've never seen so many different outfits before, so much richness, luxury. It overwhelms me. *I can't do this.* I turn around, terror gripping me, but Will is already shutting the door, cutting me off. I'm trapped.

My legs wobble, and I look around wildly. My wig slips, and I reach up to adjust it.

I spot someone standing up at the long table at the opposite end of the room. Socrates waves at me, and I gratefully hurry over to him.

As I pass, people murmur to each other, but the general hum in the room along with the music makes it so I can't hear them. The way they glance at me then look quickly away means I probably don't want to know what they're saying anyway.

I finally reach Socrates's table, and he smiles wryly. "Welcome to your first official festivity. You've made it farther than most Americans ever dream into the upper echelon of our society."

I have no idea what to say, so I just mumble, "Thank you, I think."

He gestures to the seat next to him, and I collapse into the uncomfortable wooden chair. A few moments later, white-dressed waiters, all young with dark hair and dark eyes, bring out trays and little tables and start to serve the meal. Even though the food smells great—some kind of soup with beef and mushrooms—I'm too nervous to do more than sip it.

"She is lovely," an older man with a thin mustache says, leering at me while nudging Socrates with an elbow. The gold etched nameplate in front of his seat says he's Ferdinand Caringer.

I open my mouth to say that I do, in fact, have a name when Socrates pinches my arm. Apparently, it's like the farm, and I just need to shut up and act like part of the scenery. So much for Absolution equaling freedom.

"Yes, she's perfect," Socrates murmurs.

My cheeks grow warm as another stranger turns to assess me through narrowed eyes. "A girl this time, eh?" The man cocks his pale blond eyebrows suggestively. "I heard she's a troublemaker. Is that right, old man?"

"Yes, but trouble is far preferable to boring." Socrates smiles benignly.

Hello? I'm still here. I shoot Socrates a look, but he shakes his head. *Fine.*

After dinner and a chocolaty desert, the room quiets once more. Because I was so focused on getting to Socrates, I didn't notice a small stage surrounded by deep burgundy curtains in the front of the room. On it stands a polished wooden podium.

A short, balding man climbs up onto the stage, reaches the podium, and clears his throat. His voice grows immediately louder, as if there are some sort of invisible speakers.

"Good evening, distinguished and celebratory guests. I am Mr. Atkins, and I'll be your speaker for tonight. This is the eve of a new era when one of our most venerable personages, Socrates, accepts a new Second. Throughout his many lifetimes..." An image of my cousin's lifeless body waking up as Thoreau comes to my mind. "... Socrates has spearheaded some of the greatest peacekeeping efforts throughout history. Never one to shirk from adversity, he is set to speak before Congress regarding the controversial Free America Act." *What is he talking about? None of this makes sense. Maybe I should have paid more attention in school.* "Please give a warm welcome to the first of the Firsts, Socrates."

Mr. Atkins steps back, gesturing with his hands, and Socrates stands up, squeezing my shoulder reassuringly, before adjusting his tie so it's straight before taking a step leaning on his old twisted cane. That's when I notice Ben's not at his side. The dog's absence feels wrong, like he should be as permanent a fixture as Socrates's cane. *Huh, must have left him in his room.* I suppose this isn't the most dog-friendly place. Although Socrates sways as if he's having a hard time staying upright, no one steps forward to help him. *What if he falls?* Then, just as the

213

thought crosses my mind, it happens. Socrates stumbles. I look around, but no one makes a move toward him. *Fine, if no one else is going to help him, I will.* I take a deep breath and stand up, quickly walking over to him and taking his free elbow in my hand.

"You shouldn't be up here, girl, but thank you," he says, gruffly.

"Why?" I whisper, cautious of all the eyes on me, many of them glaring.

"Seconds are like little children, better to be seen and—"

"Not heard, I get that. Well, I'm not going to let you fall. So either you take my help or you take my help. Anyone who doesn't like it will just have to deal with it." Socrates shakes his head. A faint smile plays at the corners of his lips.

When we reach the stage, one of the servants standing at the edge of the steps puts out his hand to stop me. Socrates leans forward and whispers something to him. They both glance at me.

What? I drop my hand from Socrates's elbow. A couple of men from the front look as if they're going to stand up and come toward us. Socrates shakes his head so minutely that I barely catch it, and they settle back in their chairs. He smiles the briefest of smiles and nods at the servant, who steps back and glares at me.

As Socrates lifts his foot to take the first step, I feel all of those eyes on me, so I falter and freeze. *Come on. I can do this. I have to. I can't just stop now. Everyone's already staring at me. How much worse can it get?* I take a deep breath of air thick with tension and animosity. Socrates waits for me, one step up, watching me from the corner of his eye, as if he's waiting for me to make a decision. When I finally step up to stand next to him, he takes my hand and squeezes it, allowing a little smile to twitch the corners of his lips. We both climb the rest of the stairs and walk across the small stage to stand at the podium.

"Good evening, and thank you, all of you, for joining me for my seventh Acceptance Banquet. I am, of course, Socrates, and this is my Second, Mira." He scans the crowd. "Every time I choose a new Second, I wonder, will this one be different from the rest? Or will he or she blend in, mere pale facets in my long-lived existence where eventually the only recollection I have of his or her individuality is in the hall of portraits in my house? Well, from the moment I met Mira, who arrived late for her own choosing, I knew she was different."

I shift uncomfortably in my heels, drawing a sharp glance from Socrates.

"You see, she didn't want to go. She had a life and was merely biding her time until phasing out of the program in a few months. She never believed that she'd be chosen. She never thought both she and her family would be given such a great honor as this. In her mind, her future was set at the farm—leaving the program, getting married, and raising children of her own who would one day train to be Seconds themselves. Even though her cousin, Adrian, was chosen a couple of years ago, she never thought she would have the honor.

"But in an instant, her life changed. She was no longer a servant at Chesaning Farms. She was Absolved, with all the freedoms, responsibilities, and long hours of lessons that entailed. She has lived at Chesaning Farms her entire life, but suddenly, she was an outsider." He isn't smiling anymore. His words take a more ominous tone. Maybe I'm the only one who notices. I shift from my left to right foot, nerves and never having worn heels before to blame.

"Just before she was to leave, Live Once rebels infiltrated her farm with the goal of preventing her from being my Second by any means necessary."

What is he playing at here? I told him the truth! I told him that it was all a lie.

"Luckily, our nation's best were there to protect her,

and with her own strength and resourcefulness, she made it through that situation, unharmed." Unharmed? That's a joke.

I can almost hear a collective sigh of relief in the audience, as if they, too, have lived through seeing the barrel of a gun inches from their faces and being prodded in their backs by armored "rescuers." Maybe they have, but I doubt it. But they seem so happy here, so eager to watch me die. I hate them.

"Throughout all of my lifetimes, my various physical personas, and my numerous roles and purposes, I've had the privilege of choosing several outstanding Seconds, not the least of whom was my own son, but few of them have made such an impact on my own life as Mira." He smiles at me again, and when I look at the crowd, I see other people grinning, too. I try to join them, but feel more like throwing up.

Socrates puts his arm around my shoulders, leaning into me. He smells like medicine—like the kind we put on the aching joints of the horses after way too long spent in the fields—and smoke. "Those who have taken Seconds know that after a while, the various faces and experiences kind of blend together until the only one you really remember is the first."

Many members of the audience nod. Are they all Firsts? Is that possible? Will said this stupid banquet was to introduce me to the Firsts and other dignitaries. Just how many Firsts are there? Could they all be here?

"But I can assure you that no matter how many more lifetimes any of us live, no one will forget Mira." He looks down at me again, then back at the crowd. "I've always considered the Release Ceremony to be a rather private matter, with no audience present. However, I am inviting all of you, either in presence or video cast, to be there with me during this unique experience. Because, my friends, I can assure you, this one will be different. I now present to you my seventh Second, Mira of Chesaning Farms."

Socrates steps back as thunderous applause erupts, and I follow him off the stage and into groups of people who clap him on the shoulder, shake his hand, and murmur things I can't hear. Only I seem to see the fatigue in his eyes and the weariness that causes his steps to slow. I tighten my grip on his arm, but maybe we're both helping each other right now, holding each other upright. Somehow, I make it back to my seat without falling apart.

A servant walks by with a tray filled with glasses of red wine. He's a mere boy, not much older than Max, pale with long dark locks of hair parted at the side of his head.

One of my neighbors, an older gentleman with a mustache that would hold a coat up on each end cocks a finger at the servant. As the boy turns sharply, he trips over my neighbor's shoe, and the tray goes flying. One of the glasses lands in my lap, coating my beautiful dress with dark red stains that look just like blood. I immediately dab at the mess with my napkin.

The man next to me starts yelling at the poor boy. "Idiotic, stupid, lazy, clumsy fool! You're the worst servant I've ever had. I'll have your head for this. You should be put on the farms, made to work like the rest of the scum. I'm going to talk to your supervisor."

The boy cowers, head bowed. He shakes and hunches his shoulders, trying to be invisible. The man raises his fist, as if about to hit him.

I jump between them just as the man's hand starts to go down. "No, don't! It was an accident. Leave him alone." I turn my face, but the blow doesn't come. Instead, the man grabs my arm and tries to move me aside. I put my hand on his arm and stand my ground.

"What the hell are you doing, girl?" He looks at my hand as if it's diseased.

I suddenly realize everyone around us is silent. I feel myself flush as red as the wine on my dress. *Great. Just great. Good job, Mira.*

The boy quickly looks at me, the fleeting, darting look rabbits get when a hawk notices them.

I try to smile at him. He slides further behind me to escape the man's wrath. "It's okay, it was an accident."

The old man, his face an enraged deep red, snarls, "Get your hand off me." I pull my hand back, as if his arm were white hot. "Just because you are Absolved doesn't mean we're equals. You're still a rebel whore all prettied up in a frilly dress."

Out of the corner of my eye, I see the boy reach down, scoop up the tray and spilled wine glasses, and scurry away. I wish I could do the same, but I glance back at the old man, meeting his eyes.

"You think you're one of us now, don't you?" He raises his hand, looks around at all the faces staring at us, and seems to remember that we're in the banquet hall for a feast—sort of in my honor, even. He lowers his hand, scowling. "Stupid girl."

"It was just an accident. Everyone makes mistakes, even you, I'm sure." I grow bolder as I realize he's not going to hit me. His face turns an even deeper shade of red. *Why can't I keep my mouth shut?*

"What the hell gives you the right to talk back to me? I'll have you know, I'm Edridge Marshall, former President of the United States."

This is just great. So much for keeping out of trouble. With my luck I'll end up in another prison like Fullbright. Do they even have jails here in Washington? "It's only wine. I can go change." I glance down at my dress. It's ruined. "I'm sure the boy was just nervous, just like I am."

"You should be. You don't belong here any more than they do." He gestures at a couple of servants at the next table.

"Then, let me go home!" I hiss, my voice barely rising above a whisper.

"If it were up to me, you'd have never left the prison," he snarls.

One of them peeks at us, catches Marshall's glare, and quickly looks away. The way they look down is what does it for me. At this moment, I'm really seeing everything, my society, my country, for the first time. Like they really believe they are better. That they deserve to be here more than we do, and we should be thankful for even the barest crust of bread from their plates to eat. *I'm done.*

I stand up straighter in my ruined dress and stare into Edridge Marshall's eyes. We're the same height, and the deep grooves around his eyes and mouth deepen when he realizes it. "You know what? You're wrong, and I'm sick of being treated like trash. It doesn't matter if a person is born on a farm or in a city, has ancestors from Texas or relatives who've lived in Massachusetts since the Mayflower. We're all the same. We're human beings, and when Socrates gets that bill passed—"

He cuts me off. "I don't care who you are or who you're going to become, you are nothing but filth." His face gets even redder. "You Texans are nothing more than animals, the lot of you, and I was never in favor of letting you all live. You should all have been killed after the war like any beast who outlives its usefulness. If I had my way..." He takes a step closer, and I have to step back, not because of his height, but because of his girth. "... you'd never have been born."

"But I was." Anger simmers below the surface. I can feel everyone's eyes on us, on me, waiting for my reaction. In the back of my mind, I hear Mr. Flannigan's warning not to embarrass Socrates. Then I see his corpse, lifeless, falling to the ground. *This one's for you, Mr. Flannigan.*

Former President Marshall doesn't seem to notice everyone staring. "If you know what's good for you..." He shakes a fist in front of me.

My hands shake. I want to shout, yell at him, curse him out, but if I do that, I'll have proven his point, that I'm merely an animal, just like him. I close my eyes for a few seconds and try to calm my breathing. "I wouldn't be standing here, would I? I'd have run off with Tanner and Henri Lee. You'd have another Second to yell at, another person who's weaker than you to abuse when really, you're only embarrassing yourself. You call me an animal. Try looking in the mirror."

He huffs and puffs out his cheeks, hands shaking in anger.

"I don't care who you are. You have no right to speak to me or anyone else like that. I don't care if we're Texans or... or former Presidents." He opens his mouth to speak, but I don't give him a chance. "You know what? I think I've lost my appetite." With that, I drop my sopping pink napkin on the chair and head for the door. My whole body shakes, and I know that if I stop, I'm going to fall apart. So I just keep going.

Out in the hall, I wander blindly for several minutes, not sure where I want to go. I lean against the wall until my breathing evens, and I can see straight again. Eventually, I end up walking past the cafeteria. The elevator is on the other side, if I remember correctly. Great, now I'll have to walk through there in my ruined dress for everyone to see. I close my eyes. *I can do this. I can do this.*

A hand gently cups my arm, and I jump about three feet in the air. "Mira," Will murmurs, a sympathetic look on his face. *He knows. How does he know?* Was my tantrum broadcast or something? He pulls me into his arms and holds me until my body stops shaking, and I don't feel like bursting into tears. When he pulls away, he smiles, and it's one of the most welcome sights I've ever seen in my life.

"You love making a mess of things, don't you?"

"It's part of my charm."

He chuckles. "Come on. Let's get you something to eat."

A REGULAR SUPERMAN

socrates

"YOU NEED TO KEEP THAT girl in line," Marshall snarls after Mira slams the door to the banquet hall with a resounding "thunk." I decide not to get into an argument with him. He's not the most pleasant bloke, even when he's in a good mood. Were I to speak, I'd tell him I agree with her and that he's shown himself, time and again, to be a pompous ass. As liberating as that would feel, I truly doubt it would help the situation. Without me to help fuel his rage, he gives up and stomps away. *Good riddance.*

"I don't know." Aquinas peers over a steaming mug at me. His hooked, liver-spotted nose nearly curls over the edge. "I think she's something else."

"Of course." I incline my head to him. "That's why I chose her."

"Where'd you find her again?" Nietzsche asks. He studies me carefully, fingertips stroking the tip of his pointy black beard.

"Chesaning."

"Hmm. I'll have to keep that place in mind. I've always appreciated a strong Second."

I raise my eyebrows at him. "You aren't even close to your next one, my friend. You have plenty of time."

He lets out a rueful chuckle. "There is that one in a million chance you'll get that Free America Act passed. Right now it looks like a long shot, at best, but if it starts getting close, I'll have to just go ahead and find one early so I don't miss out."

"Just like Julius?" He shrugs. I've never liked Nietzsche. The personality shines through, no matter what pretty face he wears, and he does like the pretty ones.

"Stupid thing, that act. Why do you want it, anyway? I thought you liked living as much as the rest of us."

"I do. This bill, it's the right thing to do." I set my hands on my lap. They're shaking too much right now to keep them on the table or take a drink.

"Who are you trying to convince, anyway? You enjoy living as much as any of us. In fact, you've killed more than the rest, so who are you to judge where we find our future selves?"

"It should be a choice, the way it was before."

"But the rebels, it was part of their punishment." He eyes me, quizzically, like he is actually curious.

"That war has been over for more than two hundred years. The Texans should have been freed long ago and never subjected to having their children taken and killed so we can continue our immortality. We survived well enough on volunteers before."

"Traitor." He chuckles, trying to cover his anger with humor, but I can hear the venom underneath. "There are so many more of us now. We'd never make it. And to hell with anyone new joining in, that hasn't been done in quite a while."

"About forty years," I muse. "That was Ecclesiastes. After what happened with her, becoming a First suddenly lost its favor." Closing my eyes, I can still see the headlines: "First Goes Berserk: Initiates Genocide." I eye my plate, suddenly losing my appetite.

"Can you blame them? She went insane and incinerated

an entire country. Then, because she was a First, she was immune to the charges. It was a bloody disaster, literally." He cackles at his own joke. I frown. "Only thing they could do is let her live out the rest of her life and die in prison. Hardly a fair punishment for what she did."

"I need more time to do what needs to be done." I look down at my painfully old, wasted body.

"Don't we all?" He smiles. "It'll never pass, you know. No one supports it except you."

"It'll pass. It has to." Passion echoes in my voice, and I feel a renewed sense of purpose.

"And you think anyone is going to listen to you talk about getting rid of the Seconds after you've just taken one? This program is an institution, something even average Americans are proud of since it was discovered here."

"I'm not getting rid of them, just changing the way we get them. Letting the potential Seconds make the choice, not the other way around."

"I don't know, I still think you're crazy." He shakes his head, his tight white curls bobbing. "I heard you gave your girl a choice, too. Who does that anymore? You know it's not really a question. You can't give them that sort of power. What would you have done if she'd said no?"

"I don't know." I'm trying to be cordial because, no matter how I dislike the man, Nietzsche and I are brothers of a sort, after all. "Find another one, I suppose. The doctors have given me time enough for that."

"What if you couldn't? Find another Second, I mean."

I shrug again, as if it doesn't matter, though I feel cold inside. "Then I guess I'd die."

"And that doesn't bother you?" He sounds genuinely curious.

"Of course it does. Look, Nietzsche, I'm sorry to cut this short, but I'm very tired, and Ellie will have my head if I don't rest." I slowly get to my feet. The pain is much worse than it was yesterday. I thought they gave me six months? This doesn't feel like that. It feels like the end.

Ellie, sitting across the table, immediately gets up and comes over to help me. "Ready to go?" I nod. "Good, you look like you're about to keel over."

"Showering me with compliments, eh?" I allow her to lead me into the hallway, and we take the elevator to my room. When we get there, Ben greets me at the door, and I scratch him on the head before making my way over to the bureau. I pull out some plain soft real cotton pajamas and limp over to the bathroom. Out of the corner of my eye, I watch Ellie sit on the bed.

"Still in pain?"

"Always."

"Aren't you taking any pain medication? I know you don't like the patches or the implants, but maybe they would help."

"No. I take pills or nothing, and those aren't working anymore."

"Maybe you should see your doctor."

I shake my head, even though she can't see it. "There's nothing they can do for me. Besides, if they knew the state I was in, they'd have me move up the Release. Mira's not ready yet."

"Why not? You said Will showed her her cousin's Release. She knows what's coming. How much more ready could she be?"

"I know." I pause, shucking my black and white tuxedo. "Maybe I'm just getting sentimental."

"You could always let her go."

"To what? She'd be hated, persecuted, kicked off of her farm, rejected by her family. That's no life for her." I walk out of the bathroom and drop my clothes in a pile next to the bureau. Ellie shakes her head. One hand on Ben's harness, I take the few torturous steps to the bed and sit down, placing my hands on my lap. When I lift my right hand to grab a bottle of painkillers on the night stand, it shakes. Sharp pain rips through my chest, and I gasp.

When I accidentally knock it over, Ellie picks it up, opens the container and hands me a capsule.

"More," I grunt.

She taps out a couple more into my hand. When I gesture for another, she shakes her head before handing me one more. "That's it. You'll overdose, Soc."

"Then Mira would be off the hook." She grimaces and drops another pill into the palm of my hand. I clink them together. Maybe the conversation during the banquet hit me harder than I'd thought.

"What about the Act?"

I incline my head. She has a point. "There is that. Guess I can't check out before it passes."

Eliot hands me a glass of water. "Still think you're going to save the world?"

"I'm a regular superman." I try to smile up at her as I down the pills dry, and lie back on the bed. "Besides, maybe it wouldn't be so bad, especially if it's just like going to sleep and never waking up."

"Is that what you want?"

"Sometimes. Sometimes it's just so hard to keep going." I pause to breathe. The pills take effect. "What about you? What made you choose to make this one your last?"

"I guess I'm just tired, too."

BARELY

mira

tHE NEXT MORNING, I'M AWAKENED by a young boy, probably about twelve, with wild eyes and golden bronze hair. He's brought a tray of food. I rub my eyes and blearily focus on the clock—a quarter after eleven.

"You didn't call for breakfast, ma'am, but we wanted to make sure you had something to eat anyway."

"Oh, thank you." I smile. "Please call me Mira. What's your name?"

"Jacob." He gives me a wide smile revealing a missing front tooth. "This is my first week here at the Smith. I never thought I'd get to see a real live Second."

"It's a pleasure to meet you, Jacob. But if you'll excuse me..." I nod at the tray of food.

"Oh right, sure. My mum made it herself. Said she never thought she'd see one of you people in the cafeteria, either, but she was sure glad you came. She said to tell you thanks and for me not to be too annoying." He grins again, and I can't hold back a smile.

I lift the lid to the tray. Inside is some kind of wrapped sandwich that looks a hundred times better than the slop Will and I were served in the cafeteria. "Well, you can tell your mother that I definitely appreciate the food and that you haven't bothered me one bit."

Jacob bows, the grin still stretching his face, and races out the door.

I eat quickly, then jump in the shower. I've just finished dressing when someone knocks on the door. Figuring it's Will, I fling it open. "Will, I need a minute to—" But it's not Will. "Socrates, sir. What? Why?" I stumble back a couple of steps. "Good morning, sir. Please come in."

Socrates limps in, Ben at his side, and leans his cane in the corner by the door before turning to me.

"I hope I didn't startle you too much, Mira. I just wanted to thank you for your help last night at the banquet. Few people—let alone any Seconds that I can recall—would have stood up to help an old First to the podium. Especially considering who I am."

"Why? You needed help. It was as simple as that."

He shuffles over to the chair by my desk, slowly sits down, and with one hand rubs his temple, as if the very action hurts. "But you know why I chose you. What your purpose is. What really happened to your cousin. Yet you were kind to me. You helped me."

I bite my lip. He's right. I should see him as a monster. Someone evil. "But you're not..." I murmur. He raises his eyebrows, and I realize I said it out loud. "Sorry."

"I'm not what, girl?"

"Nothing." I fiddle with my hands. *Does he really want me to say it?*

"Speak up, girl," he says, not unkindly. *Guess he does.*

"A monster."

A slight smile curves Socrates's lips. "But I am. Ask any one of a million Lifers, people on the farms, or even those in the major cities. People who don't have access to Firsts. They don't know us, and if everyone knew what we did, what we do to stay alive, we'd all be called monsters. Worse even."

"Then why do you do it?"

He shrugs. "The first time? It wasn't intentional, trust

me. It was my wife's idea. She wanted our son's passing to have some use, some purpose. I just wanted to die."

What do I say to that? I look away from him, toward the tiny window opposite the bed. I can't see anything outside, but if I did, would the world look the same as it had when I first came here? Somehow, I don't think so. "Why do you do it now?"

He chuckles, following my own gaze to the window. "To make a difference." He pauses. "At least, that's what it was before. Now..."

"You don't know?" I guess, and his head turns toward me so quickly that he winces.

"You're very perceptive." He takes a deep breath. "Anyway, that's not what I came here to talk about. You helped me yesterday and I... well, Ellie calls me crazy, but I want to help you."

I laugh. "What would you do? Let me go? You can't do that! I'd be banished, killed. My family would be in danger."

"If that wasn't the case, would you want to be released?" He cocks his head at me, as if honestly considering it.

"Yes, no. I mean. No. I... I don't want to die, that's for sure, but if I am your Second, then my brother doesn't have to stand for visits any more. He can't be chosen. And the bill, well, I only know what Mr. Flannigan said." Socrates winces at the mention of his name. "But from what he said, that bill will free my people, and that's more important than my life. I... I don't want to die, I really don't, I'm terrified, but..."

He nods, as if pleased by my response. "That's to be expected. Is there anything else you need?" He cracks a grin. "I do have a little bit of pull. I'm sure I can make it happen."

I chew on my lip again, wringing my hands. Should I ask him? Should I say anything? "Can I go home?"

Socrates raises his eyebrows in surprise. "I thought you wanted to remain my Second."

"I do, honest. It's just, my brother. Tanner. My mom. I never got to say goodbye."

Socrates stays silent for a long moment. Is he thinking the same thing I am? Does he see the faces of the people he's left behind? Like Mr. Flannigan, the courage fading from his eyes just before the bullets slam into his body and he falls slowly to the ground.

"I'm sorry about that."

"Is that possible? I mean, could we go back to the farm?"

"Yes."

"Really?" Hope wells inside me. "I... I thought it was illegal."

He shrugs. "I'm a First, remember? If it means that much to you, I will make it happen."

I nod. "But... won't we get in trouble?"

He chuckles. "Don't worry, Mira. I do have a bit of clout left."

"I've never heard of a Second going back to the farm without being rejected."

"Who cares? We have the time and my schedule, as it is, is open. If it makes you feel better, I'll make the arrangements."

I take a deep breath. *Do I want to see them? What would Max think? Would he be confused even more? Does he miss me? What would Tanner think?* Worry and guilt swell inside me as thoughts of Will take over. But Tanner, he tried to save me. I owe him this much. With my decision made, I give him my answer.

"I have lunch if you're interested." Will sets a plate of food on the desk a couple of hours later. My stomach growls, but I shake my head.

"I don't think I can eat anything. Sorry."

"Nervous?"

"Yeah, kinda. Socrates says it's fine, but still... no

Second has ever gone back home after being chosen. I guess I'm just worried about how my mom will react." My traitorous stomach grows as the smell finally gets to me.

"Who's coming with us?" I ask, turning away from the food as my stomach churns again.

"Just you, Socrates, and myself," Will replies, watching me closely, concerned. "And Ben, of course. Look, are you sure you want to do this? You don't have to if—"

"Yes. My brother, Max, he's only six and..."

"And that boy, right? What was his name again?"

I scowl, tempted to toss a pillow at him. "Tanner, and you leave him out of this."

"I heard you two were supposed to marry." He arches his eyebrows at me, darkness and maybe something else seeming to cloud his vision.

"Are you jealous?" I grin, boldly running my finger from his shoulder to his hand.

Will clenches his fist and takes a step back. "Not in the slightest."

"Good, because Tanner and I... we were just good friends, that's all."

"Just friends?" I open my mouth to speak, but he shakes his head. "Look, it's none of my business." Will spins around on his heel and stalks toward the door. "Then, I'll just leave you to it, and I'll see you when the pod's ready."

I chuckle as the door shuts, almost in a slam, behind him.

A few minutes later, the boy who brought my breakfast, Jacob, comes to my room and says the pod is waiting. Will comes to my room and escorts me to the transport room. Socrates waits there, wearing a blue cotton shirt and black pants. Ben sits patiently at his side, and when he sees me, his tail swishes back and forth on the floor.

As I approach the sleek silver pod Will directs me to, my hands sweat. Will's words echo in my head. Do I really want to do this? Should I? It's never been done before. Should I be the first?

Just as I'm about to change my mind, Socrates flashes me a reckless grin and winks before climbing into the transport first, followed by Ben, and shuts the door. The machine hums on, flashes a bright white light, and then goes dark. After a few seconds, the door pops open with a slight hiss. The pod is empty, and Will gestures for me to get inside. I offer him a shaky smile as I climb over the slight lip, but his face stays blank.

When the door swings open, I'm faced with the interior of the manor's pantry. One of the house servants, Tevan, stands stiffly by the door while Socrates grips his elbow. Socrates's dog sniffs the floor, looking for snacks. Will clears his throat from behind me, and I stumble forward. He grabs my elbow to keep me from pin-wheeling out onto the floor. That would be a wonderful entrance.

Will takes my arm and leads me toward Socrates, who is talking to Mrs. Chesaning on the veranda. As we get closer, I can hear Socrates's voice, low and soothing, while she clenches her hands in front of her.

"No, madam, there is nothing wrong with my Second," he says.

"Are you sure? She's always been... well, we thought she would be..." She looks harried, her normally perfect chestnut hair askew, strands hanging around her face, her eyes, washed out but puffy around the sides. In my mind, I see Mr. Reynard shaking his finger at her and pulling out his little makeup box of horrors. Looks like she's due for a renewal.

He shakes his head. "No, she's perfect. We have some extra time before leaving for my compound, and I felt that it would do her good to see her family. She didn't get to say goodbye before she left."

She squeaks something about the short notice, but is too polite to outright object to our presence.

Socrates puts a hand on her arm. "I understand, and I apologize. I can assure you that we'll be gone quickly. We won't disrupt the workings of your farm, and I sincerely appreciate your kindness and hospitality." His voice is low, soothing, as if he's trying to project calm and relax her. *Good luck. The woman was a mess even when I was growing up. The house staff always complained about how she'd get worked up over the littlest things, like getting the exact shade of purple for her centerpieces correct. As if that really matters.*

She blusters something else, but I don't pay attention, too busy staring at the barn and the apartment building where we live. *Lived. Don't forget, Mira. You don't live there anymore.* People in the fields and the barnyard stop their work to gawk at us. I recognize them, but they look hurriedly away, as if they know me but don't want to.

Will's hand falls from my arm to my hand and squeezes it. I hold on for dear life, needing the comfort. The sinking feeling in my stomach grows glacier-huge. *Will was right. This was a bad idea.* Horrible, even.

Socrates looks over at us, eyebrows raised, then back at the farm. "Let's get on with it, shall we?" He limps into the courtyard, leaning heavily on his cane. Ben walks on his left, there in case his master needs him. Tevan follows close behind. When we get down to the yard, my mother walks out of the barn in a group of other workers and stands stiffly. *Where's Max?* Maybe they don't want him to see me. *The sister who was chosen, but came back.*

We stop about ten feet from my mother. She looks older now, her red hair frayed and frizzed, eyes lined and red. I find it amazing what a difference a few days and a lifetime can make to how I see them.

"Mom." I walk up to her, leaving Will and Socrates behind. Casting her eyes at everyone else, she pulls me into a tight embrace.

"Mira, what have you done?" she whispers into my ear. I pull away from her.

"Nothing! Why would you just automatically guess that I'd screw this up?"

My mother glances back at the barn, and I see Max's little head poking around the side. She looks past me to Will and Socrates. "Do you mind if Mira and I have a word, alone?"

"Of course." Socrates nods, gesturing to Will. The two men turn and walk back to where Mrs. Chesaning still stands.

Mom leads me around the side of the barn to a bit of shade. "You should never have come back. People are going to think you were rejected."

"But I wasn't. Honest. Socrates brought me back so I could say goodbye. I miss you and Max. I love you." Nausea rises up from my stomach when she looks away and pauses before taking a deep breath.

"I love you, too, Mira, but you don't belong here, not anymore." She walks over to an old rusty picnic table and leans onto one of the benches. I follow her, not looking back at Socrates or Will or even Max, who waits in the shadow of the barn, staring after us.

"How can you say that? I was born here. This is my home!" My voice is getting shrill, but I don't care.

"Seconds never come back, even after... everything. They *never* come back. You coming here... it's just not right." Her eyes soften, and a tear tracks down one cheek. "We love you, Mira, your brother and I, we do. We miss you, too, but you have to move on. You're Absolved now. We miss you too. Max asked about you after you left. I explained as best I could what an honor it was to be chosen, but he's too young to understand what a gift it truly is."

"A gift?" I lean away from her. "I'm going to die in less than a week. Did you know that? Doctors are going to strap me down on a table and kill me, just so Socrates can live another lifetime."

Her face blanches just a second before she looks away, wringing her hands. "I didn't... I didn't know. You've got to believe me."

"You had no idea." She won't look at me. "I guess they were right, then. They said you didn't know about it. I didn't think you'd actually allow me to be chosen if you knew."

She closes her eyes and takes a deep breath. When she opens them, she looks even older and more tired. "No. I didn't know. I... well... I suspected they might not be telling us everything."

"But you still let me go? They're going to *kill* me. How is that okay?"

"It's not, but there's... there's nothing we can do about it now."

"I can't believe this. I thought you loved me." My words hit her like a physical blow, and she clenches her fists at her sides.

"How dare you say that? Of course I love you." I shake my head and start to protest, but she holds up a hand. "Is this really the kind of life you'd want? Married to a man you don't love with children who will also have to stand in a line, waiting to be chosen? Is that what you want?" Her face gets all blotchy and red. Tears fill her eyes as she reaches out to touch my arm.

I pull away. I don't want her kind of comfort. "Maybe, maybe not. That doesn't matter. Socrates said I have a choice. He said that if I didn't want to do this, I don't have to, and you know what? He's right."

She angrily shakes her head. "Blood wins, every time. Your father and I were afraid of that."

"What are you talking about?"

"Your knack for arguing, fighting, breaking the rules." She sounds bitter, as though she's had this discussion before. "We thought it came from your mother's side of the family."

I lean back, feeling the blood rush from my head. "But you're my mother. Don't you mean from *your* side of the family?" I've never met my maternal grandparents. They were older when they had my mother and died before I was born.

"No, I mean your birth mother's family."

"Are you telling me you're not my real mother?" My mind reels, but my body is frozen. All little kids dream, or have nightmares, of finding out their parents aren't their real ones, but in reality? Never in a million years.

"I guess it doesn't matter anymore, and if you're so determined to know the truth about everything, then no, I'm not." She spits the words at me as if they're poison. "Haven't you ever noticed that you don't look a thing like your brother or sister?"

"I... well... no... but I'm not... I can't be... Rosie was my sister. Max is my little brother."

"Half-sister. Half-brother. Your mother..."

"I'm not your daughter?" *I can't believe this.* She reaches out to me again, but I step back. "Don't touch me. Tell me the truth."

"I'm sorry. Your mother died shortly after your birth. You'd be dead, too, if I hadn't agreed to take you in, so you have no right to be angry at me."

"What do you mean?" She pauses so long, eyes looking inward, that I think she's not going to say anything, that she'll let me leave without telling me what on earth she's talking about.

"I know you loved your father, and you won't want to hear this, but when he was younger, he was... well... a bit wild." One of my last memories of my father, teaching me to help birth a horse, comes to mind. He was always so careful, always trying to keep me safe. Not a wild bone in his body. "He had an affair with... with... that woman." She winces at the words, as if even now, so many years later, the thought of my father sleeping with another woman still burns her.

235

My mind whirls. *This can't be possible.* "No, he would never do that. He loved you."

She reaches for me again, the pain in her eyes so vivid I let her take my hands, too numb to pull away. "I'm afraid so. We had only been married a year and—"

"What was her name?"

"Moriah." She drops my hands as if they are scalding hot.

"Was she from here?" I feel detached. Everything makes some weird sort of sense. She's always treated me differently than my brother and sister. I thought it was because I killed Rosie. Now I know it's because I'm the bastard child of my father's mistress.

"No. She moved here just before the affair started. I don't know where she lived before, some other farm, I guess."

"What was she like?"

"How can you ask me that? Your father and I were barely married a year before I found out she was pregnant."

It hits me. The law. Adultery has particularly steep consequences. "The Chesanings found out?"

"Of course, and she was banished, as is the law. They were going to send you out with her, but the night before they took her out into the forest she begged me to take you. She knew the wilderness was no place for a child, that you wouldn't stand a chance out there."

"And you... what? Adopted me?"

She shrugs. "I knew it wasn't your fault, and I so wanted a child."

"What happened to Dad?"

"Nothing. She admitted it was her fault and claimed she seduced him." A satisfied look crosses her face, and she nods, as if justified. Is she proud of this? That a woman died?

Disgust rises in my throat. *You were my hero, Dad. How could you? She was pregnant with your kid. You abandoned her.*

As if hearing my thoughts, she continues. "You have to understand. If your father hadn't done what he did, he would have been banished, too, and then you would have died with the two of them."

"Did he love her?" The words escape my mouth before I can stop them.

Shock, then rage quickly turns her face from white to bright red again. "No! How could he? He chose *me*, us, over her. He saw the error in his ways, and we raised you together, as a family."

"What happened to her?"

"Suicide. After she was banished, she found some hemlock and swallowed it. We found out later she had connections to Live Once and was planted here to infiltrate the farm. It's kind of ironic, really, you being chosen as a Second since all she really wanted was to stop that program." She glances over my shoulder. "I know we probably should have told you earlier, but we didn't think you'd ever need to know. You have to understand, despite everything, I've always loved you."

I let out a sarcastic laugh. My mother... well, the woman I thought was my mother, loved me. Right. I mean, maybe in her own way she did, but it's not the same as all the other kids. I could never please her. Now maybe I can guess why.

"No, really. You're the most amazing daughter I could have wished for." She smiles and reaches for me.

I pull away. "That's a lie. I'm a horrible daughter. I killed my own sister!"

She looks away quickly, and something dark and slimy shivers up my spine.

"What, next you'll tell me that was a lie, as well?"

"Mira, stop, please. It happened so long ago. Don't make me talk about this." She's hiding something else. I can feel it.

"Has my whole life been a lie? No wonder you wanted me to leave and never return."

Her hand cracks against my cheek before I can react, and then her finger pokes me in the chest. "You want the truth? Well, here it is. There was a First who was supposed to come the morning after your sister's fifth birthday. His name was Nabokov, and he was looking for a young girl with black hair and green eyes. He liked them as young as possible and was coming to our farm first."

"But what does that have to do with her disappearance? That was my fault. It was so hot that day, and she wanted to go swimming, but I wouldn't go. I wanted to hang out with Tanner instead."

"If I tell you more, will you promise not to tell anyone?" She looks so miserable I feel myself feeling sorry for her, just a little bit because after she lied to me about being my mother all those years, well, it'd take a whole misery to make this right.

"Who would I tell? I'll be dead in a few days anyway." I know I'm being mean, but I can't help myself. She winces again at my harsh words. "Just, please, tell me what happened."

"We... well, your father and I met someone who said he could help. This man—I never learned his name—said that if we could arrange for the two of you to meet him in the woods by the border, his people would get you to a safe place. We'd never see you again or even hear how you were doing, but it'd be better than the alternative." She paces back and forth in front of me, not once meeting my eyes, as if I would judge her and blame her for Rosie's death the way I'd blamed myself all these years.

"And you believed him? He could have been a pedophile, a murderer, someone who sells children."

"You don't understand what it's like to be a mother and to know your children are in danger. You're right. We should have told you." She reaches for me.

I brush her hands away and shake my head to clear my thoughts. "You should have told me a lot of things. Did she make it? Is she safe?" In my mind, I see little Rosie with her long blue-black curls twirling in the wind, her hands full of dandelions. Giggling, laughing, alive.

My mother frowns. "I don't know. You were supposed to go with her, and if he didn't show, you'd both come back." She scrubs at her eyes.

"So since I didn't go, you let her go out there, in the forest, alone?"

Her face hardens. "She wasn't supposed to be alone, remember?" Anger flashes in her eyes.

I shake my head. Suddenly, I feel as if a weight has been lifted, but instead of feeling relieved, I feel tired, exhausted. *No, Mom, you're not going to pin this on me any longer.* "You know, for seven years I've blamed myself for my sister's death. And now I find out the truth, and it's *still* my fault."

"I'm so sorry, Mira. I love you, really I do."

"But if I'd gone with Rosie, she might still be alive, right?"

She shakes her head. "W-we don't know that. She might still be alive anyway. The man—"

"Yeah, because some stranger, whose name you don't even know, might have taken her. Or she could have wandered into the forest and been killed by wild animals. Or the man himself might have..." I shake my head. I can't say it. "It doesn't matter. We'll never know. No wonder you hate me."

"I don't hate you. How can you say that?"

"You lied to me about my mother, lied to me about my sister, let me feel responsible for her death all my life, and you call that love?" I shake my head, and based on the look on her face, it's as if I actually hit her.

She puts her hand to her mouth. "I think it's time for you to leave. You've caused enough damage."

"You know what? I'm glad I'm leaving. I'm glad I won't have to look you in the eyes ever again. See your lies, your hates, everything that you've ever told me that wasn't true. Even getting banished is better than coming home to you." Her face blanches even whiter. "Yes, you heard me right. I'm not doing it." Suddenly, my heart feels lighter than the air around me. I feel free, giddy even, and laugh. "I'm not doing it. As soon as I can, I'm telling Socrates the deal's off. I quit."

I turn around and leave her standing there, shoulders drooping, tears dripping down her face. This time, I don't beg her to let me stay. I don't run up to her, hug her, or tell her I love her. I'm done with that. Socrates and Will wait in the courtyard, talking to Tevan and watching this year's crop of new foals frolic in the small pasture next to the barn. A sorrel filly, Diamond, is one I birthed. Part of the training I'll never need.

When I emerge into the sunshine, all three heads turn. I square my shoulders and walk over to them, hoping they can't read the emotions on my face. *Fat chance of that, I'm sure.*

Max, jittery in the doorway to the barn, runs out into the sunshine and tackles me. "Mira!" He grabs me around my waist so tight I can barely breathe. "I missed you. Mom said I'd never see you again."

I crouch and hug him back, breathing in the little boy sweet sweat scent on the back of his neck. *Oh Max, I'm so sorry.* "I missed you, little man. I came back to see you."

"Why? Mom said you couldn't. Tommy said you were gonna die." He looks up at me, a way-too-mature sense of worry creasing a line between his baby soft eyebrows. "Are you?"

What do I tell him? Yes, I was going to die, but I changed my mind? That I'm going to see if Tanner can get him free? I tilt his chin so he looks me straight in the eyes. "Tommy's an idiot." Max grins in relief. "Of course I'm not going to die." Just saying those words brings relief, and I smile back at him. "I'm going to have to leave for a little while..."

"No!" He squeezes me tightly, and I bury my face in his neck again.

"But I'm coming back, I promise." Socrates can find a new Second. My brother, sister, everything that happened is too big, too important. I can't just bow out now. Tanner was right. I need to fight.

I set Max a little bit away from me and say, "I want to stay. Really I do, but I can't right now." I kiss him softly on the forehead. "But I promise you I'll come back. You're my little brother. I couldn't stay away even if I tried. Besides, if I did, you'd get big and strong and come after me, wouldn't you?"

He nods vigorously. "You bet."

"Now you have to be strong for Mom, all right?"

He nods again, more solemnly this time. "And help Tanner, okay? He'll need your help around the farm."

His chest puffs up with pride.

"You better get out of here, okay? Before your teacher catches you missing school."

He spins around and takes off. I guess in Max's world, everything's all right now. I wish I could say the same for mine.

Just as I head back over to Will and Socrates, I hear Tanner yell, "Mira!" He hurries toward me, sunlight glinting off his rusty-blond hair, sweat stains spotting his brown coverall. His face is bruised, his left eye black and his bottom lip split and crusted over with dried blood. A long cut follows his hairline from the left temple down to his chin. I notice a hitch in his step. There must be worse injuries beneath the surface. He slows as he reaches me.

"Mira..." Tanner pants, holding his side as if the simple act of breathing is agony and pulls me aside, taking me stiffly into his arms. I feel Will's eyes bore into me, and I force myself not to break away from Tanner's embrace. "I missed you so, so much. The whole time I was in prison, I thought of you." He squeezes me tightly. "You believe me now, don't you? You know what I was trying to do before those soldiers came. It was never supposed to end like that."

241

I lightly trace my fingers down the bruises on his face and the slashing cut. He winces, and I jerk my hand back. "I'm sorry. Are you okay?"

He laughs, a harsh, angry sound. "I'll live."

I wince. "The soldiers did this to you?"

"No, I fell down the stairs."

Never having heard this sarcastic edge to him before, I step back, unsure.

He smirks. "They *re-educated* me."

"But they sent you back. They killed Mr. Flannigan. Why are you—?"

"Still here? Circumstantial evidence at best. Personally, I think it's because killing a farmer doesn't have nearly the impact as killing someone well-known in Washington as a teacher for Seconds. I'm nothing compared to him."

"I... I'm sorry." I shiver.

Tanner shakes his head. "Don't worry about me. I'll be fine as long as I don't try to leave the farm."

"Why can't you leave?"

He pulls up his left sleeve and reveals a small silver bracelet, similar to the one Will stole from Socrates, but so tight it looks like it's melted into his skin. A red light blinks on the top. I reach out to touch it. My fingers graze its sleek surface. Although it looks cold, it's the same temperature as his body, and when I try to put my fingers around it, I can't. He flinches, and I can feel a jolt of something pass through his body. "Don't. It's no good. It's fused to my skin."

I look up at him. "What is it?"

"It's the latest fashion accessory for the criminally charged. Well, more like a warning. Be a good little Texan, and no one gets hurt."

"Is it a bomb?"

"No, thank goodness. But I was told it's a perimeter tracker and contains a healthy dose of neurotoxin to boot, so if I try to leave the farm, even one step outside the boundaries, I'm dead." He stares at his portable prison, and the tired loathing in his eyes make me want to take him in my arms, hold him like he held me so many times before. But I don't. I can't.

I fold my arms around myself instead and rub my arms in an attempt to stop shivering. "This is crazy. How can they do this?"

"Who's going to stop them? Call it what you will. They're in charge of enforcing the laws. Trust me. It didn't turn out the way they wanted for them, either."

"What do you mean?"

"They couldn't find any real link to the rebels, or I wouldn't be here." Tanner rubs my arms with his hands, up and down. "It's you I'm worried about. I wish I could help you, but I can't." He gestures at the bracelet. "I'm kinda stuck here."

I try to summon up a smile, to assure him that it's okay. "I'll be all right."

"No." His voice is anguished. "I don't think you will. The guards, they told me saving you didn't matter, that you were dead anyway. I didn't believe them but..." He takes a deep breath. "But I don't know what to believe anymore." An angry, frustrated look crosses Tanner's face, and from the corner of my eye, I see Will take a step forward.

"Tanner, listen to me, please. Socrates is a good person. Well, sort of. He's changed the world, and will do more for our people than I ever will. He will—"

"Stop. I don't want to hear any more bullshit propaganda about how wonderful that man is. I can't take it anymore." He turns away from me, and I put my hand up to stop him.

"Let me finish, all right?" I take a deep breath. "What I was going to say was that I changed my mind." The barest hint of relief flashes through his gaze, but it's quickly masked by suspicion, like he doesn't really believe me. Or maybe he's afraid to. "I couldn't tell you before, but..." The words come out in a rush. "... I decided I'm not going through with it. As soon as we get back to the Smith, I'm going to tell Socrates I want out." The huge grin on his face must mirror my own. "I'm going to live, Tanner."

"Mira, are you serious?" I nod, and a wide grin stretches his face. "I knew you'd come around!" And before I can stop him, he pulls me tight into his arms, and his lips crush mine. His mouth opens, and I can feel his tongue pressing against the seam of my lips. *I can't do this.* "Tanner, stop." I try to say, but I'm speaking into his mouth, and he's not listening. I wedge my hands up so they're against his chest and push. Hard. After a second he backs away, eyes heavy, breathing ragged.

"Mira. I'm sorry. I... I can't... I don't know what came over me."

"It's... okay," I try to smile. "Just don't let it happen again."

Just as quickly as the passion came over him, sadness follows. "It was never me, was it?"

What does a girl say to that? *No, I never loved you?* Or *eww, kissing you is like kissing my brother?* No, both are way too harsh. I try to answer him, but he smiles instead and pecks a kiss on my forehead.

"It's okay. I-I guess I've known for a while now. I thought, well, I thought after we got married it would be different. That you liked me well enough and we could make it work. I love you, Mira. I always have."

"I love you too, Tan. It's just—"

"I get it. Don't worry. You don't have to explain anything."

"No, listen to me. I do love you, but yes, it's like a brother. I know I could have a great life with you, but I can't come back here. After I tell Socrates my decision, well, there's no turning back. I don't know what's going to happen." Sure, I'll be banished, but my real mom was exiled, too, right? She might have survived if she'd not taken her own life. I'm stronger than that. I have to survive. For myself, for Max, for my sister who never should have died in the first place.

"You're right, but that doesn't mean you have to go into hiding. So many people are watching you, what you do, what you say. You could do so much for the world." He fists his left hand and slams it into his right. "And here I am, stuck at the farm. Completely useless." My eyes are glued to that little blinking light. He opens his fist then closes it again, the metal bands loosening and constricting with his movements. "You're better off with him." He nods behind me, and I turn to see Will, walking toward me.

"But I'm not—"

"Mira, are you ready?" Will asks quietly. His eyes never leave Tanner.

I glance at Tanner. His jaw is set and his eyes flinty. "Yeah, I guess so." Will offers me his arm, and I take it. About halfway back to Socrates, I turn my head, trying to get one last glimpse of Tanner, but he's gone. The barnyard is empty, vacant.

"Did you get the goodbye you wanted?" Socrates asks, one hand on his cane, the other buried in Ben's ruff.

Rosie's cross flashes before my eyes. "Would you mind if we stop at one more place?"

"Sure, that's not a problem."

I lead them across the lawn to the edge of the forest, Will constantly scanning from side to side. Maybe he thinks it's dangerous to be so close to the edge. I guess I can see his point, even though I've never felt safer.

When we get to the playground, I let out a deep breath. There is a sea of new little crosses sunk into the ground where the guards' heavy boots trampled them. The dolls and toys have been put back in the right spots, and if I didn't know better, I would never have believed that just days ago this area had been littered with the little matchsticks and overturned teddy bears.

"What is this place?" Socrates asks. His voice is low. Even he recognizes how special this place is.

"It's our playground."

When I don't say any more, he snorts, disgusted at my lack of explanation. "I can see that, but where are the children?"

"They're all around us. Can't you see them?" I gesture with my hands. "They're everywhere."

"Ben, stay." The dog whines, but sits and waits at the edge of the field. Will follows us, which is probably for the best, though a part of me wants him to stay away, as if I'm still not ready to show him this part of me. But maybe I'm wrong. Maybe sharing who I am, who I was, will help the little ghosts sleep.

We wind our way through the tiny memorials, careful not to knock any over. Even Ben seems reverent. He stays where he was told and doesn't sniff at any of them or do what other dogs do. I stop at Rosie's little cross. Someone has put a fresh bouquet of wildflowers at the base, and I finger one of the blooms.

"What happened to them?" He reaches out, fingering the dress on an ancient doll, the cloth no longer blue but a pale gray.

"Accidents, wild animals, disease. Some of them just disappeared." I close my eyes. *I'm sorry, Rosie.*

"Who is this?"

"My sister, Rosie."

Socrates's hand tenses on the head of his cane. "Did she get sick?"

"No. She was one of the ones who disappeared."

"How could that happen? Wasn't anyone supposed to watch her?"

I crush one of the tiny blooms between my fingers. "Yeah, me."

Silence. "My apologies. No one has any idea what happened to her?"

"Oh, I know what happened, all right." I can't keep the bitterness from my voice. I don't care about the promise I made to my mom. I don't care about my decision not to be his Second. None of that matters. Nothing matters except that the truth gets out about a little girl who disappeared into the forest and never returned.

"What?"

"Your precious program is what happened to her. There was a First scheduled to come to our farm. He wanted a young girl who looked like Rosie. I guess he likes to raise them himself before the Release. She was just a baby." *Should I be telling him this? What if he reports us?* What would happen to Max then? A cold knot forms in my throat, and my shoulders tense.

"So your parents sent her out in the forest to die?"

"No. Don't you get it? They sent her out there to *live*. Sure, they didn't know what exactly would happen if that First chose her, but my parents didn't want to take the chance. They didn't want this life for her." I gesture at myself, then at him. "They thought a chance, even one as slim as running and hopefully finding help, would be better than..." I look away while I'm talking, embarrassed, as though I'm betraying him somehow by laying my thoughts, my feelings all out there. *You don't owe him anything,* a little voice snips in my head. *Look at all he's taking away. If anything, he owes you.*

"Did she make it?"

I laugh. "I have no idea. I was supposed to go with her, make sure she got picked up, though I didn't know it at the time."

"I'm so sorry."

I look down at the little cross again, tracing the edge of the wooden arms with my fingers. "Me, too."

"So why did you agree to become my Second?" *Do I tell him now?* Right here in the midst of all these crosses, all these memorials? What would he do, just leave me here? Thinking of facing my mother again, I gulp. No, I can't tell him here. Best to go with the original plan and tell him when we get back to the Smith.

"At first, it was because I was supposed to. Now? I'm doing it for Rosie, for my brother, Max, and for all those kids who won't have to stand in a line ever again as soon as that bill passes. Who won't have to worry about being chosen, leaving their families, and being forced into this *great destiny*. My hope is that I'm the last kid who has to die so that your people can live forever."

"You sound very knowledgeable about the Free America Act. I thought you didn't know much about it?"

"I know enough. Look, does it really matter?" I put my hands on my knees and stand up, feeling old, maybe as old as Socrates.

"No. I don't suppose it does."

I glance at him as the sun hits the horizon. The glowing golden light casts deep shadows across his face. "Are you ready to go?"

"Yes, are you?"

I nod. "Let's get out of here."

Socrates stands up, weaving back and forth, and takes a step. Before his foot can reach the ground, his eyes roll back in his head and he topples to the ground, violently shaking. Ben races over, whining, and yips, pawing at Socrates. I roll him over on his back, feeling for a pulse.

"Socrates? Are you there?"

Footsteps pound toward me as Will leaps forward, pushing me aside, crouches down, and feels for his pulse. "He's alive, barely." He taps a button on his com unit and speaks rapidly. "Code eleven nineteen at Chesaning. I repeat, code eleven nineteen."

"I'M NOT READY."

socrates

IT'S DARK INSIDE ME. OUTSIDE me. All around me. I can't see it because my eyes won't work, but I feel everything. I can't open my eyes for the life of me. It's just too hard, too much. God, Ellie, where are you?

Voices enter the room. A doctor? More than one? I don't recognize any of the voices, and they're talking too low for me to catch more than a couple of words.

"Progressing much faster than we thought..." This voice is deep, masculine, but I can't place it. Not one of my regular doctors.

"Not much time left..." This one is feminine, gentler, younger.

"How could we have missed it?" *Is he a doctor?* He must be, otherwise he wouldn't be in here.

Hey, I'm still here! I hear you!

"Move the transfer up," the male doctor says. The female says something else, but I can't catch it. She speaks too low for me, and her words slip through my mind like smoke. "No, I don't care if he wants it or not. He'll die without it."

No! I'm not ready yet. Ellie? Are you there? Ellie! I need you! I try to gather all my strength, all my will, to merely open my eyes, move a finger, but nothing works, and the barest of efforts exhausts me. I slip away, back into the soothing, relaxing darkness.

"Dad?" A small voice rises from the darkness, and I feel myself chasing after it.

"Adam? Is that you?"

"Dad, what are you doing? You're going to kill her, Dad. Please don't do this!"

"Adam! Oh my God, Son, I haven't heard your voice in so long. I'm so, so sorry."

"Don't do it, Dad."

"Adam? Where are you?"

"Please, Dad, don't do this again."

"Adam? Adam!" His voice fades away, but the other people move closer.

"How are his vital signs?" One of the doctors taps on the panel next to my bed that controls the monitor built into the bed. I've seen enough of the insides of hospitals to know that they monitor all of your vital signs without touching your body.

"Stable, for now, but there's no telling how long that'll last."

"What should we do?"

The two voices pause. "Move up the transfer, like I said. We have to, otherwise he will die."

"What about the Release Ceremony?"

"Skip it. He's too weak. It's unfortunate, but it can't be helped." I sense the two checking me over one final time. "It's a pity," the man says. "He's done so much. To be brought down like this."

"We're not going to let him die," the woman says. "Don't talk like that. We'll move the procedure up, the transfer will go smoothly, and everything will be fine. He just doesn't have the six months he thought he did. That's all."

The other doctor sighs. "You're right. It'll all work out in the end."

A minute later, their steps fade away, and I'm left

alone with my thoughts again, slowly swirling into the blackness that is my mind, searching for my son's voice, when hesitant, lighter footsteps enter the room.

"Socrates?" Mira whispers. "Are you in here?"

Yes, yes, my girl. I'm here, I say, in my head, of course, because nothing else works.

"I... I heard the doctors." Her voice is apologetic, as if she feels guilty for something. "They said you don't have much time left."

Tell me something I don't know.

"This... this changes everything," she murmurs, and I listen as she walks over to the chair on the other side of my bed and sits down. "I... I was going to back out." Her voice is so low, so quiet, I almost miss it. She sniffles, and I imagine tears filling her eyes.

"I was going to ask you if I could back out, change my mind, and go home, even though I'd be banished. I..." Her voice cracks, and a sob breaks through. "I want to live. I don't want to die. I... I even promised my brother that I'd go back for him. That I wouldn't leave him again. I decided when I was at the farm that I wanted to get out, be free, let you find another Second. But... but now there's no time, is there?" She trails off into silence and sits there, thinking. It goes on so long I almost forget her and fall away, deeper into myself.

"But I can't be afraid." Her words are stronger now, more assured, as if she's made a decision. "There's no one else who can do this. No one else who can take my place. I... I have to."

No, you don't! I try to shout, but once again, the words refuse to leave my parched lips. I'm trapped in my own body. *You don't have to do this, girl, you can still go home.*

As if hearing my voice, she continues. "I can't go home. If I'm the only person who can help you get that Act passed to free my brother and all the other Texans, then I'll do it. I'm done being a coward. I'll be your Second."

251

WE'RE ALL SLAVES HERE

mira

NUMB, I WANDER AROUND THE Smith and eventually find myself at the pressure-locked entry to the gardens. Once inside, I make my way to the stream and sit down on the grass, putting my hands behind my head and watching the birds flap across the artificial sky. The early afternoon shadows are deep, and in the grass, little insects flit back and forth, reminding me of home. A bee buzzes near my hand, and I jerk my hand away. I know what I've got to do, but I can't do it. I can't say it. I'm too weak.

"They won't hurt you." Will's deep rumbling voice comes from behind me.

I whirl around, startled. The quickest activity I've done since we returned to the Smith. *Makes my head hurt.*

Will smiles ruefully from where he's leaning against the tall, paper-white skin of a birch tree. "They can't. These bees don't have stingers. They've been engineered to be harmless. I didn't mean to scare you. You've had a pretty rough go of it the last couple days. I bet Socrates will be fine."

"You don't have to coddle me, Will. I'm not a child. I heard what the doctors said. Two weeks, tops. What I don't get is how they couldn't see it. How with all their advanced technology they couldn't figure out his cancer was growing so fast, and now it's in all of his major organs. Even his brain is getting screwed up. He may never wake up."

Will closes his eyes. "I know. I'm just... I'm sorry."

"Stop saying that! Why does everyone keep apologizing to me!" I throw my hands up in disgust. Will puts his arms around me, impulsively, as if he can't help it, and pulls me into a tight embrace. *What am I going to do?*

"Are you okay?" he murmurs into my hair.

I pull back and look up at him. "What do you mean?"

"The farm, what happened, it was pretty rough."

I look away from him. "It's fine." *I'm fine, right? Yeah, right.*

"What happened?"

"Nothing." I try to pull free from his embrace, but he holds onto me.

"Did that guy bother you?"

"Who, Tanner?" I narrow my eyes at him.

Will's eyes grow stormy, and I fight a grin. "Yeah, what did he want?"

Part of me wants to mess with him, play with his emotions, but I can't. For some reason I feel as though I need to protect Tanner, protect what we had. "Nothing. He just wanted to see how I was doing."

"Looked like it was more than that to me," he grumbles. "Did he offer to help you escape?"

"Again?" I laugh. "How? He's at the farm, Will. I'm here."

"You never know. He's a rebel. He has connections."

I try to loosen his grip on me. "Sounds like you know something about that."

As if I were on fire, he drops me and steps away, averting his eyes. "Never mind. You don't know what you're talking about."

I turn away from him, weary of all the lies, the secrets, but also too tired to argue with him. I crouch down at the edge of the stream and pick up a smooth, flat rock and fling it at the water. It skips once, twice, three times before sinking.

"I don't know how to do this." He comes up behind me, so close I can feel the heat of his body. After a few seconds, his arms loop around my waist, and I relax back into him.

"Then don't."

"I have to. If I don't, everything will be for nothing." I take a deep breath, fear warring with a calm understanding that this may be the right decision after all.

"Is that what you really believe?"

"Yes, no." The merest whisper of the words leaves my lips, the opposite of my words when Socrates chose me, a lifetime ago. I step away from Will abruptly, bend over, pick up a whole handful of pebbles, and throw them all in the water, making a big splash. The stream turns cloudy before clearing again. Just like life. I'm a pebble in a fast moving stream, a cloudy ripple, then everything's clear again, as if it never happened. I sit down on the bank.

Will nudges me over and then joins me. The heat from his leg burns through the material of my pants. For a few minutes, we watch a pair of yellow and black butterflies flitting from flower to flower on the opposite bank.

"I've always felt sorry for them," Will says.

"Why?" The smaller of the two insects perches on a flower, while the larger one hovers around it, looking for a place to land.

"They live such short, pointless lives. In a brief time, they grow up, bring beauty to the world, then they disappear forever, and no one even remembers they existed in the first place. It's like their lives don't mean anything at all."

"Kind of like mine?"

"That's not what I meant." He takes my hands in his. "You're nothing like that, Mira."

"I want to live." I look away from him when tears burn my eyes. My hand goes to my mouth, as if to take the words back. "But this, this is the right thing to do. If Socrates can free us, how can I stand in his way?" I blink the tears away.

Will says nothing, just rubs slow circles on the back of my hands.

"I have to do this." When he still says nothing, I glance up at him.

"But," Will murmurs, and I can't move, can't look away from his chocolate-colored eyes filled with concern. Worry etches a slight wrinkle between his brows, and the familiar smile lines around his mouth are nearly invisible. He doesn't say anything else, but it's like that one word covers everything. *There's always a but.*

I need to stand up, to move. I break free from his gaze, and once I'm on my feet, I hug my arms around my waist, holding myself together. "We should head back." I laugh hollowly. "I'm just a wreck. I need to stop unloading everything on you. Stop talking about this. Grow up, and do the right thing for once."

He stands up, takes my arm, and turns me gently, so that I'm facing him. "Mira," he whispers. He bends his head, and his lips hover a breath above mine. His face is so close, not touching, but when I open my eyes, my eyelashes graze his cheek. I shiver, and finally his lips touch mine. Almost immediately, I realize this is nothing like the one-sided kisses I'd shared with Tanner. *Nothing brotherly about Will, that's for sure.* This kiss is desperate, untamed, free and unexpected like the wilderness that surrounds the farm. A fleeting sense of guilt rushes through me, then disappears as Will presses his lips more firmly to mine.

His arms tighten around me, and I lean into him, winding my arms around his neck. I shiver as the kiss deepens. A rumble vibrates up from his chest, and I think I might have answered it with a groan of my own. I can't think, only feel. What would it be like if I had a future? If

Will and I could explore this, feel this? Would we stay in the Smith in a little apartment like the one I lived in at the farm? Would I get to banter with him every evening and wake up curled in his embrace?

No, I can't do this. I push against his chest a little, feeling dizzy, as if I don't remember who I am or how to breathe. Will sighs and rests his forehead against mine, keeping his arms looped around my waist.

"Will, what are we doing? We can't do this. I'm sorry."

"For what?"

"For... this. I... we... shouldn't have..." I just gesture at him.

"You're right. You'd better get in there. We can't do this again. I'm just a servant, and you're... you're not. If someone told, I could be killed."

"That's ridiculous. You're not just some servant."

"You're wrong, Mira. We're all slaves here. Even your Socrates. None of us are free."

FOR YOU ARE WITH ME

socrates

"**I**NTERESTING WEATHER WE'RE HAVING," THE young blond-haired servant says as he wheels the cart into my hospital room. He's got piercing green eyes that remind me of the mountains around my home after the summer rains have brought them back to life. My mind is groggy, full of clouds and thoughts that might have belonged to me, but are so old, I'm not sure anymore. Dancing children in white baptismal gowns grace my dreams along with raven-haired beauties and old men with pencil-thin white mustaches. At least the old men aren't dancing.

"Yes, very," I answer absently, yawn, then narrow my eyes at the boy as his words sink in. My mind, fuzzy, finds it hard to process his words, but I still find it odd. Servants don't usually speak to Firsts.

He places the tray on my bed as it tilts automatically into a sitting position, sensing the presence of the tray. "I heard it's going to be rather cloudy and stormy."

"You don't have to do that. I'm really not that hungry."

"Oh, I insist, sir. My supervisor just ordered a new brand of sweetener, from Scoffield, England, and he wants us to treat our esteemed dignitaries, like yourself, to it."

Scoffield? Now where have I heard that name before?

"I'm sure it will taste lovely," I say.

"Thank you, sir. We take great pride in making sure all of your needs are met." That sounds strange, too. The boy is emphasizing the words, as if they have a greater meaning he wants to impart.

"I appreciate that." I smile as he sets a deep burgundy cloth napkin next to me.

"As I understand it, you have a guest coming shortly. You may want to check your food first, to ensure it's as you wish before he arrives." He nods at the tray.

Hmmm, maybe he's trying to tell me something. "Yes, I think that would be a wise decision." He smiles, bows, and backs out of the room.

When I lift up the top of the tray, a small folded piece of paper sticks to the edge, and I peel it off carefully so it doesn't rip. The paper is thin, translucent, and starts dissolving as soon as I pull it free.

Even though I walk through the valley of the shadow of death, I will fear no evil, for you are with me.

What does this mean? That I'm not alone? God, I hope not. No one should be alone in the end. Maybe that's it. Maybe I need to make sure that, in the end, I'm not alone. In my head I see a little laughing boy in a baptismal gown, waving at his father. *Are you still there, Adam?* There's no answer. *Were you ever there? Was it all in my head?*

So lost am I that I don't even hear Ellie parade into my room as if she owns the place. "Don't you even lock your doors anymore?"

"What the hell, Ellie? Is nothing sacred anymore?" I shove the note under my pillow, feeling it rip and wrinkle beneath my fingertips. "Can't an old, dying man have some privacy?"

She strokes her close-cut beard absently, and I can feel her studying me. "Well, if you just stayed in bed and out of trouble, we wouldn't be here, would we? Why didn't you see your doctor when you started feeling worse?"

"He'd just drug me and try to move up the procedure. I'm too old for treatment, remember?"

"You're a foolish old man, you know that? Besides, they've already moved it up."

"I know. I heard them talking. The funny thing is, I'm still not ready. Mira's not ready. The sands are at the bottom of the hourglass, and I still have a to-do list half-filled."

"You're not making any sense." She shakes her head and sits down next to my bed. "You've done this several times, and Mira... well, what does the girl have to get ready for? She's going to die. A day, a week, a month, a year. Extra time isn't going to help her with that. Is there anything else you're not telling me? You've certainly been acting strange lately."

"Everything is fine, Ellie, as fine as it can be." I lean forward and lift the top off the food as if for the first time. I try to smile, but just a whiff of food brings on a harsh, barking cough that wracks my body. After fumbling in my pocket for a handkerchief, I grab my napkin and cough into it. When I pull it away, the dark red cloth is liberally spotted with dark red blood. I fold it up quickly and try to hide it, but I can't fool Ellie.

She narrows her eyes. "That's it. I'm calling a doctor."

"No," I murmur, then repeat it again louder when she acts as though she doesn't hear me and starts to stand. "Please sit down. I'm dying, and nothing is going to change that. It's painful, yes, but growing old always is. You know that."

She shakes her head at me, an impossible, cranky old man. "True. We all die eventually."

"Some more than once," I quip, then chuckle. She doesn't.

I drift off after she leaves, hearing Mira's voice in my head as I sink back into the darkness.

My hope is that I'm the last kid who has to die so that your people can live forever. What if Mira's right? How

259

terrible it must be, always wondering if you're going to be chosen, hoping you'll be lucky enough to escape it, but wanting more than what you have at the farm. Wanting freedom, but never being able to obtain it, and peace, but that's too elusive as well. I slowly drift off as the thrumming of the machines lulls me into a restless slumber. *Maybe I'm not the only one who can do this. The only one who has the strength to stand up and fight for what he believes. What would the blowhards in Congress think if Mira stood up in front of them and argued for this bill? How would they react to her passion, her desire?*

When I wake up, the girl is curled up in a round metal chair next to me, the bright red cushion bunched up under her head.

She rubs her eyes the way a child would, with both hands fisted and pressed firmly into her flesh. A wave of tenderness sweeps over me, as if she were my own child. She stands up, stretches, and looks at me. "How are you feeling?"

I look away, feeling vulnerable, which is unusual for me. *Get a hold of yourself, old man.* "I've been better. You don't have to stay by my side, you know."

"I know." She doesn't say anything more, though, and Ellie walks in, two coffees in hand. I smile and hug her after she sets the steaming cups on the bedside table.

"Ellie, what a life saver! Did you sneak a file in there to break me out?"

She shakes her head. "Crazy old coot. You stay in bed." She turns to Mira, a curious expression on her face. "Good morning, Mira. I didn't know you were going to be here. Would you like me to order you something to drink?"

Mira yawns. "I'm fine. Just—"

"Keeping the old goat out of trouble?"

She snorts, and I glare at the both of them. Ellie barely hides her own grin.

I pick up my cup and hold it to my lips, letting the steam warm me. "Mira, will you excuse us?"

"Yeah, I'll just... I'll just go back to my room." Looking rather lost, she murmurs goodbye to both of us and leaves.

After she's gone, Ellie shuts and locks the door.

"Would you like me to send for that boy?" Ellie snaps her fingers. "Will, right?"

"No, I'm fine. Ellie, I don't know if I can go through with it."

"I think that ship sailed the day you selected her."

I study my wrinkled hands, knuckles swollen with age and arthritis. How they shake if I even lift them an inch off the tray. How I can barely walk, hardly even open my eyes anymore when I wake up. How nice it might be just to fall asleep. Should I tell her that? Would she smile and nod as if she's known all along? That is, after all, her choice, too. "Did you know some families would rather their children die, disappear in the forest, than have them become Seconds?"

She looks nonplussed. Does she already know? "And this surprises you?"

"Yes." She shakes her head at my blindness. "In the beginning, being chosen as an Absolved was so prestigious. It was a way to make a difference in the world."

"And you're only now realizing that not everyone feels that way?"

I frown, eyes on the bubbles popping around the rim of my cup. "No, I knew that. I suppose I just thought it was a bunch of angry protesters looking for something to argue against. Not kids. Not parents, families, on the farms, sending their kids out to die rather than be a Second."

"Well, do you see their point?"

I take a sip of coffee, only just cool enough not to burn the roof of my mouth. "Yes, but you know I've never been in favor of the government's decision not to teach the Texans the reality of project ReGenesis. To wipe its origins out of history, fuzz it up enough so they don't ask questions." I close my eyes, thinking back to all those volunteers, those

261

people who chose to be in the program. It needs to stop. The truth must come out. "This Act needs to pass. Those people, all of our people, deserve to be free."

"Like it was before the Immigration War?"

"Yes."

"And this justifies taking Mira's life?"

My mouth twists down at the corners. "I'm beginning to think we were wrong. Perhaps these children should never have been made to be Seconds."

She shrugs. "We thought it best at the time. The free citizens wanted their pound of flesh and, well, the success rate is so much better with children than with adults."

"Now who's the heartless one?" I try to smile, to belie the unease her words bring. She's right. We were so far removed from our own mortality that we saw the children as objects, a renewable resource rather than the indescribable treasure that they were and are.

She takes a sip of coffee and sets the cup back down before folding her hands in her lap. "I won't deny my part in this. We were all responsible, in our own way. Maybe it wasn't the right path, but we thought it was at the time."

I shake my head. "How could we be so blind? I sincerely thought that most of the Texans would see this as a privilege, an honor."

"Given that they don't understand what actually happens, most of them do support the program. In all societies, there will always be those who disagree with the status quo: those who fight against whatever the majority believes. Have you ever thought that maybe they're right?"

Adam? Are you there? What would you do, if you were still alive? I feel tired all of a sudden, and lay my head back against the pillow. "The doctors moved the transfer to tomorrow. They're even skipping the Release Ceremony, said it'd be too much for me to give a speech in my condition."

Ellie pauses, the silence full of things unspoken. *What*

are you thinking, Ellie? "I know." She's silent again as she studies me, letting the weight of our words fill the space between us. "Are you thinking of changing your mind?"

Am I? Should I go through with it? Mira's passion, her excitement, her vision of what the world should be like comes to mind. Could she do this? Could she handle doing what needs to be done? "I don't know. Nothing feels right anymore. We live so long, serve as a reminder of the past, to teach and guide the future, yet I have relatives all over the world, and I haven't met a quarter of them. My children might be dead, but their children's children's children aren't. I should know them, watch them grow up, but I couldn't pick them out of a crowd. I could be related to half of the world somewhere down the line, but I'm nobody's grandpa."

"Do you think you're losing too much during the transfer process?" She narrows her eyes at me.

"Perhaps, or maybe I've just reached the limit of the human capacity for memory. Maybe my mind, recycled as it is, just can't hold any more new information without tossing out the old. It's not as though there is any research to prove just how many times the human mind can be downloaded into new bodies. Even five hundred years later, it's still relatively uncharted territory."

"Is there anything I can do to help?"

"No." A coughing fit hits me, and I pull out my handkerchief and hack into it. I fold it up, hands shaking, and shove it in my pocket. Agony wracks my body as it subsides. I don't remember it being this painful ever before. Is this what it feels like to run your fingers alongside of death? Almost crossing over but not quite?

Eliot reaches over and folds my hands in hers. My vision blurs, and the person before me is not a middle-aged man with brown hair, but my lovely Eliot, rolling blue-black curls and sea-foam green eyes that dance in the sunlight, matching the waves on a peaceful ocean shore and wearing nothing but a smile.

"You know what I think it is? I think you see your son, Adam, in Mira, and it scares you. You're not a monster, Socrates. You're a human, no matter how long you've lived."

"I just feel so weak, and it's not just the age, or the cancer, or any of a million things I have wrong with me. It's inside my mind. My soul. I don't know if I have the strength to die."

She frowns, her eyes losing some of their brightness and filling with disappointment. "So you're still going through it with it."

I don't know. Am I? I stare into her eyes for a moment, then nod.

"Then maybe you are the monster that you fear." Her lips are set in a grim line, and even though I know she still loves me, a part of her hates me as well.

"Would that make it easier for you?" I ask.

She closes her eyes, shakes her head, just as an orderly in dark green comes in.

"Sir, we'd like to check your vitals. If you don't mind," he says this last bit to Ellie, who merely shakes her head and walks out the door, every step a statement of her frustration.

After the orderly, Malcom, finishes his inspection, which is as good as can be expected for a critically dying man (I can tell by his false smiles and nods), he leaves and suddenly, clearly, it comes to mind. *I really can't do this.* I'm so wrapped up in who I am, the past I've made, the people I've left behind, that I really can't. Maybe at one point in time, but not anymore. *I really am too old for this.*

My hand quivers as I reach over to the top drawer of my nightstand, pulling out the piece of paper I'd found on my nightstand the first day I arrived at the Smith.

Are you feeling lost? Alone? Unsure of your place in the world? Do you need someone to talk to? Our counselors are available 24 hours a day.

*Just dial 599 on your in room com unit and ask
for Dr. James Scoffield.*

*What if I'm wrong? What if this isn't what I think it
is?* I take a deep breath. *I guess there's only one way to
find out.*

I lean over to the buttons on the monitor next to my
bed. "I need to make a phone call."

"To whom may I direct your call?" A pleasant electronic
voice, similar to the AVAS system, asks me.

"Extension five-nine-nine, please."

"As you wish, sir."

*Am I making the right decision? What if I'm not? Will
Mira be able to do—*

"Good evening. D.C. Crisis Hotline, how may I help
you?" A young woman answers. She's not the person I'm
looking for.

"I'd like to speak to Dr. James Scoffield, please."

A pause. "Certainly, sir. I'll put you right through."

Ellie hugs me when she returns to my room. My arms are
so heavy that I can barely lift them to wrap them around
her. *Will she understand? Will she help the girl do what
needs to be done? Am I doing the right thing?*

"Have you heard the latest?" She sits in the chair beside
my bed.

"In here?" I try for a smile and gesture to my quiet
surroundings, but based on the look on her face, my
levity doesn't work. "It seems the doctors believe that any
sort of outside contact might stress me out, make things
progress quicker." A painful coughing fit emphasizes my
point. "They've cut off all contact with the outside world,
except for you and the girl."

"Well, this one's not about Mira. There was another
rebel attack last night."

265

"On whom?"

"Julius."

I raise my eyebrows. Another of the oldest of us, Julius is a Japanese physicist who named himself after the great emperor after his first procedure. "What happened?"

She purses her lips. "He had picked a young boy, Rico, to be his Second. Lifers bombed the hospital where they were."

"He wasn't at the Smith?"

"No, a private institution in Tokyo sponsored him, so he decided to have the Exchange there."

"Was anyone hurt?"

"The boy was killed, along with two doctors. Julius hadn't arrived yet. It happened right as he was getting into his transport pod."

How terrified the boy must have been, alone with the building coming down around him. "I take it the Lifers claimed the attack as their own?"

"Yes, though not the main group. They're claiming it was one of the fringe arms of the rebellion, those who live on the outskirts and aren't completely controlled by the main organization."

"I didn't think Julius was old enough to start looking for another Second."

"He told Napoleon he wanted to get his done just in case this bill passed."

"Is he going to choose another one?"

She nods. "He's already scheduling more visits, one at the same farm where he chose Rico."

I shake my head. "The boy was probably what, six? Seven? Julius had at least another decade before he'd be forced to take a Second."

"No one is ever *forced* to take a Second."

"I know that, it was a figure of speech. But no one forced the rebels to blow up that hospital, either."

"I guess they figured the price was worth it."

"Maybe we're all just a bunch of serial killers. We've merely got private sponsorship and governmental immunity on our side."

"Then, why are you doing it?" She links her hand with mine and traces her thumb along the pads of my fingers.

"Mira and I talked. She said that this Act was more important than her, than me, and that it needed to pass. It goes along with something she said at the farm about how she doesn't want any other children to have to go through this." I look down at my hands folding in my lap. Wrinkled and thin-skinned, spotted with dark patches and nearly transparent in others. They don't look like hands that can change the world.

"But you don't have to kill her to get it passed. Someone else can do it."

"Do you want to see me die, woman?" She closes her eyes, and I know my words have cut her.

"Of course not. I love you. You know that, but none of us have the right to choose one life over another."

"What if it's one life over hundreds of thousands?"

"Even then, I wouldn't want to be the one to choose. Are they really going to do it tomorrow?"

"Bright and early."

"Then there's nothing more I can say, is there?"

I shake my head. "No, I'm sorry. But thank you, Ellie, for everything you've done for me, everything you've been throughout the years. I don't know what I'd do without you."

She leans down, kisses me softly on the forehead, much like a mother would kiss her child, then walks out, softly closing the door behind her.

A sea of little crosses comes to mind, stark and sadder than anything I've seen in a very long time. A teenage girl kneels before them, tears streaming down her face. I take a deep breath and push the button next to my bed.

"I'd like to place a call to the medical center, please."

"Of course, sir." As I wait for someone to come on,

I reach over the side of the bed and dig my hands into the scruff of Ben's neck. His tail thumps on the floor as I scratch.

"Smithsonian Medical Center. May I ask who is calling?"

"This is Socrates. I'd like to speak to head physician Ronald Adams, please."

"Sure, sir, let me transfer you." The line goes silent for a few seconds.

"Hello, Socrates. This is Dr. Adams. How may I help you? Everything is on schedule for your procedure, and we're very excited to help you make this transition as smoothly and safely as possible."

"I do have one request to make, and I apologize for it being at the last minute."

He pauses. "Of course, sir. What is it?"

"I've grown partial to a particular doctor whom I'd like to have dispense my personal medication. Have you encountered this before?"

"Of course. Many Firsts favor certain physicians. What's his name? I'll let the other doctors know and clear him with security."

"Dr. James Scoffield." Sweat beads at the back of my neck. What if he refuses my request?

"Hmm. I can't say I've heard of him. Are you sure? If he hasn't participated in the procedure, we don't want to risk anything going wrong. Our doctors have a great deal of experience, but we still don't want to take any chances."

"I can assure you that Dr. Scoffield is one of the premier doctors in his field, and I would feel most comfortable having him by my side. If he were unable to attend, for any reason, I'm not positive I'd be able to go through with it."

"Then, it's done, and we'll also have plenty of other medical professionals on duty in case of emergency."

"Great. Thank you, Dr. Adams." *Can he hear the relief in my voice?* I smile, rubbing behind Ben's ears.

"No problem. I'll see you tomorrow morning, then?"

"Of course, thank you again." The screen goes blank, and I lay back on my bed, hands folded in front of me.

Ben hops up and lays his head on my lap. With one hand, I stroke the top of his skull between his eyes. It's his favorite spot. He melts, sinking into the bed. When I get to a certain spot at the base of his neck, his left rear leg kicks sporadically.

"You're such a good boy, Ben." His tail thumps. "The best friend I ever could have asked for. You've always been here for me. Helped me, the only one besides Ellie I can trust. I know—I know that it's going to be hard but..." I stop petting him, and he tilts his head to look up at me. His big black eyes look deep into my soul. As if he knows exactly what I'm going to ask him.

"You'll be—you'll be good for Mira, won't you, boy?" The dog sighs, almost as if in response, and wags his tail again.

"She'll need your help. She'll be all alone, and I won't be here to tell her what to do. She won't have anyone by her side."

I shake my head. God, if only Ellie could hear me now, talking to a dog. I look back at Ben. He's not just a dog. "You'll be her rock, won't you, boy?" My voice cracks and thick, sticky tears cloud my vision. "You'll be the best dog ever for her, won't you? She's going to need you."

Ben crawls up further on the bed so he's right next to me, whines, and licks my hand.

"I'm going to miss you too, boy." My voice cracks. "And I'm so, so sorry you can't come with me. I'm so sorry I have to leave you behind. You've been my best friend since the day you wandered up to the house. Do you remember that day? Half-grown, half-starved, and covered in cactus burrs, you still came right up to me and sat by my feet." I shake my head, a tear breaks free. Ben licks it away. His soft, thick tongue clears the pain. "I need you to be here. Be here for Mira. She'll need you. Everyone needs a good dog by their side, Ben, and you're one of the best. Right, buddy?" Ben lets out a little whine. "Definitely one of the best."

As I'm about to drift away, the monitor beside my bed slides down and beeps.

"Hello?" *Who in the hell would be calling me this late at night?*

"Good evening, Socrates, sir." The voice is modulated, as if mechanically altered. "How's the weather at the Smith?" My mind goes back to the man who brought me the contact information for the rebels. Maybe it's him. That was something the boy said, too, the one who brought my dinner, something about the weather.

"Fine, sunny and not a cloud in the sky," I say.

"Excellent. I heard it was going to rain soon." Is he asking if I still want to go through with this?

"Not for a few weeks. I—I talked to a weatherman." *Is that what they're even called anymore? I'm really fishing here.* "And he said we're all clear, right up through the Release tomorrow." I'm no good at this subterfuge. Do they have scripts for this sort of thing?

"That's what we're hoping. It's about time spring has come."

I close my eyes, and Ellie's face appears, then Adam's, then Mira as she spoke to me while I was unable to wake. "I couldn't agree more."

ALONE IN THE FOREST

mira

RIGHT BEFORE FIVE O'CLOCK IN the morning, a young man dressed like a servant comes to my door.

"Ma'am, I'm sorry to wake you up, but you are requested in the medical center." He looks down while he talks to me, his hands clenched behind his back, shifting from step to step. What is he nervous about? I take in my rumpled sleeping clothes, wild hair, and sleep-sticky eyes. I'm about the least scary person I've ever known.

"It's fine," I pause. "What's your name?"

The young man gulps. "Flynn, ma'am."

"Flynn," I roll the name around on my tongue. "Call me Mira, please."

"Ma'am, I—"

"Oh stop it. I've already been over the name thing with Will. Speaking of which..." I swing my feet over the side of the bed and stand up, yawning. "Where's Will?"

"He's, ahh, busy right now."

I raise my eyebrows. "Really?" Hurt fills me. This is it. This would be the last time I'd get to see him, and he's gone? I sigh. *Guess I don't mean as much to him as he does to me.* "Look, if you'll just give me a few minutes, I'll clean up and meet you outside my room, all right?"

He nods. "That's fine, Mira. I'll be waiting outside."

After I shower and get dressed, Flynn leads me to the Smith medical center. The room is a sterile, blinding white with a metal bed, chair, and cabinet. He picks up a thin white gown and hands it to me.

"This is an examination room. I need to leave you here when the doctors come—" A knock, a short staccato, interrupts his words. "If you'll excuse me." He flashes me a smile as he backs out. "It was a pleasure to meet you."

What an odd guy. "Umm, you, too," I say, but he's already gone.

One of the doctors, a thick, burly older man with long flowing white hair and a mustache that rivals the former president's, scowls at us. "If you're quite finished..."

"Sorry," I grumble, holding the white gown to my chest.

The doctor, whose nametag reads Dr. Bristol, looks me up and down, his eyes finally landing on the gown. "You'll need to disrobe, and change into that."

The other doctor, a youngish man with eyes too close together for comfort and a habit of squinting, looks up from the paper-thin tablet he's holding. His nametag identifies him as Dr. Cambell.

"Hello, Mira," Dr. Cambell says and smiles at me. His eyes crinkle at the corners, and he looks almost kind. As if he wasn't going to prepare me to die.

"We don't have a lot of time." Dr. Bristol taps on his wrist band. "The transfer process starts in less than an hour."

"Fine. At least turn around so I can change, okay?" Dr. Bristol reluctantly turns around while Dr. Cambell does the same, except he fights a smile.

After scanning me with a couple different handheld machines, the doctors declare me in perfect health for dying.

After the health scan, Dr. Cambell shaves my head and marks six spots around my skull for the "entry points." In my mind, I see those wicked, long needles piercing Adrian's skull.

"Will it hurt?" I ask him, my voice small.

He smiles kindly at me. "No, your First told us about your cousin's reaction to the anesthesia, so we reassessed your dosage. You won't feel a thing." I let out a breath I didn't know I was holding. At least there's that. Maybe it will be just like falling asleep. I can only hope so.

"We're done here," Dr. Bristol walks over to the door, grabbing the handle. "We'll just make sure everything is set down in the transfer theatre, and we'll come back to get you." When he pulls the door open, I see Will in the hallway.

He pushes past them and rushes into the room, closing the door behind him. In an instant, I'm in his arms. His lips crush mine, and he holds me as if I'm a life preserver, and he is adrift at sea. Maybe it's the other way around. Maybe he's trying to save *me* from drowning. I have a feeling it's too late.

Eventually, I pull away to take a shaky breath, but neither of us moves. The transfer process presses down on us, suffocating us. Tears sting the backs of my eyes, but I don't let them loose. I can't. I'll fall apart and never be able to pull myself back together. Not in time for what I have to do.

Finally, I step back and sit on the cold metal bed. *I can't do this. I can't be this close to him, feel like I'm a part of him.*

"Mira," Will whispers and sits down next to me. He grabs my hand and holds me, tracing his thumb over my knuckles.

"Do you remember what happened while we were at the farm?"

"What part?" He grimaces.

"The cemetery, right before Socrates collapsed."

"We were there for your sister, right? She died?"

I nod. "All the time I was growing up, I thought it was my fault. I was supposed to watch her, take care of her, but I couldn't be bothered, so she went into the forest alone. I failed her, failed my family, and I was a disgrace."

Will lets go of my hand to reach his arm around, looping it around my shoulders and pulling me closer.

I take a deep breath. "My mom told me they arranged her disappearance to keep her from becoming a Second. The thing is, since the Lifers operate in such secrecy, no one knows if she made it or not. They don't know if someone found her, or if she was killed by a wild animal, or anything. She just... she just disappeared."

"Do you want me to find her for you? I'll do anything you want."

I give him a sad smile. "No. I would love that, but I wouldn't even know where to tell you to start looking."

"Then why are you telling me this now?"

"Because right now, I feel like I'm Rosie, alone in the forest, and in less than an hour, I'm going to disappear. I'll vanish just like her, except that it won't be my body, it'll be my soul. And no one will shed a tear. It'll be as if I never existed in the first place." Will opens his mouth to protest, but I press two fingers against his lips, silencing him.

"Please, let me finish. Socrates is the future. I'm not. I'm just some kid picked for a destiny I never wanted and wasn't ready for. Maybe if it was another First, another time, I would have still said no, would have run away, but this is what's supposed to happen. Trust me." I sound so sure, even to my own ears that I almost begin to believe myself. Almost.

Will's jaw hardens, and he slams his fist on the bed. "I hate this! You shouldn't have to die." His words are like venom, poisonous. "Socrates is a monster. They all are. I can't just... I can't just sit here and watch them murder you."

"I'm sorry, but there's nothing you can do. Except leave."

He shakes his head vehemently. "Not a chance. I'm not going anywhere."

274

I take a deep breath, partly to think about what to say next, and partly to stop my hands from shaking. "Can I ask you something?"

"Anything." His low voice is fervent, passionate. Right now, I think he'd give me the moon and the stars if I asked. *If only that would solve our problems.*

"Will you help Socrates after... after it's done?" I ask him, hesitantly.

His mouth gapes in shock, his eyes widen, and he shakes his head. "What? No! I... I can't. Please don't ask me to do that."

"Please. Just until the bill passes."

"No! You can't expect me to see you, hear you, talk to you, and know that someone else is inside your body. I can't..."

"If this bill doesn't pass, Will, then all this is pointless." I take his hand. "Don't you see? I need to know it's going to be worth it. I... I won't be here to see it, so I need you to help me."

He shakes his head. "Please Mira, ask me anything else."

I pull out the last card I have, desperate. I have to make him see this my way, or it's all pointless. "I love you, Will. I couldn't say it before, but I do. With everything I have. But I need you to do this for me. If you care for me at all, please help Socrates."

He looks stricken. "Mira, I'm just a servant. I'm nobody."

"And I'm just a girl from Chesaning Farm, picked to be the next host to Socrates. As myself, I can't do anything, but as Socrates, I can change the world."

"Is this really what you want?"

"Yes." I smile with relief. He's going to do it. I know it. I let out a deep breath.

He kisses me softly, as if I might break, and I can see the love in his eyes. Then he leaves. I swing my feet onto the bed then lay back, my hands folded on my stomach.

Waiting for the doctors to come and get me, I start to

drift off, my mind going numb. For some reason, I think about Socrates's dog, Ben, waiting for his master to come home every day, nose in the crack of the door, but he never does.

"EVERYTHING'S SET."

socrates

aT SIX O'CLOCK IN THE morning, Ellie knocks on my door and carries in a cup of coffee. "It's all the doctors would let me bring you." She frowns and sets the cup down on the nightstand.

When she turns her back to pull a chair closer, I slip the note I've written her into her pocket. *It's better this way.* Jamming my hands back in my own pockets, I feel the soft, rounded edges of the original Ben's worn metal dog tags. It doesn't make any sense, but sometimes it almost feels like Ben is the same dog I had, all those years ago.

"Are you ready?" she asks, holding up a light-blue robe.

I slip my arms in and shrug it onto my shoulders. "Yes. As ready as I'll ever be."

She gives me a soft kiss on my forehead and helps me into a wheel chair, the same old one I used for the museum exhibit because the AI ones interfere with some of the machines down here, and pushes me toward the door. Ben gets up to follow. "Stay here, boy." My voice cracks. He whines, swipes my hand with his tongue, then sits back down. "Good boy. You're such a good boy." Ellie looks at me oddly, then shakes her head, and we leave the room.

Upon reaching the medical center, we're directed to a

private room where the servant boy from dinner stands next to the doctors, wearing the same surgical clothing as the professionals, looking confident, polished, and ready for this job. As if he's done this before. Is this James Scoffield? The man he's talking to, Dr. Adams, nods in agreement with everything he says.

Ellie stops, gives me a hug, and whispers, "I love you," with tears in her eyes.

"I love you, too." I smile back at her, my own eyes misting.

After she leaves, the doctors check all my vitals and *tsk* at my overall poor health, which is to be expected, I guess.

Right over the little scars from last time. After that, I sit in one of the chairs, in too much pain to get up onto the table.

The doctors finish their assessment, and on their way out, James Scoffield gives my hand a squeeze and whispers, "Everything's set." *Is it? Am I ready? Is Mira?*

NO ONE'S PRISONER

mira

"**S**OCRATES WANTS TO SEE YOU," a young servant girl with freckles dotting her slightly upturned nose says, coming into my room without knocking. I jump. *Thanks for the warning.*

I follow her to another room just like mine. Socrates waits in a chair, a light blue robe billowing over his thin, bent frame. The girl leaves, shutting the door behind her.

"Sit." He pats the bed.

I sit down. I don't look at him. I can't. He stares at me so deeply that I'm uncomfortable and start to fidget. His pale blue eyes glow and look right through me.

"You know," he says, "the hardest part of waking up after a transfer is remembering your name. When I wake up, it's like I'm reborn. It can be very disorienting. I can't speak, I can't move, and I can't focus on anything. My senses slowly come back to me, but it's strange because I'm in a new body, and everything works slightly differently. After I've had a few minutes to catch my bearings, the doctors ask me my name."

"Why would they do that?" A sharp pain stabs me in the chest. Why is he telling me this? It's not as if I'll be alive to see it.

Socrates shrugs. "It's tradition. In the beginning, there

was a high failure rate. Half of the time, if the Second woke up, they were still in their own bodies or both of them could be present, and the procedure would be considered a failure. If the failed Second was lucky, he or she would never wake up at all."

"What happened to them?"

"Things were different back then. Failed subjects were usually taken to labs to be tested and examined to see why the procedure didn't take. If the Second were physically fit enough, the procedure would be attempted again. You see, in the early days, it was all volunteers, so no brilliant minds were lost." His gaze leaves me and turns inward. "I came close to being labeled a failure myself a couple times."

"Why?"

"I forgot my name, believe it or not. It's strange. You wouldn't think you'd forget that. But that first conscious thought is often very confusing. Unfortunately, that's the most important test you have to pass, even though it's not very scientific."

"Then, why do they use it?" I look down at my hands, folded in my lap, then at his, twisted and unnaturally bent with age.

He chuckles. "Partly because that's just the way they've always done it. Tradition. But another part is the audience. The important people watching the procedure aren't going to sit around all day for tests to be done. Asking your name is just a preliminary thing, so they can slap a success label on you and laud it to the presses. The real tests come later, which compare the new First's memories with the actual historical accounts. There's no test that can say with one hundred percent certainty whether an Exchange is a success or a failure, but it'd be nearly impossible for a Second to know the detailed questions they'll ask. So the first thing I say when I wake up is always, 'I am Socrates.'"

"What's it like? Dr. Cambell said it was like going to sleep but..."

"He's right. The drugs are strong and take effect quickly. The reversal drugs work just as quickly." He pauses. "You know, you can still back out if you want to."

"Really? You'd let me go?" Hope, something I can't afford to feel right now, springs up in me. *Why is he asking me this? Does he want me to back out? Does he want me to say no, I won't go through with it?*

"You're no one's prisoner, Mira. If you don't want to do this, I won't force you."

I close my eyes and see my sister, younger than when she disappeared, smiling, waving her little chubby baby arms. I hear my mom say, "It was her only chance, Mira. There was no other way for her to escape." I see my brother, Max, clutching his newly tattooed arm to his chest as he stands for his first visit.

"No," I whisper. "I don't want to change my mind."

"Okay then." He puts his hands on his knees to push himself up, and just as he trembles to his feet, there is another knock.

Two doctors, one of them Dr. Bristol, the other named Dr. Scoffield, walk in. "Everything's ready, sir, if you are." Dr. Scoffield eyes me curiously.

Socrates glances at me. I gulp back the bile in my throat and nod. "We're ready," he says.

With Socrates in a wheelchair, we go with the doctors down a long hallway to a large, round room labeled as the transfer theatre. Adrian's face flashes through my mind. *What was he feeling in these last few minutes? What was he thinking?*

A door bangs shut behind me, and Will rushes over to us, pulling me tightly to him. His eyes are full of agony.

"Mira," he whispers and kisses me, his lips molding to mine perfectly. I think of the people around us. The doctors, Socrates, but Will apparently doesn't care. He doesn't even act as if he sees them.

After a moment, Socrates clears his throat.

Suddenly embarrassed, I jerk away from Will. "I thought you were gone for good."

"Never." He gives me a reckless, carefree grin. "I was an idiot. I didn't think I could handle it, but it's not about me. It's about you." He grabs my hands, and pulls them to his lips in a quick kiss.

"Are you going to be there? While it happens, I mean?"

"Of course! Unless you don't want me there. I asked Socrates's wife, George Eliot, and she arranged it. Said something about how it's never been done before, having a servant in the audience." He flashes me another grin, but this one is sadder, like he's feeling the pain of my death before I even die. Relief swamps me, then I feel guilty. Why? Shouldn't I spare him? Tell him not to come? It's not like he hasn't seen this before, but still. Am I different? I'd like to think so. If I'd known, in the beginning, could I have pushed him away, separated myself from him enough so he didn't get hurt? One look in his eyes and I see what must be reflected in mine, because he gives me another quick, passionate kiss. No. Whatever we feel, whatever we felt, it was meant to be. Just like this. "I'll be there, Mira, I promise. Even if I can't be in the same room, holding your hand, I'll be there."

"Thank you," I whisper into his ear. Socrates coughs again, so I pull away from him, leaving a respectable distance between us.

"I love you, Will."

"I love you too, Mira. I will always love you." Who ever thought *forever* would be so short?

We kiss again, then he walks away down the hall, and just before he turns the corner, he looks back, and I see pain chasing the bravery from his face. He doesn't want to be here, doesn't want to see this. But he's doing it, for me. Then he smiles, and I hold that image in my head as Socrates and I are led into the medical theatre. The same room where my cousin died.

I point at the big machine humming softly in the center of the room. "Is that the machine that does the actual transfer?"

Socrates nods. "Yes, it will upload and store my mind while yours leaves your body. After restarting your heart, the machine will download my mind into your body, and the doctors will administer the drugs necessary to revive me."

There are several orderlies and doctors in the room, moving so efficiently they're a blur of motion. We are directed to our appropriate beds, and a thought strikes me as I push myself up onto the thin mattress. Is someone making a video like they did of my cousin's transfer? Will a future Second have to watch me die like I did Adrian? I put a hand to my head, telling myself to be strong.

"Mira," Socrates calls out, grabbing my attention. "Remember what I told you."

Why? Is that important? Does that really matter? Maybe he just wants me to remember that it's not going to hurt. *Yeah, right.* Like it didn't hurt my cousin? Deep in my chest, I feel a crack in my calm façade. Fear breaks through, and I shake.

"Lie down, please," an orderly with kind brown eyes and curly brown hair says. His nametag reads Martinez. He looks so calm, so normal. *How could you?* I want to ask. How can you do this? How can you work here, knowing that whoever the kid is, he or she is going to die? "It's going to be okay." *Liar!* I want to slap him, punch him, push him away, but I don't. It's almost as if I'm not a part of my body anymore, like they're already disconnected.

I just lie down like the good little lamb that I am, and Martinez secures soft fabric cuffs around my wrists and ankles. "So you don't fall off the bed," he says, even though I don't ask.

He puts a little silver gun with a pink pad to the back of my wrist and pushes the button on top. The instant pain surprises me as a tiny needle finds its way into my vein. He attaches the other end of the needle to the clear tube hanging from the stand next my bed then covers me with a thin white blanket. Just like my cousin. I close my eyes. *This is really happening, isn't it? I'm really going to die?*

I glance over and watch the same thing happen to Socrates, except they don't tie him down. *I guess you don't have to tie down a dead body.* The young blond doctor, Dr. Scoffield, walks in. He scans the room and then walks over to Socrates. They talk quietly, but with the buzz of the electronics, I can't tell what they're saying. A couple other doctors glance at the stranger, but he ignores them.

Martinez taps my arm to get my attention. "Sedatives will be administered through your IV. The first will relax you, and the second will make you just go to sleep, so you won't feel a thing."

"Promise?" My voice comes out shaky, and I sound more like Max when he's scared than Mira, the seventeen-year-old almost-adult. Maybe Max and I aren't that different after all.

He smiles benignly. "Don't you worry. Everything's been calibrated just for you." He flips a switch next to one of the bags, and the colorless liquid moves sluggishly down the tube. When it reaches my hand, I feel coldness seep into my veins.

After Martinez leaves my side, Dr. Cambell comes and attaches little round pads to my head. This is it. "These probes will connect your mind to the computer right next to you," he says, matter-of-factly, though his eyes are pained, as if he doesn't enjoy his job. *Tell you what, Doctor, you and me both.*

Martinez walks over carrying a wicked helmet-like contraption, all shiny steel, and I shiver. It looks so much bigger in person than it did on Adrian's video. Do all Seconds feel like I do? Terrified? Frozen with fear?

By the time they lift my head and gently place the

helmet on it, I'm already feeling woozy. Dr. Cambell reaches toward my head, and I know he's going to insert the first needle. He presses a button, and a lancing, sharp pain shoots hot and fast into my skull. I jump, screaming. My tongue feels thick in my mouth, so there isn't any sound. Then he pushes another button. The next one hurts even more, and I fight the restraints, wrenching my arms back and forth, fighting to get free. *I changed my mind! I can't do this! Please, let me go!* I scream again as he pushes another button, and white hot agony stabs into my skull, but again, no sound comes out. Is this what they meant by making sure I don't feel any pain? Just shutting me up enough so no one can hear my screams?

Martinez wipes at something hot dripping from one of the wounds in my head. "Hold still, or you'll break off the needle, and they'll have to do it over again."

I freeze in panic. Would they do that? Stab me with more needles, right on top of the old? One look in Martinez's eyes, and I know it's true. Not because he'd want to, but because he'd have to. Maybe he doesn't have a choice, either.

Another button. Four down, two to go. Dr. Cambell continues, as if it doesn't matter that each needle is poker-hot agony. Tears pool in my eyes. When he finally finishes, Dr. Adams fiddles around with the computers for a few minutes before the one who put the helmet on me comes back and stands next to the rack with the clear bags on it. He puts his fingers on a little valve.

"Ready?" he calls.

I don't say anything, but he isn't really asking me anyway. I squeeze my eyes shut as tight as I can and ball my fists, trying not to panic. Somewhere off to the side, Socrates says, "Yes," and I feel a cool numbness fill my body.

I can't do this. I want to live a long life or even go home and spend one more day sitting by the stream. I want to watch Max play in the mud or catch fireflies in old jars.

I want to scream, cry, and shout. I want to laugh, kiss whomever I choose, and marry the man of my dreams. I fight the straps, wrenching my arms. I widen my eyes, shaking my head as best I can, searching for someone to help me.

Dr. Scoffield meets my terrified gaze and nods, smiling slightly. What does that mean? That he's acknowledging my existence? That he knows I'm afraid? Terrified? Is it some sort of message?

Martinez walks over and hands Dr. Scoffield a syringe. "This will ease his transfer into the main computer. As soon as we give the signal, slowly inject this into his I.V."

The doctor nods again, but when the orderly turns away, he slips his hands in the pockets of his scrubs. When he pulls them out again, there's a syringe in his hand, but it's different, smaller. *What's going on? What did he do?*

I open my mouth to ask, but no sound comes out. My eyelids quickly grow heavy, and my tongue is a dead weight in my mouth.

Okay, so I'll close my eyes for a second. Just rest them a minute. *That's it, then I'll find a way to fight the drugs, break free. Do whatever I can. Whatever I... can? What am I doing here? I shouldn't be fighting this. I'm doing this for Max. For Rosie.*

I feel myself drift and try to open my eyes, but I can't. It's that darkness, the heavy blackness I can't do anything about, that scares me more than anything else that's happened so far. Even those awful needles, at least I knew those were coming. But this blackness? It's absolute, and I don't think I'll ever be able to escape. I try to move my arms, my feet, my head, even a finger. I can't. Everything is just dead weight.

I feel as if my body is shaking, but I know I can't be moving at all. I'd know it if my body was moving, right? Yes, I'd have to feel it. But I can't really feel anything anymore.

So cold now. Tired. Is this what death feels like?

REST NOW

socrates

"**d**AD? ARE YOU THERE?"

"*Adam?*"

"*I'm here, Dad.*" Warmth fills me.

"*Adam! I can't believe it.*"

He chuckles, a familiar, aching rumble in the back of my head. "*I'm not going to leave you.*"

"*Thank you. I... I don't want to be alone.*"

"*You're not.*" He pauses. Did I lose him again? Panic sets in.

"*Adam?*"

"*I'm still here, Dad.*"

Relief. Thank you, God. "*Am I?*"

"*It's time for you to rest, Dad. You've helped enough.*"

"*But I haven't. I haven't really done anything worthwhile.*"

I feel a rush of warmth, like he's hugging me. "*You had me, right?*" he says, impishly.

I can feel the humor in his voice. "*You're right. You were the best thing that ever happened to me, but I was a terrible father.*"

"*No, you weren't. You were the best Dad a kid could ever ask for.*"

"*I forgot who you were!*"

"*That was an awful picture. Don't worry about it.*"

"*But I do. I worry about many things, actually.*"

"*Like Mira?*"

Mentally, I nod. "*Will she be able to handle it?*"

"*She has to. It'll be tough, but she's the best one for the job.*" His voice sounds farther away.

"*Adam?*"

"*I'm still here, Dad.*"

"*Don't leave me.*" Even thinking the words is a struggle. My mind feels thicker. It's getting harder for me to think, to reason.

"*I won't. Rest now, Dad. Everything will be all right.*"

"*I will. I love you, son.*"

"*I love you too, Dad.*"

MY NAME

"**S**IR, WAKE UP. CAN YOU hear me?" A voice, fuzzy in my ears, slowly reaches through the haze like a hand grasping at fog. Why can't they just let me sleep? "Can you hear me, sir?"

I wrench my eyes open, blink painfully against the bright light then scrunch them shut again.

"There you are, sir. Open your eyes again, please." The voice sounds relieved. Must be that it's happy I'm showing signs of life.

I blink again, and a round face smiles at me. "Sir, can you hear me?"

I make some sort of noise and try to move my head, but it's stuck. There is something around my skull, holding me still. I try to scream with the pain, the agony of movement, but I can't. I can't do anything. Darkness swims in front of my vision, even with my eyes open. Then suddenly, it's gone, and someone dabs at my face with a cool, wet cloth. I try to move my hands, but they're stuck too, though they don't hurt the way my head does. Vague shapes move across my vision, and whatever's holding me down loosens.

"Sir? Is everything all right?"

Who is he calling sir? I nod anyway, and the young man smiles again. I struggle to sit up, my head swimming. A dark fog clouds my sight.

"Slowly, please, so you don't black out." The man wraps his arms around me and helps me to a sitting position.

"Good." He studies my face closely with bright green eyes, peering into mine, as if trying to see into my soul. "My name is Dr. James Scoffield. I'm here to help you." *Scoffield. Scoffield. Why does that name sound familiar? Do I know this guy?* Something in the back of my mind bugs me, like I should recognize him, like it's important, but I can't shake the memory loose.

"Everything checks out, Dr. Scoffield," says another doctor, standing in front of a machine in the middle of the room. I can't read his nametag, but he looks familiar, too.

"Good," Dr. Scoffield says. "Okay, sir, this is important. Do you remember what your name is?" He looks at me closely, as if this is some sort of test that I have to pass. Or fail. *Who cares what my name is?* My head's killing me, I feel as if I'm going to throw up, or pass out, or both, and he's asking me what my name is?

He asks me again, and I almost say the first name to come to my mind, but he shakes his head, so minutely I almost miss it. *Nope, guess that's not it. But who am I?*

Memories rush through me, a little dark-headed boy, a sister who... disappears? A young man with rugged good looks and a deadly bracelet wrapped around his wrist. I know him too, somehow. Then there is another young man who filled my heart with passion and a will to live. Something about butterflies, and bees without stingers. Little crosses getting trampled and kids disappearing. What was I supposed to remember? Dr. Scoffield asks me again. *Oh yeah, my name.*

Dr. Scoffield takes my hands in his and squeezes them gently. His are warm and firm, comforting. I glance across the room and see someone dressed in green cover... an old man with a blanket. Who is...? Socrates? Is it... is he dead?

And I'm... not? How could this happen? Why? I'm not supposed to live.

Was this his plan all along? Is that why he told me

what I needed to remember and what happened to those who failed? Did he want me to take his place?

I turn away from Dr. Scoffield and stare right at the curved glass wall. *Remember, Mira. There's an audience, Will, watching my every move. I have to make this good, or I'll never get away with it.*

"My name is Socrates."

ACKNOWLEDGMENTS

I've heard it said that writing itself may be a solitary practice, but the actual process of publishing a book is anything but. I never realized how true that was until my first book was published.

First and foremost, I'd like to thank my wonderful husband, family, and friends. They've supported me through years of talking to myself and scribbling fragmented ideas down on napkins and receipts. Better yet, they've only called me crazy once or twice.

I'd also like to thank the wonderful people at Red Adept Publishing, especially Karen, Michelle, and Kris, who all helped mold this behemoth into a novel worth publishing and endured countless emails and conversations to accomplish that goal. I'd also like to thank Lynn for believing in me and my book and helping me grow through this process to become a much stronger writer.

ABOUT THE AUTHOR

Chanda Stafford teaches middle and high school English. She loves traveling and currently lives in Michigan with her husband and a menagerie of rescued dogs and cats.

When she's not reading or writing, Chanda enjoys old zombie movies, authentic Italian food, and comic books.